for Mo,
who cared for my
dear mother so
kindly,
love and ~~best~~ wishes,
R. S. Charles
10.02.10

X

J. Snider
X

9 | 0770342096
Sasha

Whispering Palms

R. S. CHARLES

Eloquent Books

This novel is a work of fiction. Any similarity to persons living
or dead is purely coincidental.

Eloquent Books
An imprint of Strategic Book Group
P. O. Box 333
Durham, CT 06422
www.StrategicBookGroup.com

ISBN: 978-1-60860-949-9

Printed in the United States of America

Book Design: Judy Maenle

Chapter 1

"Montgomery. You really will have to do something about that dreadful woman!" shrieked a predictably outraged Lady Laetitia Lascelles as she burst open the door, completely unannounced.

"I didn't hear you knock, ol' girl," mumbled Monty with an air of disinterest. "And which dreadful woman would that be?" he mused, nonchalantly looking up from his morning newspaper. "There are so many on the Island."

"Don't be obtuse, man!" retorted the distinguished visitor. "Firstly, I don't need to knock. You're a public servant! And secondly, you know damn well to whom I'm referring! That bloody tart who parades up and down the beach every day, wearing next to nothing and flaunting herself to all and sundry. It's an utter disgrace!"

"Lottie, I'm the Governor of this Island, not some errand boy. I have far more important matters to concern myself with," he yawned, before continuing to puff noisily on his pipe. "I'm intrigued, however, that you see me as being a public servant. I'll have to remember that one! Anyway, why don't you do something? You're hardly the shy, retiring type!"

"Damn it man, that's not the point! It's up to you to maintain standards. The place will be overrun with floosies if we're not careful. But it's plain to see that she's got even you under her spell as well! Huh! Typical man! Well you haven't heard the last of this. And I'm sure that Daphnee wouldn't be too pleased either to learn that you condone such behaviour!" she bellowed as she slammed the door and flounced off down the hallway, leaving Monty looking somewhat bewildered, unable to think of an even vaguely suitable facetious response.

Lord Meadows and Lady Lascelles had been sparring partners for years. Both from old English aristocracy, she saw it as

1

her duty to monitor moral standards on the Island, and he saw it as his duty to ignore her. "She's just having a bad day again," muttered the Governor to himself, and instantly forgot the episode which had unnecessarily interrupted his morning coffee.

The Island in question was exotic and alone, small and remote. Nestling anonymously off the southern coast of a sprinkling of larger Caribbean islands, it had enveloped itself in a rich variety of lush, sprawling flora and fauna. Surrounding, sparkling, clear blue seas gently lapped against the white, sandy shores and craggy cliff boundaries, helping to secure its envied seclusion.

The climate was perfect; hot, but not too humid. Mild rain storms interspersed the mingling seasons, usually disappearing as fast as they came. And sheltered by its fortunate geographical location, the Island's prevailing winds were usually light and pleasant, providing a much appreciated gentle circulation of air.

Few real locals actually lived there any more, and those who did inhabited the less salubrious side. The developed quarter, on the other hand, had strong colonial influences and, though it was now 1986, still seemed to exist in a time warp from the 1950s.

The Island was a hideaway for some, a home for others, but everyone had a past and everyone had a reason to be there.

The 'Royal Palms', formerly a grand residence of Victorian gentry, had been an imposing feature of the shoreline since that era. Immersed in a history of mystery and intrigue, it doubtless had many an interesting story to tell. Now, however, some say against its will, the draughty old relic had been tastefully refurbished into a deluxe hotel and provided a lively social centre for the small, privileged, bohemian community.

Redesigned to allow the intrusion of a few decadent contemporary facilities, it specifically catered for the rich and anonymous, appealing to those who expected and demanded a lifestyle of envied luxury. By and by, however, it also lured some of the Island's more undesirable characters into its clutches, often for reasons best not to reveal.

Part of the hotel complex was the adjacent gourmet restaurant, 'Le Paradis Gastronomique', boasting top quality food and drink which one could savour in an intimate ambience of fancy furnishings and unrivalled splendour. Besides offering patrons the invitation to over-indulge in culinary delights and alcoholic beverages, the secluded corners of the classy venue had also become a popular haunt for a far more compelling daily pastime, the opportunity to dish the dirt on everyone else, in utter comfort, of course!

The only other such amenity was a rather down trodden beachside café, frequented solely by the echelons of the small society who were unable to afford to dine or enjoy liquid refreshment in the more up market watering hole.

* * *

The balcony doors of the plush first floor hotel suite facing the beach slowly opened. Raoul, wearing just a flimsy sarong, ambled on to the decking, leant on the beautifully carved wooden balustrade, and took a deep breath of sea air. "It's going to be another glorious day," he yawned, as he surveyed the stunning vista in front of him.

"Come back to bed!" murmured a sleepy voice from inside. "We've got all day to enjoy it."

"Morning Raaa!" trilled a woman's voice seductively from the hotel's private seafront garden below. The smiling face of bikini clad Della Dubois was alluringly looking up at him from under one of the colourful umbrellas which hospitably offered shade to the hotel pool sunbeds.

"Using my private facilities again, Mademoiselle Dubois?" flirted Raoul, raising his eyebrows with a saucy grin.

"Oh, I'm sure we could find somewhere much more private than this," replied the gin soaked voice, invitingly.

"You think so?" asked Raoul with a chuckle, purposely posing provocatively to show off his hairy chest and manly physique. "Shame I'm off limits."

"Who are you talking to?" shouted the voice from inside, sounding increasingly more agitated.

"Not that slut again, I hope? I've told you not to encourage her! Anyway she's banned! Tell her to sling her hook!"

"It's only a harmless bit of fun," reassured Raoul. "She knows the score." He silently blew the bleach blonde a kiss, rubbed his hand slowly across his groin, turned around, and went back into the hotel, closing the wooden shutters gently behind him.

"One day!" pouted the busty beauty softly to herself, as she eased back onto her sun lounger. "One day!"

Raoul was one of the males on the Island seen as somewhat of a 'catch', but officially he was spoken for. That didn't, however, deter several Islanders from targeting him for their sexual desires and, as a born flirt, he openly enjoyed the attention.

The only child of elderly Catholic parents, Raoul von Reissmann, now 34, had been brought up in England by his flamboyant, ex-socialite French mother and destitute father of German nobility. The couple had met when young, during the war, fallen in love, and then been forced to shelter as refugees in England shortly afterwards. To avoid any undue attention or suspicion, and for the sake of safety, they claimed his father was Dutch, having changed the 'von' in their surname to 'Van'.

By the time he was born, Raoul's parents' original lifestyle had sadly plummeted, and the family lived modestly, and somewhat reclusively, in a Council dwelling just outside London. Both his mother and father took whatever work they could, scrimping and saving to ensure that their son was well educated. They tutored him at home, and selflessly supported him through a scholarship to Boarding School.

From early childhood, Raoul soon became naturally proficient enough to speak both his parents' languages faultlessly and with little real effort. The first class Honours degree in Business he later obtained from Oxford University was the icing on the cake and the key to many convenient doors which would soon begin to open for him.

Working as a skilled interpreter with an outgoing, sociable nature, he became swiftly noticed by those who mattered, making several useful contacts in high society. Little did he know that those early days were to lead to an interesting, if somewhat turbulent, future?

* * *

"Oh do come along!" barked Sadie irritably, as she marched across the beach for her regular morning constitutional with her two elderly dogs. Wearing her renowned fawn tracksuit and beige plimsolls, her striking silver hair made her a familiar and instantly recognisable sight on the seafront.

At 56, she had already turned into a bitter spinster lacking sympathy for anyone, except, seemingly, her long standing companion, Olivia Van Leiden, an ailing older widow of considerable wealth, who had moved to the Island for health reasons and brought Sadie, a retired nurse, with her. They had been friends for many years back in England, and Sadie had been her equal until her father had suddenly died and left her not only penniless, but with considerable debts, reducing her to instant poverty.

Despite being of strong character, Sadie Finch had no life of her own and was, to an extent, browbeaten by her friend who now had the upper hand, doing her a favour by 'employing' her. Sadie's only consolation was her frequent indulgence in a modest form of clairvoyance. Apparently, certain feelings and senses encouraged her to endure her current lifestyle in the firm but unspoken belief that Mrs. Van Leiden's days were numbered and that she would inherit both her money and her substantial estate. After all, she had no-one else to leave it all to. Then, and only then, would Sadie really be able to live again!

"Morning, Sadie!" echoed a well spoken female voice across the mildly wet pathway which the receding tide was just beginning to reveal. "You seem in a terrible hurry this morning."

"Oh, Harriett! Yes. Didn't see you there. Sorry! Deep in thought, I'm afraid."

"Yes, yes, so I see. At that pace you could have very nearly knocked me over, and you know I'm rather fragile at the moment. I have to be so careful. My back has been giving me such jip recently. Could have been a nasty accident! Do watch where you're going in future," pleaded Harriett in her inimitable, clipped English accent, perfected over the many years of her career in broadcasting for the BBC World Service.

"Off to the Orphanage today?" enquired Sadie with a wry smile.

"No, I'm going over to the Church to meet Father Antonio and Dr. Tremaine's wife. We need to talk about fund raising."

"So that's why you're all dolled up," teased her friend as she admired Harriett's white, cotton trouser suit with matching silk neck scarf, sun hat and stylish sandals. With her auburn tinted hair, gold framed spectacles and attractive skin tones, the former radio celebrity remained a model of sophistication and elegance, and still enjoyed many an admiring glance. "Fund raising indeed," mocked Sadie with a grin. "Whatever next?"

At that point, without any warning whatsoever, Harriett Haversham suddenly flung her arms up and gave Sadie an almighty blow to the head, almost knocking her over. This was promptly followed with a few powerful, but badly aimed kicks. She then fell to the ground and flailed helplessly around, uttering the most revolting obscenities that her normal impeccable manners and refined conduct would never dare to have suggested. Slurred speech, unsteady deportment; for all intents and purposes, Harriett seemed drunk as a Lord. Such a spectacle would be most frowned upon. Most frowned upon indeed!

Luckily, Sadie knew what was happening and instantly rummaged through her bag for some sweets, a biscuit or something with sugar in it. Unfortunately, she had nothing, and was forced to cry for help while trying to prevent Harriett from both harming herself, and lashing out at her in the process. Meanwhile, Sadie's dogs had begun to howl and bark and scamper about, causing uproar, and Harriett's Scottie had fled in terror.

"What's all the commotion?" shouted Raoul, hastily covering his modesty with a towel as he burst open the balcony doors.

"Oh, it's only that silly cow having another one of her turns," replied Della Dubois disinterestedly. She then shamelessly flaunted her assets as she slowly turned herself over on the sun lounger to tan the back of her body, which was by now completely naked.

"Aren't you going to help?" asked a somewhat concerned Raoul.

"Nah! Just let her get on with it. That'll teach the posh bitch to take her medication. She's always forgetting. Besides, Sadie's there. She couldn't be in better hands, now could she?" Della laughed sarcastically.

"Looks like Sadie's got her hands full!" observed Raoul anxiously, ever the gentleman.

Just as he decided to get dressed and go to the rescue, Father Antonio and Mrs. Tremaine were hurriedly arriving on the scene, having witnessed the whole affair from the churchyard garden. The Doctor's wife looked stunned as Father Antonio gently enticed Harriett to calm down, offering her a soft drink he had rudely snatched from a concerned waiter watching at one of the poolside tables. The priest seemed to have such a natural, soothing effect on the female in distress.

Unbeknown to most people, however, there was a guarded history between these two associates. They had, in fact, first crossed paths in Italy over thirty years previously, when Harriett, a devout Catholic, was on a pilgrimage, and before the handsome young trainee had taken Holy Orders. She'd carried a torch for him ever since, and it seemed more than just coincidence that she had decided to settle on the Island where he had been born and subsequently returned to, as the community's only cleric.

"Sip it slowly, my dear," whispered Father Antonio tenderly. "It's alright, Hattie. I'm here now. There's no need to worry." Harriett allowed herself to drift gently into the pastor's arms and, with the help of the others, he slowly got her to her feet and supported her to one of the benches lining the sandy alley.

About ten minutes later, Harriett, still dishevelled, dazed and confused, blankly began to look around and then gradually became more coherent. "Oh no, not again!" she sighed. "Sadie, did I . . . ?" she asked hesitantly, as she noticed her friend's freshly blackened eye. Sadie nodded, for once somewhat sympathetically. "Oh, I am so sorry. Do forgive me. What on earth is the matter with me lately? I haven't the slightest idea! I can't apologise enough," whimpered Harriett, shaking her head in dismay.

"I'll live!" grunted Sadie stoically, wiping sand off her clothes.

"This damn malaise! I just don't know when it's going to strike next," she sobbed repentantly.

"Well it wouldn't be a problem if you took your bloody medication like you are supposed to," roared Della Dubois, who couldn't resist chipping in, and was by now sipping a large gin. "We keep telling you, but you won't listen! One day you're going to do yourself or somebody else some real harm, and what's worse, you probably won't even know anything about it. Mark my words!" nodded the sun worshipper with a knowing air of conviction. "Mark my words!"

Harriett just looked up in utter bewilderment, not knowing quite how to respond.

* * *

"Of course, you know there's something going on there," confided Kittie to her sister Clarrie as they both relaxed in their favourite corner of the hotel beach garden.

"Where? What do you mean?" questioned Clarrie.

"Her and him!"

"Who?"

"Toni and Harriett! They knew each other before."

"But I thought he was born here."

"He was! He lived on the poorer side of the Island for most of his early life. Then, both his parents died. It was in that terrible storm. He was still very young, so his grand-parents, who were Italian, encouraged him to go and live with them in Rome. While he was there, he met Harriett. He was in his early twenties. She was a 'debutante'. They had an affair!

"But, he's a priest," observed Clarrie, interrupting to show she was carefully following another of her sister's interminable monologues.

"This was before! Now do listen! His grandparents were very religious and put pressure on him to take Holy Orders. Said it was God's Will that he should return to the Island and start an Orphanage for other children who had lost parents. In the end, he was forced to choose; Harriett or the Church. You can see who won. She's never forgiven him and she won't let it go. That's why he drinks so much. He's never been sure he made the right decision . . . And that limp . . . ? Gout! Too much communion wine, if you ask me," blurted Kittie knowledgeably, hardly pausing for breath in her unflinching judgemental tone.

"But, how do you know all this, dear?" asked her sister inquisitively.

"I make it my business to know, Clarrie. I make it my business! Could be useful one day. Forewarned is forearmed!"

Just as she'd finished speaking, the bushes behind their bench seemed to rustle clumsily. They both thought this unusual as there was no wind to speak of. Clarrie was sure she had also heard footsteps on the gravel pathway, fading gently away into the distance, but, being partially deaf, did not wish to appear foolish to her sister, so said nothing.

Every community had its gossips, but these identical twin sisters, of debatable age, from the more wealthy side of the Island, knew more than most; one by enterprising choice, the other by passive obligation.

However similar in looks, they were dissimilar in character. Kittie was a forthright, interfering trouble maker, whereas Clarrissa was meek, mild and always saw the good in everyone. Usually they were together, but when apart, no-one could ever really be sure who was who.

Chapter 2

"Never put the milk in your cup before the tea, boy! It's what common people do!" boomed Lady Laetitia across the hotel's Salon de Thé.

"Ye, Ye, Yes, mamma," softly replied the young man, nervously shaking the cup as he proceeded to switch round his intended actions.

Poor Alistair! 29 years old, and he was still completely dominated by his mother. His shy, introverted manner had prevented him from making any real friends, only polite acquaintances who spoke to him like a pet, merely out of respect for his mother's considerably influential position on the Island.

Instead, his world revolved around his writing. Alistair spent hours and hours just writing; nobody knew quite what. A diary? A novel? What? It was a complete mystery. He lacked the confidence to mix openly, but, wide eyed and alert, the astute young man always appeared extremely well informed about whatever was going on in and around the busy community.

Some laughingly referred to him as the 'eyes and ears' of the Island, simply because his unbearable stammer made it uncomfortable or embarrassing to engage him in any sort of dialogue. Anything resembling a conversation seemed quite out of the question! Constantly scribbling away must have been the most satisfying fashion for the studious fellow to express himself. Though was there any point? No-one ever actually got to read what he wrote.

Had it not been for Alistair's unfortunate disposition, the slim, bespectacled young gent with the concealed physique of a seasoned swimmer would doubtless have attracted far closer attention from quite a selection of suitors. As it was, he could only dream of the romance and intimacy he craved.

In his ever inventive quest to communicate, Alistair had, however, picked up the invaluable art of being able to read people's lips. He was quite gifted in this respect, and had initially acquired the skill to make things easier for his dear departed father who lost the ability to use his voice in his later years due to a sudden baffling illness, apparently caused by some sort of trauma.

His mother, meanwhile, had missed the point completely. She merely enunciated every word she uttered to the poor man, louder and more slowly, until one day, in a rage of utter frustration, she gave up speaking to him altogether. The fact that she assumed her browbeaten husband was also deaf allowed him the amusing and convenient excuse to ignore her too!

"Ma, Mamma. Ha, have you n n noticed the, the . . . ?"

"Come on boy! Spit it out!" impatiently interrupted his mother in her thunderous tone, drawing even more unwanted attention to their daily ritual of what was meant to be peaceful and relaxing mid morning tea in the hotel lounge.

"The yacht moored out in the bay!" blurted a reassuring voice eagerly from behind. "Good Morning Lady Laetitia! Good Morning Alistair!" beamed the tall, well dressed gentleman with an air of distinction and confidence.

"Ah, Sebastian! Good Morning to you," gushed the widow to the hotel proprietor. "So nice to see you. Are you doing your rounds?" she enquired attentively. "Well, I'm sure you don't need to. The place looks splendid, as usual. On top form! A credit to you!" This rarely displayed effusive praise from one of the Island's most fussy females was both questionable and unnerving.

Unabashed by her overpowering, and strangely complimentary demeanour, Seb persevered.

"Yes, it's been out there for a few days now. No-one knows to whom it belongs. They don't seem to want to come ashore and join us though, for some reason."

"It's like being bloody spied on!" chipped in the familiar, gin soaked voice of Della Dubois, as she traipsed through Reception in a bikini and flip flops. "And they've got no business to!" she continued emphatically, spoiling the air of tranquillity and causing other guests to exhibit noticeable discomfort at her uninvited arrival.

"And what business do *you* have here, Miss Dubois?" enquired Sebastian, with more than a slight hint of annoyance.

"Wouldn't you like to know?" she replied belligerently. "Perhaps, I'm just visiting."

"The hotel or any guest in particular?" the owner sternly enquired. "Do please remember we have a dress code. And you know that the staff are not to receive social calls during working hours, don't you?"

Della Dubois ignored Sebastian's reproach, and gently began to massage her shoulder before brazenly announcing with a wicked grin, "Oops! Oh dear! How embarrassing! My bra strap has just snapped." She then clumsily cupped her now visible left breast, as she fumbled down to Alistair's eye level in an attempt to hold on to it. "Better go! Wouldn't want to appear indecent in such distinguished company or surroundings," she sniped with a smirk. "Bye Ali!" The tease laughed as she seductively blew the impressionable admirer a kiss and dawdled her way provocatively towards the exit through the French windows.

Instead of shrivelling up in discomfort, as one might have expected, Alistair appeared calm and composed, and there was even a suggestion of a grin from the corners of his mouth. That is, until he saw the reaction of his mother.

"Frightful woman!" burst out Lady Laetitia, indignantly. "Got the morals of an alley cat. You just make sure you have nothing to do with her, Alistair. Do you hear me? Nothing whatsoever!" ordered his mother with a forbidding frown that left him in no doubt that she meant it.

"Y, Y, Yes m, mamma," he nodded obediently.

As she rose irately from her chair to leave, Laetitia pulled Sebastian firmly by the arm to one side. Her mood seemed to have abruptly changed. "I think we're going to have to do something about that little madam before she goes too far!" she forcefully whispered in his ear. The unfaltering tone in her voice reflected a disturbing note of sinister conviction.

"Yes, I'm afraid we may very well have to," muttered a pensive Sebastian softly to himself, as his eyes closely followed the unwanted guest's lingering departure. The hotelier had long harboured his own strong, personal reasons for disliking the flighty female, and the look of contempt on his face only served to make such feelings even more publicly obvious.

* * *

Raoul enjoyed his lunchtime strolls. These were the few occasions where he could leave the complex and just wander wherever the whim took him. He'd completed his hotel duties and now was his time to relax, on his own.

As he headed through the grassy, palm lined lanes, he began to hear the strains of loud, lazy music blaring from the open door of one of the more dated wooden built villas, just off the beaten track. "Edith!" he thought to himself. "Why not? Haven't seen her for a while."

Whistling, he wended his way up the sandy front pathway to the entrance, completely missing his friend who was lounging in a wicker chair in a secluded and shady part of the garden. "Edith! Edith! Où es-tu donc?" he shouted expectantly.

"Over 'ere." replied a gravelly female voice with an unmistakable French accent. Turning around, he spotted a brightly coloured headscarf which could only belong to the petite, jazz singer from Marseille.

"Qu'est-ce que tu fais là?" he asked, as he cheerfully approached.

"Raoul, 'ow the 'ell do you expect ma bloody English to improve when you still insist on speaking to me in French?" she joked, puffing lingeringly on a long cigarette which she smoked stylishly through an expensive and quite distinctive holder.

"Is that you?" he suddenly enquired with great interest, "singing on the record. Is it one of yours?"

"Wish it bloody was! Hah, mon ami, you are so ignorant about jazz," she playfully rebuked, raising her eyes toward heaven. "That is none other than Billie Holiday. You must 'ave 'eard of 'er! She's one of the greatest!" Edith lit another cigarette and poured herself some gin. "Tu en veux?" she asked, offering him the bottle.

"Non, merci." Raoul shook his head. "I'm fine. It's too early for me. Besides, 'you know who' wouldn't like it!"

"And who the 'ell is going to bloody tell 'im, ah? Not me! Not you! So who? Live a little, eh!"

Raoul just chuckled to himself. Edith was a most likeable lady; so amusing, even though she did not mean to be. But, close as they were, he knew he had to watch what he said. The chanteuse had an unfortunate habit of allowing her mouth to run away with her at times, blurting out confidences and saying things she later bitterly regretted. Occasionally, her uncontrolled drinking and her dubious smoking habits made her a bit of a loose canon, so one had to tread carefully.

To most people, Edith was somewhat of an enigma. Though in her early fifties, she looked much older. Her tight head scarves, fashioned in the shape of a turban, hid any hair she had, and gave her a very high forehead. Her facial skin seemed ravaged and rough, no matter how much make-up she wore, and did little to complement the chic image of a former star. She also loved to worship the sun, which Raoul concluded wasn't exactly the kindest pastime to protect the ageing process of a woman's skin.

After some further ribbing about being unsociable, Raoul finally gave in and accepted a glass of iced water with some lemon. When his host lifted the carafe to pour him the drink, he noticed that it had been carefully keeping some documents in place on the garden table. They were face down, so he was unable to satisfy his nosy nature. Raoul tried to appear disinterested, but his constant straying eyes almost immediately betrayed his curiosity. Edith was no fool and consequently rested her elbow on the papers as she continued to pour. Then she swiftly placed the glass container back where it was obviously most needed.

The atmosphere seemed a little tense after that, so they carried on chatting idly, both pretending the uncomfortable moment had not reared its head.

Edith's present persona was dubious, and doubtless fashioned by the life she had lived before she came to the Island. She had told Raoul that she used to be a street singer on the rough French docks, earning barely enough money to eat. She'd often slept rough, and self indulged in drug abuse. As a consequence, she suffered the physical mistreatment from others which usually accompanied that kind of lifestyle.

Even during the brief time she enjoyed fame, her celebrity status was not enough to protect her from being used and manipulated by ruthless managers. She claimed to have been too weak to speak out and seek help then. Rather strange for someone with a temperamental side which gave clear signals never to dare intimidate her.

Apparently, when the fleeting diva had managed to siphon off enough cash from her agent to be able to change her life, which was, by all accounts, not really that long ago, she had left France under a cloud and 'escaped' to the Island. Sometimes she tended to misuse English words, but yes, this time she appeared to have got it right. That was the exact word she used, he recalled to himself. But why this island? It's not exactly on the map. Perhaps that was why!

The young man was still intrigued. What were those official looking papers? He couldn't just come right out and ask. That would be rude and might stretch their friendship a little too far. Dare he ask for another drink in the hope that something might give the game away? Imagine his fortune when an unexpected gust of wind started blowing the bottom corners of the sheets high enough for him to catch a glimpse.

Edith's eyes were closed as she revelled in the warmth of the sun's soaring rays which had now infiltrated their shade. Raoul felt guilty about his duplicitous thoughts, as he deliberately kept his companion talking to allow his fingers to deftly stray to the edges of the pages. He had just managed to ascertain that they were documents in English, and they did look official, when

15

he felt Edith's penetrating gaze focus on him. "You only 'ad to ask," she curtly snapped. "They are the deeds to my property. Solicitor's rubbish, that sort of thing. Be my guest. Take a look!" she offered indignantly. Was she bluffing or was she telling the truth? Raoul did not wish to insult her by finding out, so he made light of the situation, saying that he could never understand such unintelligible English either. They both laughed albeit in a somewhat strained fashion.

Raoul slowly sipped his ice cold lemon water and somewhat uncomfortably began to question his ungentlemanly behaviour. After all, he did have a soft spot for his flamboyant friend. But he tried not to think about her too deeply, because so many things just didn't add up. Yes, there were old records beside her gramophone with her name on them—'Edith Maureau.' But the labels were incorrectly spelt. She had always signed herself 'Moreau'. He had just seen her signature on the documents, the ones she couldn't understand. When he tentatively asked about the mistake, she laughed that only someone as pedantic as he would notice such a minute and irrelevant printing error. But was that the reaction of a real 'star'? Usually such people had egos, didn't they?

Yes, she could belt out a jazz tune, and on the occasions she had performed on Cabaret nights at the hotel, she was given standing ovations. Nobody denied she could sing. But there were flaws in her story. It frustrated Raoul. He was her special friend, her confidant. He wanted desperately to trust her. Edith had always been honest and open with him, or so she said, yet she remained guarded and a very private person to everybody else on the Island.

And though Raoul loved to converse with her in his mother's language, he was somewhat suspicious, both of Edith's French and her constant wish to avoid using it, supposedly because she wished to improve her heavily accented English.

Above all, she reminded him of his mother, whom he loved greatly, and this unsettled him.

"Eh bien, il faut que je parte," gasped Raoul as he looked at his watch.

"But you've only just bloody arrived," replied his friend, raising her hands in acceptance.

"I know, but it was just a quick visit. I'll be back again sometime. You know I will. Besides, I want you to sing at the hotel again. We'll arrange it."

"Raoul, before you go, 'ave you seen my reading glasses?" she asked, flicking idly through a fashion magazine which she had carefully placed over the corner of the documents. "I am always losing them. I 'ave got about six pairs, all over the 'ouse. I cannot find any!"

Raoul smiled, stood up, and gently lowered the spectacles resting on her forehead down in front of her eyes. "Ah!" she exclaimed, as if she'd just discovered the elusive answer to a crossword puzzle. "That's better! I can see now!" The visitor dissolved into laughter and kissed Edith twice on one cheek and once on the other, alternately, and then raced off down the path before she had time to even get up from her chair. "Au revoir! Raoul!" echoed briefly into the breeze as Edith took another sip of gin and puffed smoke into the air.

* * *

"You're late back," stated Sebastian, purposely looking at his watch as Raoul strolled through the hotel lobby, hands in pockets.

"No later than normal!" he replied indifferently.

"Will you do a shift on Reception? One of the girls has gone home sick."

"Can't you do it? I've got plans," Raoul whined.

"What plans?" asked Seb.

"I promised I'd go through a few things with Dimitri."

"In that case, you can definitely cover Reception. You can see him any time," barked Seb with a look that could kill.

"Oh I will!" teased Raoul. "I'll make sure of it."

"And make yourself decent! We've got standards to uphold," shouted Sebastian as he went in to the office, slamming the door.

17

As well as being annoyed at his unanticipated, enforced labour, Raoul was beginning to realise that he now possessed an ever growing tendency toward laziness where the hotel was concerned. He decided, nonetheless, to do as he was bid without further protest. He really had no option.

Luckily, the reluctant receptionist's overwhelming boredom was quite soon unexpectedly broken. His renowned curiosity had been instantly aroused when his wandering attention had fleetingly been inadvertently drawn to an unfamiliar silhouette on the opaque glass of the office partition. Someone was sitting in one of the plush chairs overlooking the poolside, reserved only for special visitors. The door had momentarily opened, and then quickly closed again. There was no-one scheduled in the appointment book. What was Sebastian up to?

Raoul's lingering thoughts were inconveniently interrupted by a deep voice in lazy, broken English. "So we go now? You want me, yes?" He looked up at a swarthy, handsome young man with a tanned face and long, jet black hair tied back in a pony tail. It was Dimitri. Not only was he the hotel pool life-guard and masseur, but he also did odd jobs around the complex when required. His inappropriately bare, muscly chest and tight revealing swim shorts were already inviting disapproving looks and comments from guests in the lobby.

"Can't!" blurted out Raoul, somewhat off guard. "Last min-ute change of plan. We'll have to . . . get together some other time." Dimitri reacted with a predictable snarl of annoyance. "And I've told you before; don't come into Reception unless you're properly dressed!" he instructed the employee, with a look which was stern, yet unconvincing, to say the least.

"Whatever you say!" responded Dimitri through gritted teeth. "But now you wait your turn."

"And you do as you're told if you want to keep your job!" reprimanded a flustered Raoul, looking nervously around to see if his authority had been compromised.

Dimitri openly seethed with wounded arrogance. As a parting shot, he menacingly growled, "I no like being made fool of. And no forget I have more than one boss who need my . . . eh . . . services." He then made his way in the direction of the hotel bar, where an adoring, young blond was patiently waiting and watching, with more than a passing interest.

At that moment, the office door closed again. Sebastian swiftly ushered his mystery guest through the staff exit before turning to meet Raoul's instant eye contact, and face like thunder, across the lobby. Raoul wasn't going to give his partner the satisfaction of enquiring what was going on, so he picked up the telephone, quickly dialled a number, and turned his back toward Seb as if the call was of a private nature and not intended to be overheard.

Finishing the apparently secretive conversation, Raoul smiled and replaced the receiver. Through the mirror in front of him, he casually acknowledged a familiar guest who was at a table, writing. "I'm going for a haircut," he announced, as Seb approached with a guilty look that only Raoul knew. "Just rang Elise. She can fit me in now."

"But there's no-one to do Reception," complained Sebastian.

"Oh, I'll close it for an hour. We're not bloody servants, here to wait on them hand and foot. I'm sure no-one will mind . . . There we are!" he said proudly, as he produced a familiar sign printed off from the typewriter; "Reception is now closed. Please ring for service in the event of an emergency only."

"You'll hear that from the office. We're not expecting any new arrivals," he assured Seb, and quickly made his way down the marble steps to the hotel's beauty salon in the basement.

* * *

"You look pissed off, Ra," smiled Elise Beauchamp in her usual bubbly tone that would normally make everything instantly better.

"Yeh, think Seb's up to something," he declared thoughtfully.

"Probably just your imagination," she reassured.

"So, what's the latest?" Raoul asked rubbing his hands with glee.

"Oh, couldn't possibly say. What about client confidentiality?" grinned the beautician.

"You're a hairdresser, not a bloody Doctor!" he exclaimed. "Besides, I'm your Boss. You can tell me anything. It's your duty. Do you really think I came down here for a haircut. Now dish the dirt!"

"Well," started Elise in hushed tones, "you know . . . " And with that, all that could be heard was the occasional gasp, fits of giggles and embarrassing silences as other clients passed by and Elise had to respectfully bid them farewell, usually just before she let off a string of obscenities about them.

"And how's Curtis? You two still head over heels?" probed Raoul.

"Oh, probably up to some shady deal somewhere," she sighed. "I don't expect too much, so then I'm not disappointed. Come to think of it, I haven't seen him for a couple of days. And I'm still waiting for him to put a ring on my finger."

"Life's one long wait," Raoul announced philosophically. "And half the time, if we knew what we were waiting for, we probably wouldn't wait after all!" he continued.

"Bit deep for you, that, Ra," Elise joked.

Confidante to men and women alike, 29 year old, dizzy Elise, with the enviable figure of a well endowed model, was a former hairdresser and beautician to the stars. That is, until she ruined a major celebrity's hair and had to do a moonlight flit to the Island to escape the blaze of disastrous publicity and the threat of being sued.

Some said she had a similar appearance to Della Dubois at times, but her naturally blond hair, a colour which, being a hairdresser, she often changed to suit her mood, was much longer. Putting her hair up, however, revealed the tattoo of a scorpion at the nape of her neck, reflecting the sting in her tail.

Clients told her confidences they wouldn't even tell their own mother, trusting her to keep those secrets guarded . . . . But did she? Though Elise was one of Raoul's closest friends, she insisted, even to him, that she was not a gossip and would only ever pass on 'common knowledge'.

They were just finishing his 'consultation' when the telephone rang and Elise was called to the front desk. Raoul hung around. What was happening appeared of interest. Elise seemed to be trying to plead profusely, but was unable to get a word in. She was spluttering, flustered and embarrassed, and moved from one foot to the other, rather like people often do when they are desperate to go to the lavatory. Her sign of deference indicated that she was either speaking to someone superior or to someone who had some kind of hold over her.

Flushed and tearful, she came off the 'phone and scuttled hastily into the back room. Raoul went to the door. He was about to go in when he heard the flinging of objects splattering against the wall, followed by a kick and a heavy thud. "I'll have that bloody bitch!" she screamed with resolve. "And I'm sure if I don't, I know someone else who will."

Raoul considered it best not to enter, nor to enquire further, but all the same, his inquisitive nature had again been aroused. "See you," he muttered disconcertedly with a quick wave to Elise's next client as he left the Salon. A red faced Alistair had already had his hair washed by the apprentice over twenty minutes previously. Staring into the mirror adjacent to the Reception desk, he was still patiently sitting in the chair, waiting for the hairdresser to attend to him. His blond locks were now bone dry, and he looked rather uncomfortable, and perhaps somewhat unnerved or even annoyed. You couldn't really tell with Alistair, he gave nothing away.

Raoul had a guilty afterthought. He felt that as 'management' he'd better apologise on Elise's behalf, so he returned and told the young client that the stylist wouldn't be long and that she had 'women's problems'. This, for some reason, made Alistair appear even more unsettled. Without a word, he bolted from the chair, ham fistedly pulled off the towels from around his shoulders, and headed unapologetically for the stairs, leaving a flustered Raoul to clear up.

Such a reaction from the normally mild mannered Alistair was quite out of character. What was going on? He obviously had a lot more on his mind than the inconvenience of an unnecessarily long wait at the hairdresser's.

Chapter 3

"How the bloody hell am I supposed to produce gourmet dishes wit' staff like you morons?" screeched Ryan O'Rourke, throwing a dirty saucepan on the freshly mopped floor of the restaurant. "Half of you got no idea what you're supposed to be doin', even though I've shown you at least umpteen bloody times. And you expect me to actually serve this disgustin' crap you're comin' up wit'? I wouldn't give it to my dogs, let alone the Island's most distinguished . . . "

He was interrupted by Grace Elisabeth Hickory. "Mister O'Rourke," she drawled, with distinct disinterest. "You better check yourself, or you ain't gonna have NO staff to help you with any relunch, if you ain't careful."

"Re-LAUNCH!! Grace Elisabeth, re-LAUNCH!" emphasised the new, temporary Head Chef with his arms in the air.

"Well that too!" grinned Grace Elisabeth winking to some of the other volunteer helpers, proud that it hadn't taken her long to learn how to press all the right buttons.

Grace was one of the original Caribbean inhabitants and was highly respected by both the local work force on the Island and employers alike. She had gone into service at the big house, as then was, at a young age and cleverly worked her way up to Senior Housekeeper at the now luxury hotel. Privately, she hated these 'rich, arrogant foreigners' who had taken over, exploited and spoilt her homeland, even though they had improved its small economy and her own status. Publicly she thought it prudent to 'keep her place'.

At 62, she had amassed a wealth of history about the secrets of the secluded Island and its various residents, but she considered it best to use this information wisely, as and when it was needed.

"Le Paradis Gastronomique" had attracted wealthy lovers of good food for years. The fastidious members of the community jealously wished the establishment to enjoy exclusivity, but visitors from all over the globe had begun to stumble upon the secret hideaway and had been spreading the word. Needless to say the aspiring, young Irish chef was not content to remain in the shadows either. He was keen to 're-establish the restaurant's culinary profile on the Island' and his own reputation, of course! But such folly could attract unnecessary attention and not everyone was pleased.

Temperamental and flamboyant, O'Rourke had very recently been underhandedly headhunted by Sebastian and encouraged to move abroad to take over the hotel's jewel in the crown. His hasty appointment had been announced by the owner as a move to avoid some very heavy British tax bills, but there had been no consultation, and subsequently there was talk!

All at once, work stopped and everything came to an abrupt halt. "He's on his way!" shouted Grace Elisabeth with glee, and everyone ran out of the kitchen on to the back lawns.

"What the hell's goin' on now?" gestured a baffled O'Rourke, rolling his eyes. "And what in the name of Jesus is that almighty din?"

There was a continuous vibrating rumble, accompanied by the whining of what sounded like propellers struggling to slow down. Then, gasps of anticipation were audible from the gathering throng as a series of bumps across the turf and an ear piercing screech eventually led to a dull thud.

"Hola amigos! Ees me again!" announced a booming voice as the noise, which resembled a tin can being opened, followed by a creak and a bang, finally faded into the dust. When visibility resumed, the smiling face of a middle-aged Spaniard, with a large untidy moustache, beamed to an adoring crowd offering a spontaneous round of applause.

"I do wish he'd learn to fly the darn thing properly," mused Lord Meadows.

"Oh he can fly it alright. It's taking off and landing he's not so good at!" laughed his friend, Maggie Maynard, making one of her rare appearances away from her dog walking chums.

"The Colonel would have a bloody fit! How is he nowadays, by the way?" enquired Monty, with an air of compassion.

"Oh, not so bad, you know. Bit of arthritis here and there. Poor ol' chap is still housebound though, unfortunately."

"You still painting, my dear?"

"I'll say! I've got some very interesting scenes of the Island under my belt," boasted a proud Maggie. "And I capture exactly what I see at the time. You know, rather like a photograph."

"You're early!" was Sebastian's rather unfriendly greeting to the celebrated visitor.

"I know Señor. Zer ees preediction. Very bad wezzer on ze way, so, Elroy, he come early. Island need supplies and post. Elroy, he come! He stay couple days zees time. He bring lots."

Workers from the hotel and restaurant needed no encouragement to begin tucking in to the stash of goodies on the 'plane, boisterously unloading everything from fresh meat to Elise's latest fashion hair products. Everyone seemed to be thoroughly enjoying themselves amidst the complete shambles of what should have been an operation of military precision. In fact, the scene had all the finesse of a car boot sale.

Elroy was a likeable rogue and provided a vital scheduled lifeline with the outside world once a month. More importantly, he collected and brought the post. "I only 'ave two mails," he announced apologetically, shrugging his shoulders. "One for Señor Raoul, and one for Señorita Dubois." Both parties had by now arrived and grabbed their letters quickly to avoid them getting into the wrong hands.

"Señor Raoul, your letter, she has black borders. Ees bad news, no?" The European custom of sending black edged envelopes usually announced a death, but Raoul did not seem unduly bothered.

"Maybe. I'll read it later, in private," he confided discreetly in a concerned Elroy, not wishing to make too much fuss or attract

24

Seb's attention to it. He casually slipped the correspondence into his inside pocket and hurriedly went back into the hotel.

Raoul knew what was in the letter. He'd been expecting it. He had specifically instructed his contact to place the information in such an envelope, in order to explain it as the death of an elderly German aunt if Seb asked. In truth, he had actually hired a private detective back in Britain to dig into Ryan O'Rourke's past. He neither liked nor trusted the newcomer and was suspicious of his motives and relationship with Sebastian.

Having gone into the office for some privacy, Raoul made sure he was alone, locking the door and pulling the drapes before unceremoniously tearing open the letter. Though quite lengthy, the contents had been compiled in note form, as a report;

RYAN O'ROURKE.

"Born 1952. Brought up in southern Ireland. Five sisters. Only son of farmer and his wife. Lonely child, but related well to sisters. Father a tyrant and bully, expecting boy to take on more and more farm duties as he grew older.

Youngster only interested in learning how to cook from talented, but over protective, mother who trained in service before marriage. Husband thought son's desire to become chef was effeminate. Tried to block any ambition to leave and seek a future in big wide world . . . ."

"I didn't want his bloody life history; this is no good!" fumed Raoul.

"At 16, ran away from home to London. Penniless and homeless, fell into clutches of manipulative pimp who realised and abused youth's sexual preference. O'Rourke lured into providing 'personal services' as only means of earning enough money to survive."

"This is more like it!" Raoul rubbed his hands jubilantly.

"Boy's determination to make something of his own life justified the means to achieve it, at any cost. Soon learnt duplicitous tricks, persuading 'special' clients to lavish him with financial gifts in exchange for exclusivity.

At 20, started work as junior chef in top London restaurant, 'The Gourmet Paradise', after recommendation from mystery wealthy businessman. Talents and flair soon recognised; fast tracked his way into buying own small, but stylish, restaurant. Financially backed by same unknown benefactor." Raoul's mood darkened as he read on. The penny was beginning to drop.

"Much acclaimed, O'Rourke's standing in world of haute cuisine grew and grew. Became award-winning celebrity chef by 28th birthday."

The report finished with some personal observations from the sender. "To this day, evidence suggests that O'Rourke has no idea of the identity of his sponsor. All business conducted through third party. Likely he has moved to the Island because British newspapers were beginning to dig into his shady past."

The detective concluded with the necessary niceties; "I hope this information is of use. Should you wish me to pursue the matter further, please contact me? I acknowledge, with thanks, receipt of your deposit into my bank account."

"Mystery benefactor!" scowled Raoul, screwing up the letter and stuffing it angrily into his trouser pocket. "No bloody prizes for guessing who that is or why!!"

Back in the kitchen, the hive of activity had resumed with the din of pots and pans clattering all over the place, a loud Irish accent barking orders, and the smell of sumptuous food wafting through the air.

"Everything o.k.?" shouted Seb from the swing door at the entrance, not venturing in for fear of spoiling his white, cotton suit with the odour or stain of food.

"Everyt'ing's just fine. No problem!" reassured the busy chef.

"So you don't need me then?" asked Sebastian.

"Well, not right now," smiled Ryan, coyly adopting a puppy dog pose, just waiting to be petted.

Feeling an uncomfortable presence behind him, Seb instinctively turned around and bumped right into a simmering Raoul who had just witnessed, at first hand, what he surmised could only be a flirtatious interlude. "This looks about as organised as a piss up in a brewery," Raoul criticised, barely containing his rage.

"Give him a chance," reassured Seb. "I don't know why you've always got such a downer on him."

"Nor do I yet," muttered Raoul to himself as Sebastian walked away. "But you can bet your life when I do, there'll be big trouble."

* * *

Della Dubois placed the mail that she had just received carefully onto the lounge table in her living quarters; some ramshackle rooms behind the beach café which she ran and owned. She stared carefully at the envelope, but the look on her face did not betray whether she was too afraid or too excited to open it.

With a sudden determination, she seemed to pluck up courage. She quickly retrieved her sharpest knife from the kitchen drawer, made sure the windows and blinds were closed, and that there was no draught, then very, very deftly slid the knife along the top edge of the envelope. She gently proceeded to shake it until the contents slowly eased onto the silk scarf specifically placed on the table below.

"Well, what have we here?" she schemed, rubbing her hands. Three pieces of overlapping newspaper awaited her examination. The sheets were of different sizes and seemed like cuttings. The one on top was in Italian, and looked as if it had been photocopied from a very old source. "Mmm, I shall need help with this one," Della sighed thoughtfully. "My Italian isn't up to much. The picture says it all though. All I need is a few key words. A dictionary will suffice, I think." Her face beamed in triumph.

The second sheet was a genuine tabloid piece with the headline; "Missing nurse suspected of poisoning wealthy aristocrat."

"This gets better and better," she smugly muttered to herself.

And finally, there was a large page from an English daily newspaper with a small, somewhat insignificant looking article ringed in red. It related to someone's sudden disappearance after a house fire at premises Interpol had been keeping under surveillance. Apparently, there had been a seizure of a vast quantity of drugs, and the key witness for the prosecution in the trial had taken flight.

An accompanying note, badly spelt, and written on a scruffy scrap of paper read; "This is for you. Hope its wat you want, now were qwits. Thats it now. No more." The accompanying signature was illegible.

"So, where shall I start then?" the sassy, bronzed blonde eagerly pondered. "I know . . . With them all!" Della deviously laughed, coughing and spluttering after another gulp of gin and a forceful drag on her wilting cigarette.

Chapter 4

It was a beautiful evening. There was a gentle breeze and the air was pleasantly fresh. The descending sun was still smiling hazily in the sky against a backdrop of lazy, lapping waves from the deep blue sea forming fleeting patterns on the soft, white sands. People had already started mingling in the magnificently decorated marble hotel Reception area and champagne corks and the tinkling of glasses echoed through the lobby above the noise of polite, light conversation.

A string quartet was carefully setting up between the plants and palms in the corner of the terrace, while the 'native' Islanders were gleefully preparing for their barbeque on what was normally considered to be the hotel's private beach area.

"Let's hope their damn steel band doesn't drown out the sound of our musical entertainment," commented Lady Laetitia acidly as she arrived. "I'm expecting something far more genteel! In fact, I really don't care much for music at all when I'm dining. I find it intrusive and inappropriate! How can one converse properly with a din in the background?" Totally unaware that she was merely talking to herself, she painstakingly proceeded to negotiate the steps to the lounge area, being very careful not to ruin her glittering ball gown or allow her tiara to dislodge her carefully coiffured hair.

"Oh, do come along boy!" she barked as Alistair trailed behind somewhat reluctantly. He hated these formal occasions. He always felt out of place. But with his crisp dinner suit, contact lenses, fresh tan and carefully styled hair, he had already begun to turn heads.

"Who's that dear?" Clarrissa asked her twin sister from their seated vantage point on the terrace.

"Alistair Lascelles!" she replied curtly.

"Who?"

Kittie shouted her answer again, even more tersely, which signalled to Clarrie that she had better not ask too many questions because her sister did not like to repeat herself.

The tall, spindly, old fashioned twins were wearing their usual liberally applied make-up, which regrettably only accentuated their unappealing bony faces. Sporting exactly the same unflattering boyish haircuts, they once again appeared in identical outfits; rather conservative blue dresses with lace trimmings and low heeled shoes. In fact, it was most disconcerting how everything about them matched, except their intellect, that is. One was rather simple, the other highly astute, but which was which?

Sadie Finch came striding resolutely along the terrace in a beige, cotton trouser suit and flat, white sandals; the only hint of colour was a green scarf draped in the shape of a tie round her neck.

Closely behind her, Harriett Haversham appeared. She really had made the effort. Immaculately made up, hair in curls, nails freshly manicured, and wearing a beautiful, low cut sequined evening gown with an elegant silk shawl covering her shoulders, Harriett was dripping in jewellery and looked every inch the former media celebrity. Luckily, she still had the figure to carry it off, and was given several admiring glances by adoring males. However, within herself, she did seem somewhat preoccupied. Her mind was definitely elsewhere.

"Where's Mrs Van Leiden?" she asked Sadie rather rudely as she finally caught up with her.

"Not very well this evening. Wanted to stay at home," was the immediate grumpy response, indicating it was really none of Harriett's business.

"Shouldn't you be with her?" she clumsily inquired without thinking. Sadie's powerful glare said it all, and Harriett quickly retreated into the group of guests behind her. She had an unfortunate habit of unintentionally upsetting people by saying the wrong thing, and then worrying about it afterwards.

"Alright ol' girl?" asked Lord Meadows as a dawdling Harriett nearly tread awkwardly on his toes by slowing down without warning.

"Oh, Monty! Daphnee!" she enthused, as if she hadn't seen them for years. "How lovely to see you both. Oh don't you both look fine!" She then blurted out what was really on her mind. "I think I've just said the wrong thing to Sadie. She looks to be in a foul mood and I shouldn't like to put her out. She can be very difficult when she wants . . . "

Harriett's whining worry was soon lost in the sound of gasps as a black Mercedes limousine with a flag on the bonnet regally drew up at a snail's pace. "Who's in there?" asked Clarrissa excitedly.

"How do you expect me to know? Somebody with more money than sense, I shouldn't wonder," sneered Kittie, as if she had a foul smell under her nose.

"I bet they're famous or even royalty. Someone off the yacht in the bay," continued Clarrie, with child-like enthusiasm.

"Don't be ridiculous! Who'd bother to come here in an automobile? Everyone's within walking distance of the hotel," sniped her tetchy twin.

The darkened windows hid the figure inside until the uniformed chauffeur got out and respectfully opened the door for the 'celebrity'. The first glimpse was of two highly polished pink, strapless high heels on the end of two very long tanned legs. Next, a female form in a short, black, tight fitting, low cut designer dress topped with a gold necklace emerged, her face hidden by sunglasses and a red silk head scarf.

It was harder to identify the mysterious guest in the fading light, but as soon as the headscarf and sunglasses came off, and the dulcet gin soaked tones announcing, "Now that's how to make an entrance!" filled the air, followed by a brassy cackle, everyone knew it was the very vulgar, but very voluptuous, Della Dubois.

"Close your mouth, dear!" whispered Alicia Tremaine nonchalantly to her husband. "Do remember she's a patient!"

"Mmmm, the ass with class!" teased Dimitri with a lustful grin, as he lounged suggestively over his personally reserved table on the cleverly lit poolside area.

31

"Hi, honey!" she raucously responded, waving a black glove. "You're looking drop dead gorgeous yourself!" Dimitri knew this already, of course. Brazenly basking in his own simmering sexual presence, he readily lapped up drooling and admiring glances from a selection of rather unlikely sources.

"Just look at her! Who on earth does the preening peacock think she is!" hissed Lady Laetitia to the small clique surrounding her.

"What's that, ma dear?" enquired Monty who was giving the floorshow his full attention.

"I'm talking about Bella Budois, making an unnecessary spectacle of herself again," she griped, even louder.

"Della Dubois, Lottie. She's called Della Dubois."

"Never presume to correct me, Monty!" barked the angry aristocrat. "Purposely getting someone's name wrong shows one's supreme and utter indifference toward them. It's a very useful art. Perhaps you should cultivate it some time!"

"Who invited her?" Sebastian indignantly asked joint host, Raoul, who had already begun meeting, greeting and circulating at the start of the evening.

"It's 'open house' isn't it? Everyone's welcome!" declared his partner unapologetically. Seb just scowled. No further words were needed.

They both looked the part, in their crisp, white shirts, red bow ties, black evening suits and unflinching sparkling smiles, as they skilfully worked their way around the lounge. The grey highlights in tall, slim Sebastian's short, blond, wavy hair shimmered to compliment his suave, debonair appearance. At 46, he had quite a distinguished look about him, and was generally considered to be the quiet, astute, level headed one.

Raoul, on the other hand, had inherited his father's intelligence and diplomacy and his mother's sociable, outgoing nature and Mediterranean looks. The unfortunate, faint scar he sported on the swarthy, olive skin of his left cheek made his upper lip curl slightly. To some, it gave an impression of arrogance, but to others he just looked rough and ready, yet, perhaps, all the more striking. Few knew the origin of the facial blemish. Fewer still knew it secretly assured unspoken membership to a very exclusive and very influential international fraternity on whom he had yet to call.

Tonight, Raoul's smart attire somehow managed to overshadow his normal thuggish appearance. Sporting closely cropped hair with a dark, bristly shadow around his chin and a fresh tan, he assumed a more dashing air. His newly grown, perfectly groomed moustache suitably completed his smouldering veneer.

Well liked for his sense of humour and basic outward benevolence, Raoul was one of the more popular members of the disparate community. However, simmering within was a bitter, vitriolic streak, only ever witnessed by those whom he allowed to get close. When they were alone, Sebastian, especially, regularly had to endure others being verbally torn apart in their absence during venomous bouts of spite and frustration; a regrettable indiscretion Raoul would have done well to curb.

"I've bloody had enough of this farce already!" hissed Seb's partner restlessly, as they both smiled and took another glass of champagne from Grace Elisabeth's tray. "I could be elsewhere enjoying myself!"

"It's all good for business," reassured Sebastian, raising his glass to some of the on-looking guests.

"Whose business?" snapped Raoul. "And while we're about it, I think it's about time we discussed the exact details of Mr. O'Rourke's involvement in OUR business, don't you?"

"This is neither the time nor the place," insisted Sebastian, as he sidled towards a rather uncomfortable looking Father Antonio to avoid Raoul's further questioning. "Foot playing up again tonight, Father?" sympathised Seb, patting the cleric gently on the shoulder.

"Yes . . . yes . . . something like that," replied the priest somewhat dismissively, as he eased his way past.

"Edith! Edith!" Raoul beckoned excitedly to his friend as she arrived, glowing as if she had just stepped out of the pages of a Parisian fashion magazine, in her matching shimmering gold jacket, knee length skirt, head scarf and high heels. "Thank God, you're here! Now perhaps we can liven up this boring little shindig."

"Bonsoir euh, cheri!" she whispered rather distractedly, hesitantly glancing around as they exchanged kisses on both cheeks. "Where's the bloody booze?" she nervously gasped as she retrieved her trademark cigarette holder from her accessorized clutch bag and began to light her first cigarette of the evening.

"On your own, Elise?" taunted Della Dubois knowingly, as the stylist arrived. "We must have a drink together later on."

"I shall look forward to it!" glared Elise who briskly whisked herself off to the 'Ladies' to freshen up. The delectable Miss. Dubois then proceeded to boisterously circulate, making sure she brushed very closely by Raoul as he, too, mingled. She whispered something in his ear, kissed him on the cheek provocatively, attempted a quick fondle, smiled tauntingly at Seb, flicked her hair and moved on. Raoul shrugged his shoulders.

"Glad to see someone's having a good time," was his placating remark to an unmistakably fuming Sebastian.

"Don't you think some people are behaving rather oddly tonight," observed Clarrissa, thoughtfully.

"No more than usual," replied Kittie. "In what way?"

"Well," Clarrie began. "Sadie Finch has got a face like thunder, which does not go with her lovely silver hair. Harriett Haversham and Father Antonio are both looking most ill at ease, and seem to be going out of their way not to be seen together. And our French singing star who never misses a chance to perform, looks as if she doesn't want to be here . . . So does that beautician girl, come to think of it! And, as for Mr. Sebastian, he's doing his best, but he's definitely not himself."

"Poppycock! It's just your imagination, Clarrie. You've had too much sherry."

"You've also been a little abrasive yourself, Kittie, dear," her twin ventured bravely to remark.

"Must be something in the air then, that's all I can say," was Kittie's distracted response. Her eyes then darted towards Della

Dubois who was cussing loudly, unsuccessfully trying to light a cigarette, and shrieking with laughter in a cosy corner with Raoul. The host had by now left a jittery Edith, drinking on her own, to find someone more animated to socialise with.

Meanwhile, Harriett had unobtrusively retreated to the nearby Chapel where she was finding solace anxiously going through her Rosary beads. She had turned pale and looked most upset. Having noticed her absence, Father Antonio had furtively followed, and quietly crept into the pew behind her. They both knelt in silence for what seemed like eternity. Then Harriett sat up, and without turning around, softly spoke. "It's all over Toni. Someone knows."

"Yes, Hattie, it appears they do," he whispered, deep in thought. "I've had an illegibly scribbled letter myself."

"But how . . . ? Who? Why interfere with us? Whom have we upset? Is what we've been doing so wrong? Everyone's got a right to love. What's it got to do with anyone else?" whimpered Harriett, wiping stray tears from the rouge on her cheeks.

"My dear, we knew it would happen one day. I'm a Catholic priest and Catholic priests don't marry . . . even in secret," reasoned Father Antonio with a heavy sigh. "I'm surprised we've kept it private this long. In a way it's a relief. All those clandestine meetings. You, not being there when I needed you. Me, being unable to touch or to kiss you when you were so close to me. It's all been such a strain."

"So what happens now?" sobbed Hattie.

"Well, we're not giving in to blackmail. After all, what proof have they got? So let's just take it one step at a time. We don't know who it is yet. Maybe we can reason with them?" shrugged Antonio half heartedly.

"Oh, I think we've both got a pretty good idea who it is!" assured Harriett through gritted teeth, and she's not going to get away with it. Not if I've got anything to do with it!"

"Be careful, my dear. I must advise care and caution," pleaded the priest.

"Oh I'll be careful alright . . . not to get caught," whispered Harriett defiantly, as she suggested that they make their way separately back to the Reception, having, for once, exhibited a rarely seen, yet uncompromising, steely determination.

As the Church bell struck eight, there was a loud gong. "Ladies and Gentlemen, Dinner is served! Please make your way into our Restaurant, following the seating plan on the chart at the entrance," announced Sebastian ceremoniously.

"Seating plan? Seating plan?" I shall sit where I damn well choose!" defiantly declared Lady Lascelles as she sedately followed the other guests into the Dining Room.

"I knew they'd like that. That was my little contribution," smirked Raoul proudly. "Now I'm beginning to enjoy myself!"

After the initial hustle and bustle, people began to seat themselves in their designated positions, with just a few crafty changes of name cards being surreptitiously swapped around on the larger round tables. Beautiful arrays of tropical flowers complimented the place settings, and natural fragrances, after shaves and perfumes filled the air. It was, however, the unmistakable aroma of lavender drifting through the hall which was most noticeable.

The complimentary wine began to flow, and everyone seemed more at ease as choices for the starting course were made and people were soon eating. Conversation on most tables was stilted and polite. Raoul had deliberately done his best to ensure that guests were strategically placed to avoid cosiness.

He enjoyed watching Lady Daphnee being painfully civil to Della Dubois while her husband practised his schoolboy jokes on Mrs Tremaine and Maggie Maynard, both of whom treated him courteously and kept his wandering hands at a distance. Lady Laetitia was sandwiched between Dimitri and Dr. Tremaine, with Kittie and Clarrissa twittering away across the table to each other. For once, she did not have much to say for herself apart from the occasional, "And that Greek charm won't work on me, young man!"

Alistair, on the other hand, was secretly enjoying the tender caresses of a scarlet woman. Seated on his left, Della Dubois' right hand was gently massaging his thigh and roaming up and down his inside leg. "My, Alistair, you are a big boy!" she softly whispered in his ear. "I can see I've neglected you for too long." Though excited beyond belief, Alistair sat motionless, like a statue, carefully trying to avoid the gaze of his mother who was already totally displeased at this "ridiculous seating plan business". Her blood boiled visibly at the proximity of her son to the tarty temptress.

The only table that did seem fairly animated was the largest one consisting of Harriett Haversham, Sadie Finch, Father Antonio, Sebastian, Elise Beauchamp and Edith Moreau. Raoul became instantly curious. He was sure that he couldn't have put such an unlikely clique together. They all looked most suspicious. Gasps and whispers, the occasional raised voice and frequent, furtive glances around the room came from almost all the guests in the huddled circle as they practically ignored the mouth watering hors d'oeuvres in front of them and remained deep in desperate debate.

"What's that all about?" Raoul inquisitively asked, beckoning Grace Elisabeth to his side. She shook her head and shrugged her shoulders. "See if you can find out. But, Grace, don't be too obvious," he added.

The senior housekeeper knew her craft. She sidled around the tables, smiling and asking if guests wanted their drinks refreshed, as was her duty. When she came to the big table, she took her time, but her professional manner was such that no-one thought to stop the conversation or even suspect that her presence would be of any threat.

Continuing her rounds, Grace unobtrusively made her way back to Raoul who was waiting impatiently tapping his fingers on the bar. They stood together in a business like manner and surveyed the dining room, conversing as if they were discussing arrangements. "Well . . . they all seem to be moanin' about Miss Della," Grace dutifully began. "Sayin' how her behaviour is lettin' down the Island and they ain't gonna stand for it no more! They already complained to Lord Monty, but he just say she's part of life's rich travesty, whatever that mean."

"Tapestry, I think you mean, Grace," corrected Raoul.

37

"Well that too," she nodded. "Anyway, he ain't gonna do nothin'. I think he's quite fond o' that little lady, but they don't seem to know why!"

"Do you, Grace?" mused Raoul, studying his finger nails with deliberate casual interest. "Do you know why?"

"I ain't sayin' nothin'," she replied with a firm shake of the head, "'cos I ain't right sure of my facts. But I tell you one thing, Mr. Raoul, it ain't what people think it is, and that's for sure!"

Ever intrigued, Raoul resolved to mingle once again. He had deliberately arranged not to place himself at a specific table during the evening's events as he needed to be 'floating', a condition not wholly unfamiliar to him, largely as a result of his old school friend, Dr. Tremaine's, generous prescriptions, one might add. This, he termed, his medication. It allegedly controlled his occasional bouts of deep depression and mood swings, the causes of which were unclear to anyone else but himself. He did insist, however, that he 'did not do drugs' or overindulge in alcohol. He had managed to steer his alcoholic mother off the booze during his late teenage years. This had left deep and lasting images and he wasn't about to relive them.

The main courses were served and applauded, as were the sumptuous desserts, and during coffee, Rory O'Rourke was ushered out to take a bow for his breathtaking efforts which he graciously allowed his 'talented' staff to help take the credit for. Sebastian then openly hugged Rory in front of the guests as a gesture of thanks. To some, such unchecked affection was sending out definite signals, signals paving the way for further mischief! Raoul merely looked on with derision. The chef's false modesty and subsequent familiarity with Seb only fuelled the fire.

The 'Relaunch' had been a huge success and, no doubt, news would spread far and wide, bringing in more business to boost the Island's little economy. But not everyone was pleased. The thought of a possible influx of unchaperoned strangers snooping around the cobwebs of the close knit little community was already ruffling a few feathers.

By now, an uninhibited Della Dubois was really entering into the spirit of things, brazenly enjoying herself with the help of a constant supply of boozy beverages from her nearby 'friends'. Her uncouth language was fast becoming more and more unladylike until Lady Laetitia had had enough. Unapologetically, she rose abruptly from her seat and began to approach her prey in her usual bulldozing manner. Looking down her nose, she deafeningly offered Della one of her inimitable gems. "Foul mouthed people embarrass others. They aren't educated enough to use language properly. They possess a limited vocabulary and are totally unable to appreciate the value of words, their use, or their true meaning! You appear to be in that category, Miss Budois!"

There was silence. A dazed Della steadied herself, momentarily considered the comment, laughed right in Laetitia's face and then retaliated. "Really . . . ? When I want your opinion, I'll bloody ask for it! Now piss off and mind your own business, you pompous, interfering old witch!"

A towering Lady Lascelles instinctively raised her hand in anger, but then thought better of it, in such a public arena. Instead, she simply lifted her head in a dignified manner, turned around, and, nose in the air, flounced off in a blaze of contempt. But Della Dubois had made a big mistake, and that little contretemps would be something she would live to regret.

Still the centre of attention, unexpectedly, and somewhat unsteadily, though certainly undaunted, Della rose from her table and teasingly challenged those who dared to join her skinny dipping off the jetty. Gasps from some guests at her continued audacious, inappropriate behaviour were rivalled by cheers from others, mainly males, who were egging her on. Removing articles of clothing as she excitedly ran through the restaurant exit on to the beach, Della stumbled her way to the end of the raised platform leading to a deeper part of the beckoning sea.

Before anyone could join her, the voluptuous, fun loving party girl had splashed her way into the water and was swimming rather erratically out to a driftwood raft about 150 metres away. Anxious onlookers sighed with relief when she finally reached safety. Others offered vocal encouragement as she shamelessly started dancing around naked on the precarious platform, singing and waving a scarf in the air.

Then it happened; all of a sudden, without warning. The waves on the still evening seas rapidly became uncontrollably agitated. The lonely raft helplessly began to bounce increasingly more and more violently in the swirling waters.

From nowhere the deafening noise of a droning speedboat engine drowned Della Dubois' piercing screams as she realised it was heading straight for her. Within seconds it had passed. The driftwood had been sliced into countless floating pieces.

As the waters eventually calmed, silence filled the diesel fumed air. Only debris remained, bobbing up and down in the sullen sea. But to everyone's horror, there was conspicuously no sign whatsoever of the spirited, drunken swimmer.

Chapter 5

In disbelief, the commotion began. A cacophony of chaos ensued. Volunteers started to swim as fast as they could, heading for the floating driftwood which had splintered and splayed its way over the watery expanse where the raft once stood. Splashing aimlessly about and diving down into the depths, some of the Island's stronger swimmers frantically began a disorganised rescue operation.

Local fisherman, who had been enjoying the barbeque on the beach, suddenly found themselves haphazardly rowing around in a vain attempt to find their favourite Island pin up girl. Luckily, the clear, starlit sky and the strong moonlight made visibility easier.

Back on shore, the beach was littered with observers from the hotel and restaurant. Everyone gave the impression of being horrified, eager to establish exactly what had happened. Speculation had begun. Had the flighty floozy drowned? Was it just an unfortunate accident? Could someone have innocently or deliberately instigated Della Dubois' spontaneous wish to go skinny dipping? And, how come the speedboat suddenly appeared from nowhere? More to the point, to whom did the craft belong? But, the burning question on everyone's lips; who had actually been at the helm?

Panicking onlookers emotionally voiced their own fears, but some bystanders were silent. They just watched and waited. They had their own sinister and personal reasons for wishing to discover the ultimate outcome of this tragic event.

Furtive, guilty glances anxiously flitted between those guests from the big table, as they lingered, whispering in the shadows of the swaying palms. Raoul was playing detective, desperately trying to piece together who had already left the scene and when. Who was looking guilty, smug, pleased? He couldn't really tell.

No-one gave themselves away. One thing he knew for sure; all was not as it seemed.

Suddenly, the noise of the same speed boat engine was again heard in the distance. It was coming nearer. Everyone feared carnage as it approached swimmers, rescuers and boat crews. The closer it got, the more the boat decelerated, until it moored neatly alongside the jetty. The sinister helmsman was covered in a dark cloak, but stood his ground as everyone ran mob handed towards him.

Just as things were about to turn nasty, the cape was stylishly thrown off and there was a clustered gasp of incredulity. "And THAT is how to make an exit!!" triumphed a grinning Della Dubois with a taunting cackle that echoed relentlessly through the air.

There was a mixture of nervous laughter, cheering and raging contempt as she jumped on to the jetty. Certain Islanders found it almost impossible to hide their extreme anger, but considered it best not to make their feelings too public.

Someone dared, however! "Cheap, scheming, little slut. Risking people's lives. Won't get away with it next time," scowled the muffled voice, through clenched teeth, as the ominous threat disappeared back into the bewildered throng. "This time she has gone too far!"

Apparently, Curtis Parker, Elise Beauchamp's American partner, had helped Della Dubois in her latest attempt to be more spectacularly outrageous in her behaviour. He had been wheeling and dealing out on the yacht moored off the Island for several days, and involved in some heavy gambling. He had won the speedboat and, not wishing to miss a chance to utilise his vengeful sense of humour, had connived with his amorous admirer to stage some 'entertainment' guaranteed to enrage several prim and proper personalities he'd just been itching to get even with.

* * *

The following day began in silence. The birds didn't seem to want to sing. There was no wind, and even the waves appeared reluctant to dare make an unnecessary splash. A strange atmosphere languished in the air.

Slowly, the early risers began quietly undertaking some of the necessary clearing up activities, trying not to wake the more hung over revellers from the previous evening.

"Was that a dream last night?" Sebastian asked the Governor's wife who was already taking coffee in the hotel lounge. "Or did that flighty piece make fools out of us all again with her audacious antics?"

"That was certainly no dream Mr. Torrington-Chambers," replied Lady Daphnee curtly. "That was very real! The quicker she's removed from this Island the better. One way or another!"

With that, she got up, gave Seb a knowing stare, and brusquely left the lobby.

"And where did you disappear to last night?" Lady Laetitia demanded of her son at another table, during their regular morning refreshment in the hotel lobby.

"I, I n . . . needed s . . . some air after all that ex, excite, excitement and co . . . com, commotion," he finally explained. "So I w . . . went for a w . . . walk."

"With whom?" demanded his mother in an astonished, yet stern, tone of voice.

"On my own," he quickly blurted out, responding without his usual stammer.

Little did his mother know, that her precious son's drunken stroll had ended up in the dunes, where, paralysed with temptation, in the tranquillity and complete darkness and privacy of the grassy slopes and whispering waves, he had voluntarily been taken advantage of by a stranger. Without resistance, Alistair had enjoyed a long sensual, sexual encounter and breath taking massage which now, in his thoughts, seemed to merge into the qualities of an erotic dream.

The excitement and danger of anonymous sex, where no words were spoken, within a hazy feeling of semi drug fuelled euphoric ecstasy, both thrilled and frightened him. Someone had at last enjoyed the pleasures of his taut swimmer's build. It had been a very strange experience. Did it really happen?

* * *

Della Dubois was feeling quite pleased with herself, basking in the early morning sun, as she ostentatiously paraded across the soothing sands. "This should be interesting," whispered Raoul hoarsely to someone lounging half naked on the bed in his hotel apartment, while he endeavoured to perch precariously over the exquisitely ornate balcony balustrade on the upstairs terrace. "The ubiquitous Miss. Dubois and Sadie Finch are heading straight on course for each other!"

As the two women realised a confrontation was inevitable, they both slowed their pace, but then came within spitting distance. Sadie looked very threatening and prodded Della Dubois forcefully in the shoulder several times, obviously making a very strong point. The younger woman responded in a manner which suggested that she had the upper hand.

What was being said was hushed, but very meaningfully meant from the body language involved. Raoul strained to hear, but to no avail. Frustrated, he leaned further out, almost falling over the rail.

Sadie was obviously issuing a warning which had been treated with laughable contempt. All Raoul could make out was the last word, ending in 'male', as Sadie pushed by Della, almost tripping over her dog as she did so, and continued her walk with an angry stride.

Surely they couldn't be arguing over a man, Raoul thought to himself, and continued to ponder. He turned to relate his thoughts to his visitor, but the bed was empty. The bird had flown. Should he get involved and ask his flighty friend what it was all about, or stay well clear? After all, he really had enough on his plate at the moment with his own particular mission.

Later that morning, an obviously thrilled Sebastian came bouncing up the driveway with a big smile on his face, and a package under his arm. "And what have you been up to?" asked Raoul with a blasé air of mistrust.

"Been out to Colonel and Maggie Maynard's place," was the response.

"Does her husband actually exist, or is he a figment of her lurid imagination? I've never seen him!" sniped Raoul, with a disdainful smirk.

"Oh, he exists alright," replied Seb with an enigmatic smile. "Yes, been looking at some of Maggie's artwork. She's done some good stuff, you know. In fact, I've bought a couple. They'll look great in Reception! Local artist and all that."

"Let's have a look then," sighed Raoul with distinct disinterest.

With boyish pride, Sebastian eagerly began to unwrap the brown paper covering the two medium sized canvass pictures. Raoul knew Seb had a penchant for art, but didn't really credit him with much taste. This time he was intrigued. Both the colour paintings, in oil, depicted scenes on the Island, and even Raoul had to admit that "they had a certain something." But he didn't quite know what!

"That's obviously 'Cuddlers' Cove'," Raoul observed. "Quite lifelike really, I suppose. Must have been in winter she painted that, though. Those red flowers only bloom at that time of year . . . And that courting couple kissing remind me of someone. Wouldn't have picked black for the chap though . . . Yes, she's mucked that up. He looks as if he's wearing a frock!"

"Don't be picky. She's a good amateur!" defended Seb enthusiastically.

"The one of the beach and the nude female bathers rolling around is a bit racy," enthused Raoul.

"But, the long haired girl looks more like a man. The voluptuous blond seems familiar," he commented thoughtfully. "Still, they'll brighten up Reception, perhaps! Hope you didn't pay too much. I'll get Dimitri to hang them later," nodded Raoul with a cursory wave as he scurried off for his lunchtime break.

"Don't bother, I'll do it myself, now," offered Sebastian, unable to contain his passion.

The proprietor was really no handyman by any means, and as he struggled to place the paintings in their chosen positions, watched by a curious Della Dubois, on the pretext of her interest in art, he clumsily hit his thumb with the hammer and the picture crashed to the floor, landing at the feet of a tense looking Dimitri.

The odd job man had already overheard Seb's earlier conversation with Raoul, from a corner of the Restaurant during his coffee break, and had been showing more than a passing interest in what was going on. His eyes studied the illustration closely as he rushed to pick it up. "Here, I help," he said somewhat uneasily. "But, look! It's damaged," he instantly observed, pointing to a slit in the canvass which his finger nail seemed to be making worse as he lifted it.

"Funny. That must have happened when it fell. I didn't see the tear before," mused Sebastian, becoming mildly ill tempered.

"Oh I did!" chipped in Della Dubois.

"I take it to repair, and hang it for you later," gestured Dimitri, snatching the painting away somewhat hastily, as though he did not wish any unwanted observers to see it.

"Thanks," replied a bemused Seb.

"Was there something, Miss. Dubois?" whispered the hotel proprietor unwelcomingly to the loitering female, obviously annoyed at being shown up, especially in front of her.

"No, I'm fine, thank you," she replied condescendingly, in her usual irritating tone. Knowing, however, this was not the time to outstay her welcome, she slowly made her way through the lobby out into the hotel gardens.

"Could you just put the other one up for me then, before you go?" a slightly helpless Sebastian asked Dimitri.

"What other one?" enquired the Greek, somewhat mystified.

"The one on the . . . That's strange. I left it on the chair, there. Where's that gone then? You can't leave anything lying around nowadays. Surely, no-one would want to steal a simple scene of Cuddlers' Cove, painted by an amateur. It's not worth anything. It's just a picture," mumbled a distracted Seb in disbelief as he looked around Reception, acknowledging Father Antonio who was just leaving. The only other person around was Alistair, busily engrossed in his writing, as usual. "Hardly big time criminals, either of them," reflected Seb, as he scratched his head.

"You no having much luck with these paintings, eh?" commented Dimitri. "Perhaps they no meant to be for the eyes of everyone after all!"

"Telephone call for you, Mr. Sebastian," announced one of the secretaries from the office, obviously flustered.

"Go," motioned Dimitri. "I sort all this out later. No worry."

* * *

Since the previous evening, Edith had been on Raoul's mind. She wasn't herself, and he felt guilty leaving her the way he did. Still, she couldn't have stayed long, and she didn't even give them a song, half heartedly pleading that she had a sore throat. Frustratingly, Raoul wasn't able to telephone his friend as she didn't possess such a luxury, so he decided to trek up to her villa to see her in person.

Her front door was open, but there was nothing unusual about that. There was a woman's voice belting out a jazz number from the lounge. She must be alright, she's singing, he thought to himself. "Edith, ça va?" shouted Raoul cheerfully as he entered the sitting room. The unexpected sight that greeted him soon took the smile off his face and made him shiver with trepidation.

Edith was slumped back over the settee, clutching an empty bottle of red wine in one hand, and a used bottle of tablets in the other. He feared the worst. He knew she had been uncomfortable the previous evening. If only he had taken the time to speak to her to find out why.

Steadying his impulse to panic, Raoul rushed over and ham fistedly felt Edith's pulse. He couldn't be sure . . . Was she dead?

Chapter 6

As Raoul nervously examined the body, the front door of the villa creaked slowly shut, and he heard footsteps scurrying down the path. He was too shocked to get to the window quick enough to see whom they belonged to. He was also unexpectedly startled again as Edith suddenly began to feebly splutter and cough. She was alive!

"Edith, qu'est-ce qui s'est passé?" he blurted, trying to encourage some explanation. Her pale face looked blankly at him. Continuing to comfort her in French, he hoped for some reaction to her mother tongue, but disappointingly failed to inspire any coherent response.

Somewhat clumsily, Raoul then gently tried to raise Edith's head. This was probably quite the wrong thing to do, but he knew nothing about first aid, and he had to do something. Blood trickled onto his hand. It was soon clear that both the scarf, and curiously, the skin at the nape of her neck, were loose. Carefully easing her head back onto the sofa, he knew one thing; he had to get help, and quickly! But, where? How? Edith's villa was quite secluded and remote. He couldn't just leave her, barely conscious, on her own, could he?

Trying not to panic, Raoul ran to the front door and was instantly unable to believe his eyes. Dr. Tremaine was hurrying up the path on his bicycle. "How did you . . . ?"

"No time for that now!" immediately responded the Doctor in a business like manner. "There's no time to lose either!"

Since there was no hospital on the Island, the GP was the only hope for medical problems or emergencies. "I've radioed the mainland. There's an air ambulance already on its way. The weather's still o.k. so it should be here soon."

"She's been drinking, and the pills, surely . . . ?" Dr. Tremaine stopped his former school friend before he said any more.

"She's had a nasty knock on the back of the head. That's what I'm really concerned about!"

Edith drifted in and out of consciousness and mumbled incoherently, but in perfect English, without a trace of a foreign accent. Raoul looked mystified. Jimmy Tremaine remained calm and did what he could to make Edith comfortable and stop the flow of blood.

"What's going on, Jimmy?" he asked, looking the doctor straight in the face.

"I can't tell you, Raoul, I just can't, but we've got to get her off the Island as quickly as possible, and with as little fuss. This was an accident; she fell, alright!" he insisted, putting his hand firmly on a bewildered Raoul's shoulder. "Keep this to yourself. For Edith's sake. An accident . . . She fell . . . Nothing else!" he repeated coldly.

It all happened so quickly, and was so bizarre, that Raoul wondered if he was in his own nightmare and about to wake up at any moment.

As the noise of the helicopter propellers drifted away into the distance, Jimmy Tremaine led Raoul out of Edith's house, pulled the front door shut and accompanied the flustered res- cuer down the path. "Here's a prescription," said the Doctor, giving Raoul a knowing look. "These will help you calm down. You must be traumatised. Go to my wife at the Surgery. She'll dispense them for you. Take a few. Have a sleep and put this unfortunate accident out of your mind."

"But, what about Edith? She's my friend. I need to know."

"She's safe now, and in good hands. If she really is your friend, be content with that. Now go! And you know what to say. An accident! Ok? Don't mention anything unless you really can't avoid it." The medic then hastily got on his bicycle and disappeared as unexpectedly as he had arrived.

"What the hell are they mixed up in?" Raoul asked himself, remembering that it was he who had persuaded a discredited Jimmy Tremaine to come to the Island in the first place. Bring- ing his wife, a trained chemist and dispensing pharmacist, was an added bonus which more than suited Raoul's own ulterior motive.

49

Though the couple had been disinclined to leave their home in England, they really had no choice. It was an offer they just couldn't refuse. They had generously been promised a new life by their old chum on the tucked away Caribbean isle, and financial support. All the GP had to do was keep Raoul's 'medication' flowing on demand. It would seem all above board. Keeping it in the family, so to speak, no-one would ever be any the wiser.

Still extremely confused about Edith's plight, Raoul realised that there was nothing else he could usefully do to help her now. Reluctantly, he took Jimmy's advice and headed off in the direction of the Surgery, desperately trying to make some sense of the whole distressing affair.

* * *

"What time do you call this?" bellowed Sebastian as Raoul drifted aimlessly into Reception for the afternoon shift. He soon calmed down as he saw how pale and dazed the younger man looked. "Are you o.k.? You look as if you have seen a ghost. What's . . . ?"

"Yeh, yeh I'm fine. Don't fuss!" replied a tetchy Raoul, not wishing to explain. "I'm just a bit off colour, a little woozy, that's all. I'll be fine after a lie down. I simply need to rest." Sebastian had seen it all before.

"How many times have I told you about taking too much medication and mixing it," scolded the hotelier. "Get upstairs! You're an embarrassment. I'll speak to you later." Raoul didn't argue. He did as he was told.

"I tell you there *was*!" insisted Clarrissa as the sisters pretentiously sipped their afternoon coffee in the hotel Reception lounge. "A helicopter! It landed over past the dunes and then took off again. Did you see it Mr. Sebastian? And that yacht, that's gone now too. Perhaps it was watching something."

"Or s,s, som, some . . . one," boldly observed Alistair Lascelles, who was busily scribbling away notes at a nearby table.

"Don't take any notice of my sister, Mr. Sebastian. Yachts, speedboats, helicopters; whatever next?" chipped in Kittie, ignoring Alistair's remark and making derogatory gestures about her twin.

"What indeed?" contemplated the proprietor pensively, as he made his way purposefully into the office.

When Raoul came downstairs after his nap, rather than improving, his mood had darkened considerably, and the sight of Rory O'Rourke slipping into Sebastian's office was all he needed to publicly vent his feelings. He flung open the door, without knocking, and was greeted by the sight of Seb sitting at his desk with Rory's arm over his left shoulder. "Caught in the act, ay?" he bellowed, unashamedly drawing attention from startled passing guests.

"What the . . . Keep your voice down," pleaded Sebastian as he jumped up from his chair.

"There are residents just outside in Reception."

"And I give a shit?" roared Raoul, unflinchingly.

"Calm down! What on earth's the matter with you?" continued Seb, white as a sheet. "I really will have to talk to Jimmy about your mood swings and medication."

"I've got you two sussed," waded in Raoul once again, in an aggressive rage. "Old friends aren't we? Not just here by coincidence, are we, O'Rourke?" Rory looked mystified.

"I'm just signing my contract. The Relaunch went so well. Seb's making me permanent Head Chef now."

"Yeh? I bet he is! Still providing the same services as you used to before?"

"Have you taken complete leave of your senses? What are you talking about?" interrupted Sebastian.

"Do you want me to spell it out? I know about your seedy little antics before you came over here, O'Rourke." Rory went pale.

"I've . . . , I've left all that behind me now. That's history. Everyone's entitled to a past. I've been given a fresh start," he whimpered, retreating from the desk.

"And a convenient one at that, wouldn't you say?"

"I don't know what you mean," shrugged the apparently baffled chef, in his soft Irish lilt.

"So it's just a coincidence you're working for 'sugar daddy', again? Are you providing free dessert with your bloody main dish as well?" spat Raoul as he gripped Rory by the collar.

Sebastian physically intervened. "STOP! STOP right now! You've got it all wrong, Raoul."

"Do you deny knowing this 'young man' who used to call himself a 'masseur'?" Raoul thuggishly prodded his finger into Seb's chest to ram home his point.

"No!" replied Sebastian calmly, raising his hands in admission. "No. I know him alright, but not in the way you think. Rory looked dumbfounded.

"But I, I don't remember you," he stumbled defensively.

"Well, who do you think has been financing your fast track career and restaurants, lover boy, Santa Claus?" mocked Raoul in disbelief.

"I, I was just told it was a mystery benefactor, and not to ask any questions. I must admit though, I did assume that it might have been one of my grateful old regulars who'd popped his clogs and left me money or something," the youngster mumbled back, deep in reflection.

"He's right!" chipped in Sebastian, with a heavy sigh. "Yes, I am his mystery sponsor. It was me who set him on the road to success and financed his training and restaurants, but he was never meant to know."

"Oh yeh, that figures, but you decided to just keep him nearby for services rendered, huh, in case you felt like second helpings?" glared Raoul, still beside himself with rage.

"I did it because I owe him my life!" responded Sebastian softly, but deliberately. Even Rory looked shocked on hearing this startling piece of information. His vacant expression was a picture.

"Oh, come on! Not even HE believes that tripe," laughed Raoul. "Just look at his face!"

Sebastian turned to Rory and looked him straight in the eyes. "You see, it's all been my way of thanking you." O'Rourke continued to appear astonished, thinking he was being used as some sort of pawn in a domestic argument.

His heart pounding, Seb collapsed into a nearby easy chair to steady himself, and began to gradually explain. "Think back to one wet winter night in London . . . , about sixteen years ago. It was late. You witnessed a vicious attack in a Soho back alley. But, instead of walking the other way, like everyone else who didn't want to get involved, assuming it was some gangland feud, you risked your life and came to the aid of the poor sod left for dead in the gutter. You telephoned for an ambulance, waited, and made sure the victim was cared for. You didn't ask questions or take advantage of his obvious, yet incoherent, concern for anonymity after leaving such a dubious dive in the early hours of the morning. You just did what any upright citizen should do. You were a Good Samaritan. Think hard! Recognise me now? That chap was me!"

The Irishman stared hard at Sebastian. "Funnily enough, I did t'ink you seemed a bit familiar the first time we met . . . , at the interview . . . in your office . . . the other day, but I just dismissed the idea. Do you know, I've never t'ought any more about that incident. I was living rough at the time. It was dark. I didn't take much notice. I'd seen it all before. I just did what anyone else would have done."

"But no-one else did. Did they?" Seb reasoned. "You did. Only you had the guts to risk your life for me. That's why I decided that I'd make yours worth living for you . . . , if I could. It's a small price to pay."

There was a stunned silence. Although Raoul was still infuriated, he knew Sebastian well enough to sense that he was telling the truth. He was that kind of man. This was just the sort of overblown gesture he would have made.

"So then, gentlemen, that's that cleared up," concluded Seb, rather formally, appreciating that the atmosphere was still intensely strained. "And we'll say no more about it. Petty jealousies pale into insignificance in the circumstances, wouldn't you say? At least I'm still here, and alive, but I'm not worth squabbling over!"

He looked over to Raoul who just nodded, somewhat shame-faced, but secretly he respected Seb all the more for his unself-ish kindness. Rory needed to reconcile the whole affair in his own mind, and was about to question the issue when Sebastian announced, "That's an end to the matter then," opened the office door, and headed towards Reception.

Raoul gave Rory a stare that was both apologetic and venge-ful, but then hastily departed, leaving the Head Chef completely at a loss. As far as Raoul was concerned, the unwelcome intruder still posed a threat and he wouldn't rest until he was sent pack-ing. And he didn't care how!

Exhausted, mentally and physically, and still with ruffled feathers, a rattled Raoul slumped into the cosy hammock oppor-tunely placed for reflection in a shady corner of the tranquil garden. The comforting sun inspired him to begin to relax, while his thoughts drifted fondly back to the time he and Sebastian had first met.

As a well regarded interpreter in London, the linguist had begun working for Seb, a high flying entrepreneur, as his Per-sonal Assistant in the lucrative family business. It wasn't long before he assumed control of all the company's European com-merce deals, and began to travel with his employer on foreign trips, for both work and pleasure.

Quick to realise the potential to raise his own personal status and achieve a better, secure lifestyle, Raoul gradually became more and more invaluable to the mild mannered gentleman from very wealthy aristocratic roots, and artfully began to endear himself as a firm friend.

The couple struck up a close working relationship, contrived by Raoul, which developed nicely into a partnership and even-tually, though the P.A. was not totally that way inclined, drifted into becoming something more.

Initially, Sebastian's lifestyle had to be kept a secret from his powerful high society family, but gradually it became clear, especially to those who saw themselves as elder executives within the business, that Raoul was more than just his right hand man. In the absence of Sebastian's divorced parents, who initially founded the firm, and now lived separate, extravagant, carefree lives of their own, guardians stepped in.

Not wanting any scandal, senior directors dismissed the threatening employee from their high profile establishment, without warning, and continued to force Seb to accept the attentions of wealthy female suitors, in whom he clearly had no interest.

Uncharacteristically, Seb eventually stood up to his controlling dynasty. They had already hatched a plan to banish him and pay him off, if he persisted with his 'ludicrous perverted lifestyle'. He had to choose; his family and full inheritance and support, or Raoul who was already suspected of being a gold digger out to besmirch the Company name and its standing within the world of aristocratic commerce.

Seb, a hopeless romantic, felt that he had not only found a friend in Raoul, but a soul mate. For the first time in his life, there was someone just for him. Flattered and infatuated by his close companion's misguided attentions, Sebastian remained true to his heart, and decided to accept the more than generous financial pay off from his relatives. Though exiled, he would at least be able to fulfil his dreams and live his life with Raoul.

Missing his errant parents terribly, Sebastian had always insisted that money never meant that much to him; it was people who mattered. But, was he really going to be able to dispense with the elite and envied lifestyle that the family fortune could have ultimately afforded him?

Chapter 7

The church clock chimed ten. It was another warm, beautiful morning, with just a gentle breeze. You could hear the reassuring sound of the waves gently washing over the rocks below the cliffs at the end of Mrs Van Leiden's garden.

"Sadie, we're going to be late if you don't hurry," shouted the wealthy widow who had made a special effort to look her best that day.

"I'm coming Olivia. Aren't you in your wheelchair yet?" sniped her busy companion. "Come on! You know you can do that without my help," she jollied her along.

"Oh must I?" she whined pitifully. "It's so much easier when you support me."

"You mustn't rely on me so. You never know, I may not always be here," said Sadie somewhat reflectively.

"Of course you will!" laughed Olivia, dismissing such a notion.

They were soon on their way, with Sadie pushing the outmoded wheelchair up the gentle, pebbly slope towards the main complex, and Mrs. Van Leiden shading her face under one of her selection of fancy parasols. The Governor's office was only ten minutes away and was the Island's venue for anything of a legal or administrative nature.

The two women were warmly greeted in the hallway by Lady Daphnee who doubled as the Governor's secretary, as well as wife. "Good Morning, Ladies! If you'd like to follow me, the Governor is ready for you."

"I'd like to speak to him alone," announced Mrs. Van Leiden unexpectedly.

"You never told me," snarled Sadie with slight indignation.

"Oh, I'm sure I did, dear. Anyway, I don't have to tell you everything."

"Well, am I expected to hang around here all morning?" asked her carer rather resentfully. "I've got the dogs to walk. It's past their usual time already."

Sensing a potential atmosphere, Lady Daphnee diplomatically intervened and offered to guide Mrs. Van Leiden, and even see her home afterwards. This was quickly agreed and Sadie marched off in a mood, mumbling to herself. "Poor Miss Finch, she hasn't been herself lately, you know," confided Olivia sympathetically, as Daphnee wheeled her carefully down the winding corridor.

They stopped outside a big oak door. Lady Meadows knocked and they entered. "Mrs. Van Leiden to see you, Governor," announced his wife ceremoniously. The couple were both well educated people and believed in a bit of formality when necessary. Daphnee stood beside the Governor until Olivia's smile made it clear that she was not about to speak until they were in private. "Iced tea?" she then awkwardly asked on the pretext of trying to mask her faux pas. Both declined. "I'll leave you then," she smiled, as she went into the adjoining secretary's office.

"Well, what can I do for you, Mrs. Van Leiden?"

"Look at me, for a start!" she answered softly. Monty seemed somewhat bewildered, ill at ease.

"Beg pardon," he snuffled, choking on his pipe.

"I said, look at me!" she repeated coldly. "Look me straight in the face. Have I changed so much?"

Lord Montgomery still appeared vague. "Oh come on, Monty! I'm not sure whether you're being obtuse, or whether you really don't recognise me. All these years we've lived in such close proximity, and you have no inkling? I can't believe it! Still, your attention span never did last very long!"

Before the Governor could rebuke Mrs. Van Leiden's apparent rudeness, she helpfully jogged his memory. "Perhaps, you remember me better as 'Livvy'."

Monty Meadows coughed so hard on his pipe that Daphnee scuttled in from the adjoining room.

"Everything alright, my dear?" she asked apprehensively. Her eyes strayed uncomfortably into those of her husband who continued to splutter before promptly looking away in embarrassment.

"Perhaps a glass of water?" Olivia suggested with a half smile.

As the Governor slowly retained his composure, he dismissed his wife with a wave of the hand and slowly stood up, turning self consciously to the window. "Yes, that's right, look away," declared Olivia icily. "But when you turn around, I'll still be here. Not quite the same as when you were a dashing young attaché and I was a mere impressionable secretary in Brussels, though. When I turned around, pregnant, with your child, you definitely weren't there!"

Monty momentarily froze; then sheepishly manoeuvred to study the features of his former lover. Her face was a little more wrinkled, and her former golden locks were now finer and grey, but there was no mistake. It was her! It was Livvy!

"Well I never . . . ! Unbelievable the tricks life plays on one," he observed out loud, after several painful minutes of deathly silence. "How did you . . . ? Why didn't you . . . ?" he fumbled vulnerably.

"Never mind all that now," interrupted Olivia brusquely.

"But . . . , it was only one night," he reasoned, shaking his head in disbelief.

"Yes. So it was! One dance, one drink, one meaningless sexual encounter with one promise of everlasting love and affection, and then . . . one child. And where were you? 'Posted overseas'. Your chums clammed up. No clues, no answers. I had to get on with it on my own. Not easy in those days, I can assure you!"

Monty restlessly shuffled about his office, giving 'Livvy' sideways glances as he did so. He couldn't look her in the eye. "You say a child? What child?"

"Yes, ironic, isn't it," she continued. "Now, you're the pillar of the community, the Governor of the Island, the enforcer of moral standards, and you're not even married to that woman you call your wife. She's no more a 'Lady' than I am . . . ! And now you have an illegitimate child too. Oh, don't look so worried, man. I'm not here to reminisce and I haven't come to shop you either. What would be the point now, at our age? What would I have to gain? I've got enough money. What I haven't got, unfortunately, is my health, and you can't help me there. There is something you *can* do for me, however, and I want it carried out to the letter. Understand! To the letter! You at least owe me that."

Lord Montgomery conceded with a reassuring nod, and listened intently to Mrs Van Leiden's demands. "I am entrusting you with my Will. It is to be read out, exactly as written, at my funeral, whenever that may be. Only those invited are to attend, and you are to pay special attention to the part where my child is named . . . Yes, I said MY child. I am not naming the father, but you will finally discover who your child, now also living on this Island, is too, and you can then act according to your own conscience. It's up to you whether you make yourself known or not. BUT, if there is any deviation whatsoever from my wishes, I have instructed, let's just say a friend, to uncover the evidence that will incriminate you. Your instructions are in this envelope!"

"Livvy," said Monty reassuringly, "you look as fit as a fiddle. None of this may ever be necessary."

"Indeed," she replied with a sigh. "I may outlive you yet. However, provision must be made for our child and I'm planning ahead, so don't patronise me."

"And how do I know that it's MY child?" challenged Monty, half heartedly appearing to suddenly be affronted.

"You don't! But you can call my bluff if you like, it's up to you! Now call your 'wife'. She's seeing me home."

Almost instantly, Daphnee came into the main office, with her light shawl and hat, ready to wheel Mrs. Van Leiden home. "Productive meeting?" casually enquired the Governor's wife.

"Oh yes dear, very," smiled Olivia sweetly, giving it the 'dear little old lady' routine. "Just a bit of boring legal business, that's all."

As the ladies chatted amicably going down the pebbly cliff side path leading to Mrs. Van Leiden's house, Daphnee appeared to hit a stone with one of the wheels, lose her footing, and fall, forcing her to let go of the wheelchair, leaving Olivia speedily tumbling forward towards the edge of the precipice. Onlookers gasped in horror. No-one was near enough to help.

"That'll teach you, you bitch!" Daphnee whispered softly to herself, as she pretended to try and get up. "It'll also teach that fool, Monty, not to leave the intercom on! He's got some explaining to do."

Just when the wheelchair got within feet of the edge of the cliff, it gradually slowed down and stopped. Olivia had found an emergency brake. She held up her hand to relieved spectators to signal that she was alright. Foiled, Daphnee cursed bitterly.

By this time, Sadie, who had also witnessed the affair from the front bay window of the house, had come running out towards Mrs Van Leiden, feeling equally cheated that her 'employer' had survived what could have been such a useful accident.

As she drew closer, however, the colour really did drain from her face. She could see her 'friend' sitting motionless, eyes open, head back, staring straight ahead of her. Sadie quickly felt her pulse and gasped. Olivia really was dead! She had had a heart attack!

* * *

Within hours, news of the tragic accident had begun to circulate around the Island. Dr. Tremaine had officially pronounced Mrs. Van Leiden dead, and Lord Meadows was breaking into a sweat in his office at the thought of the administrative tasks that awaited him, as well as the emotional repercussions of their strangely recent meeting.

What was he to do? Risk it? Bluff it out and go through the normal formalities of an accidental death; funeral arrangements, public announcements, death certificate and such like? Or should he fulfil the promises he had made to his former lover only hours earlier, and carry out her wishes 'to the letter'? He stared at the sealed envelope on his desk and then, after some deliberation, decided to put it away.

Before Monty could manage to fiddle with the elaborate combination of the safe, unimaginatively hidden behind a picture on the wall, his door creaked open and he felt the presence of someone standing over his shoulder. He recognised the perfume and slowly turned round. It was his wife.

"Well! What are you going to do?" she smugly enquired.

"I'm sure I don't know what you mean, my dear," he spluttered, with his familiar nervous cough providing him with the opportunity to bury his head in his handkerchief.

"My darling Monty," she responded complacently, "next time you have a private appointment, switch your intercom button off first. It was a good job it was only me in the secretary's office, otherwise half the Island would know your sordid past by now," she continued, gradually raising her voice as she swiped him across the head with a magazine.

"So, so you heard? You know?" he asked, aghast. "Oh my God! You took her home. You were pushing the wheelchair. Dear Lord, you didn't . . . "

"Murder her?" whispered his wife calmly. "You'll never know, will you? It was a tragic accident. There were enough witnesses. Besides, she died of a heart attack. I couldn't do that now, could I? And Monty, even if YOU don't wish to know the identity of your child, I do! So I suggest you give me that envelope, and we'll take it from here, together!"

Chapter 8

It was six fifteen in the morning. Sebastian was first down to Reception, still yawning, but very aware of the sombre day ahead. Raoul closely followed, still getting dressed as he did so. Some of the cleaning staff were just making final adjustments to the flowers and rearranging the lobby to give a suitable ambiance for a meeting place prior to a funeral. No-one spoke as a mark of respect. The smell of ground coffee wafted from the kitchen area, and there were croissants available for those who wished to eat before the ceremony.

The clock struck half past six and mourners were beginning to gradually arrive. Dressed in black suits and ties, the gentlemen all looked very dapper. It was still the custom on the Island for female mourners to also be attired completely in black, and outfits ranged from the plain to high fashioned elegance as the ladies took the opportunity to try and outdo each other, even in these circumstances. Hats and veils that had not seen service since the last funeral had been retrieved, brushed off, and cleverly accessorized for maximum effect. Dual purpose, dark sunglasses were shrewdly being worn both as a fashion statement and to mask the reactions of the mourners, ranging from grief and sorrow to utter boredom and inquisitiveness.

"Funny old business, this," insisted Clarrissa to her sister. "I've never been 'invited' to a funeral before."

"There must be a reason for it," responded Kittie. "I wonder what it is."

"I didn't even know her that well," chipped in Maggie Maynard.

"Husband not with you?" asked Mrs. Tremaine.

"No. He wasn't invited, funnily enough. He wouldn't have come anyway. He doesn't get out of bed before noon."

"Well at least she was thoughtful there," reassured Clarrie. "A funeral in the full heat of the day would not have been any fun," she innocently confided. "Not that it's meant . . . to be . . . , of course," she hesitated, somewhat embarrassed at what she had just said. "Well, you know what I mean!" Kittie was too busy watching everybody else to rebuke her sister, so just rolled her eyes in derision.

Father Antonio arrived in full ceremonial robes at five minutes to seven precisely; and exactly five minutes later the Church bell began to ring, solemnly calling mourners to the funeral.

Ironically, the only full stretch limousine on the Island, previously used for lascivious fun by Della Dubois, was now taking Olivia Van Leiden to her final resting place.

As the day began to awaken, Father Antonio slowly led the cortege up the narrow, winding, sandy pathway to the Church graveyard, where the service was to be conducted in the open air, as requested. The solitary bell continued to ring at short, regular intervals.

Sebastian and Raoul walked immediately behind the car, followed by a sniffling Sadie Finch, who, at times, could not contain her grief, real or otherwise. Lady Lascelles, Alistair, Harriett Haversham and Lady Daphnee came next, walking at a snail's pace, with Maggie Maynard, Kittie and Clarrie, closely on their tail. Elise Beauchamp and Grace Elisabeth Hickory lingered respectfully behind the stragglers.

" 'Ere wait for us!" shouted a familiar voice as Della Dubois, struggling in stilettos, came running up the pathway, still buttoning up her tight black blouse which outlined her ample bosom and nearly reached the hem of her black mini skirt. With her was an unshaven Dimitri, whose greasy, scraped back, black hair, tied in a pony tail, and open shirt did not really give him an appropriate image for such an occasion. "Nevertheless, they must have been invited," pointed out Clarrissa, as others began to react in disgust at their lack of reverence.

The religious part of the service was quite quickly dispensed with in the shade of some much appreciated trees. As instructed by Mrs. Van Leiden herself, there were no hymns, just a few prayers to send her on her way, and a reading from the Bible.

The mourners were each invited to throw some sandy earth onto the coffin, as it was gently lowered deep into the ground. As they did so, everyone questioned the reason for their own presence at the event. Sadie Finch was Olivia's only true companion; the others were merely acquaintances, if that. Nobody else really knew Olivia Van Leiden. Just why were they there?

When it appeared that the Ceremony was coming to an end, Lord Montgomery, who strangely had already been at the grave-side before the coffin arrived, cleared his throat to speak;

"Ladies and Gentlemen, Thank you for attending the funeral of Mrs. Olivia Van Leiden.

Many of you only knew her by sight, in a rather casual fashion, as a fellow member of the Island community. But, on the very morning of her tragic accident, she came to my office and spoke to me privately about her Will and her personal wishes for funeral arrangements, whenever they should be necessary. Unfortunately, fate intervened all too soon, in the cruellest of ways, as it often does, and not even Mrs. Van Leiden realised the imminence of her actions."

At the mention of the word 'Will', everyone's ears pricked up, and those who had been less than enthusiastic about attending the occasion seemed to show a greater interest and reverence; some even managing a sniffle or two to highlight their grief for their dear departed 'friend'.

"Mrs. Van Leiden wished me to open this sealed envelope in front of you all, as I am responsible for the legal administration on the Island," he continued formally, holding up a large brown packet. "And to read exactly what is written, as it is written. I have no previous knowledge of its contents."

The Governor began to nervously tear at the top of the envelope, while the small congregation stood silently in anticipation of what they were about to hear. Some of the ladies began to gently flutter their fans in front of their faces to disperse the heavy air and create a slight breeze.

Lord Meadows cautiously tugged at several pages of what looked like handwritten parchment paper, until he was finally in a position to put everything in order, and ready to begin. Sweating profusely, he wiped his forehead with a cotton handkerchief. Some of those present could endure the waiting no longer and restlessly began to fidget and cough impatiently.

"This is the last Will and Testament of Olivia Van Leiden.

I have lived among you, on our small Island for many years, and have always been treated in a polite and pleasant manner by all concerned. I have, however, always considered myself to be on the outskirts of the community, somewhat of an outsider, and have made few real friends. Being somewhat restricted in my wheelchair, I have had very little opportunity to visit many of you, or attend the various social gatherings which have taken place. Unfortunately, only a few of you have ever taken the trouble to come to see me, yet there has regularly been an open invitation to do so. I hope you do not begrudge visiting me on this last occasion, therefore.

I have always observed, and taken a keen interest in those around me, and have, therefore, as you may expect, built up quite a comprehensive picture of most of you, without your knowledge, of course."

At this stage, certain individuals began to feel rather uneasy. Furtively, they glanced around at each other. There was an obvious air of nervous embarrassment and apprehension. Eyes met uncomfortably across the open grave, which the gravediggers had been instructed not to touch, until they were told to do so.

"I thought that might get your attention, but don't worry, because most of my secrets, and yours, will go with me to my grave." There seemed to be an overwhelming sigh of relief. "But, if you are troubled, think about what it is that you have to hide and why," Olivia's thoughts continued.

"I have asked the Governor of the Island to act as Executor of my 'Will', which is now to be made public to you." All eyes became fixed on Sadie Finch, who could not help but stand proud in grief, ready to become the main focus of attention. "This is, however, my second Will, because the first was changed in the light of some recent information." Sadie's face went pale with uncertainty and anxiety. What had Olivia discovered?

Lord Meadows read on; "Formerly, my finances and estate were to be shared among two recipients, albeit unequally. Now, everything I own will go to one person in this gathering . . . MY CHILD."

There were gasps of incredulity. Mrs. Van Leiden didn't have a child; everyone knew that. She was a childless widow when she arrived on the Island. Sadie, bewildered and weak, had to be supported by Sebastian. She had known Olivia for thirty years. She was aware she had married late in life, but there had never been mention or sight of a child.

Grace Elisabeth's eyes met Father Antonio's, briefly, and then swiftly moved on to Lord Monty's. The Governor remained composed, lowered his head and averted his gaze, staring but not seeing. He then slowly looked up again, and proceeded.

"Knowing that this information may not be believed, I am not prepared to name the father, but he too lives on this Island. His identity can be vouched for by Lord Meadows, in whom I have confided and provided proof. He is, however, sworn to secrecy and can only verify any such claim, should it be made." All eyes were on Monty who slowly nodded his head, feeling the weight of Daphnee's piercing stare aimed directly at him.

At this stage, the proceedings began to degenerate into a free for all, with jostling, shouting and shrieking, until Lord Meadows resumed order some minutes later, reminding those present they were in a cemetery, at a funeral. Several of the more astute mourners had already started to work out who the 'child' might be, and dreaded their conclusions. The possibilities were too unthinkable to say out loud.

Continuing to perspire uncontrollably, with a mixture of nerves and the effects of the rising heat of the day, Monty bravely resumed, though somewhat hesitantly and hoarsely; "I . . . hmm . . . I spent several years trying to trace my child. Unfortunate circumstances had previously forced me to put the infant up for adoption, because I was sadly not in a position to be a mother. The trail of heartache eventually led me here, to this Island, where I have been a guardian from a distance. I did not interfere in my child's life, and beg forgiveness for not making myself known or trying to put things right. There would have been no point. My offspring and I would not have seen eye to eye. It would have been too late, and caused too much pain and anguish for all concerned.

It is up to the father now, should he outlive me, to bear the burden of watching over our child. It is also up to him whether he wishes to make himself known."

By now, the penny was beginning to quietly drop with some of the more astute mourners until Sadie, unable to control herself any longer, hysterically shouted, "It's HER. My God, it's HER!" as she lunged forward at a strangely subdued Della Dubois.

Sebastian, instead of physically holding Sadie up, was now holding her back; restraining her from doing herself, or the object of her anger, any harm. "Montgomery! Is she right?" challenged Lady Lascelles, in a voice which commanded immediate silence and respect.

Apprehensively reading on, the Governor slowly bowed his head, wrestling to believe the words on the paper before him. "Yes," he eventually muttered nervously. "Yes, she is right. The recipient of Mrs. Van Leiden's whole estate is DELLA DUBOIS!" Confirming the news, he once again lowered his tearful eyes to the grave.

"Then God help us all!" muttered Laetitia, "She's one of the most despicable people it has ever been my misfortune to meet. Give her a fortune and there will be no redemption!"

For a moment there was a stunned silence. Everyone was shell shocked . . . until; "YIPPEE! All that money! Just think what I'll be able to do now! The influence I shall have! And money talks," screamed the voluptuous vamp in an excited, though rather childish, mocking tone at the bewildered group of Islanders. "It also commands respect," she added, in a sombre, more deliberate fashion, seen by some as a veiled threat. "So, you lot who've been looking down your nose at me for so long, you'd better have a double brandy at 'Mummy's' wake, because you're going to need it ! Unfasten your girdles girls, 'cos you'll soon be gasping for air!"

"Callous cow!" muttered Kittie. "Not a thought for her dear, departed mother."

"Well, I suppose she was just an acquaintance like anybody else," replied Clarrie in thoughtful defence. "She didn't really know her, did she?"

"You won't get away with this, you hard nosed, little bitch," shouted Sadie, still beside herself with rage. "I shall contest this Will."

"Well, your crystal ball never saw that one coming. Did it?" laughed Della Dubois raucously in reply.

"No, but has it dawned on you that you've been blackmailing me all this time with your own money!" seethed Sadie, whispering right into the new little rich girl's face, well out of earshot of the others. "Ironic that, and after today's events, nobody knows what's round the corner, do they?"

"No, they don't!" responded the heiress in an equally menacing manner. "And even though I don't need your money anymore, I can still watch you squirm, just for the fun of it. You never know when my mouth may run away with me."

"Think I care!" lashed out Sadie. "I've got nothing to lose now, so watch your back."

"Oh, by the way," snarled Della Dubois with a devilish grin, as she flounced off, by now in her bare feet, carrying her high heels. "As a token of all you did for my mother, I'm prepared to give you at least a week to sling your hook out of my new home. After that, I'll have you thrown out!" she menacingly warned, looking confidently straight at Dimitri, who had apparently, suddenly and voluntarily, assumed the protective role of her 'minder'.

Lord Meadows again tried to regain control, but several 'mourners' had already begun to depart in disgust, and the funeral had disintegrated into verbal fireworks. He nodded to the grounds men to cover the coffin. "Just as Livvy would have wanted it," he quietly sighed to himself. "Going out with a bang, figuratively if not literally! Good-bye, my dear," he whispered tenderly, as a tear rolled slowly down his cheek. "I'm sorry!"

"Bit late for all that sentimentality now, isn't it, Monty?" commented Daphnee tersely, feeling a strange mixture of sympathy and anger towards her husband, as she pushed past him to leave.

The Governor tried to formally conclude the ceremony by stating that anyone with any just cause to oppose the Will should present themselves at his office within the next two weeks. "I'll be there in the morning, and you'd better have some answers," shrieked Sadie as Sebastian and Raoul escorted her through the Cemetery.

The Island was rife with gossip and conjecture for the rest of that day. People scurried busily from one to another, offering their personal thoughts and opinions about the latest state of affairs. Sadie was afforded sympathy by some, but generally there was anger and suspicion in the small community. The discovery that certain Islanders seemed privy to more confidences than they had been letting on did not bode well. Could anybody be trusted?

Skilfully playing one off against the other, the gossips would now only be content with the answer to one single question. Who WAS Della Dubois' father?

Chapter 9

First thing next morning, true to her word, Sadie Finch was impatiently waiting in the hallway of the Governor's office. "She's been here for over an hour, pacing up and down," warned Daphnee, as Monty slipped in through the side door.

"Oh dear, I'd better see her right away then and get it over with," he decided. "By the way Daphnee, where were you yesterday night? I waited at dinner for you."

"That's my business!" she curtly replied.

"The Governor will see you now, Sadie," announced Lady Daphnee apprehensively as she showed her into his office. The frustrated visitor discourteously brushed by Lady Meadows without a word, and pushed the door open for herself. Simmering with rage, she then stood in front of the carefully positioned desk, glaring at Lord Meadows. "Well!" she spat. "Are you in on this little charade too? You should be ashamed of yourself! You're the Governor of this Island, and you represent all that's right and just, or you should do!"

"Haven't had time to calm down yet then, my dear?" Monty nonchalantly chanced his arm.

"Calm down? Calm down?" she slowly raised her voice. "I suppose you are going to get a nice little backhander from that flighty piece too. Or perhaps you'll be paid in kind," she taunted. Monty spluttered and shuddered with embarrassment at the thought of that particular issue. "She probably thought up this whole scam and blackmailed poor Olivia into making that so called 'Will.' What dirt did she have on her then? And more importantly, what has she got on you to make you go along with it?"

"Sadie, Sadie, Sadie, you're barking up the wrong tree," snuffled Monty through his handkerchief.

"You knew that inheritance was mine. Everyone knew!" she continued, banging her fist on the table.

"And so it was, my dear," admitted Monty, "in the first Will."

"What do you mean?" asked Sadie incredulously. "In the FIRST Will?"

"Mrs Van Leiden became suspicious a while ago, when you were withdrawing too much money from her bank account. She was very upset. She had trusted you with access to her funds, and couldn't believe that you would repay her by ripping her off, so she reluctantly decided to alter her Will. She really had no intention of even acknowledging that Della Dubois was her daughter before that. She was merely going to leave a small amount, anonymously, in trust. In fact, she disliked her intensely, but felt that as her biological mother, she should make some contribution to her life."

"Well, well, that frivolous, little bitch has well and truly stitched me up. I was only withdrawing extra amounts, here and there, because SHE was blackmailing ME in the first place."

"What about?" tentatively enquired the Governor.

"That's of no consequence now, but since you represent law and order on the Island, I am making an official complaint that I was being blackmailed by Della Dubois. It's up to you to investigate the matter and therefore annul the second Will. I bet it wasn't even witnessed, and if it was, I should very much like to know who by!" ranted Sadie furiously.

She then shrewdly took a more intimidating stance. "If you fail to act, I shall have no hesitation in contacting the Authorities on one of the bigger islands, and I don't have to spell out the implications of that now, do I?" she casually threatened. "It will cast a big shadow over your ability to independently control this community. And who knows what skeletons they'll find in your cupboard. One thing's crystal clear. There's certainly more to this than meets the eye and I intend to find out what, and do something about it, one way or another." After her tumultuous tirade, Sadie savagely swung open the Governor's office door and stormed off down the corridor.

"The plot thickens," commented Daphnee glibly as she slowly sidled in through the secretary's entrance, making it clear that she'd heard every word. "And I don't give much for your chances of coming out of this unscathed!"

"Well it's a good job I've got you by my side then, isn't it my dear, 'LADY' Meadows," asserted Monty, obviously shaken. "Or have you forgotten how your life would change too?" Daphnee thought a while and then replied pensively.

"Yes, I suppose I had better stick with you on this one, though Lord knows why! So, we need to do something constructive, and quickly. At the moment, all that conniving cow, Della Dubois, is thinking about is the money, but it won't be long before she tries to establish who her real father is. Then she'll try to squeeze him dry as well. In fact, she may have more intelligence than we give her credit for and be working it out already."

"But what can we do? After all, she's my own flesh and blood. She's . . . my . . . daughter," shuddered Monty unpalatably.

"Oh, don't go all moral on me now," replied Daphnee. "Remember who you're talking to! We're talking survival of the fittest, or at the very least, damage limitation. She'd have no qualms in bringing you down, so we'd better come up with a plan . . . and fast."

* * *

Della Dubois pretentiously paraded through the Reception of the Royal Palms Hotel with Dimitri struggling behind her, laden with suitcases and bags. She had quite an air of her own importance and waved staff aside as she swept up the stairs as if she owned the place.

"What the bloody hell's she doing here?" barked a stunned Sebastian through the open door of the office.

"That's not the kind of language our guests pay to hear," mockingly rebuked Raoul, busily on duty at the desk.

"Well they'll hear a damn sight worse if you don't answer my question!" continued Sebastian as he furiously got up from his desk and moved towards his partner. The mere mention, let alone the presence, of the woman seemed to bring out the worst in the normally mild mannered Seb.

"She's booked the Penthouse Suite?" announced Raoul calmly.

"And who on earth let her do that?" snarled Seb, closely studying the reservations diary.

"I did! Forgive me, but this is a hotel, n'est-ce pas?" stated Raoul rhetorically.

"Yes. But not for the likes of her! We have standards to uphold. We don't want her lowering the tone. Besides, she hasn't even got the bloody money yet, and she won't have, either, if I've got anything to do with it."

"What's it got to do with you? It's not like you to meddle in other people's affairs," noted Raoul.

"I want her out of here as soon as possible," ordered Seb forcefully. "You checked her in. You get her out. Tell her we're double booked or something. And, Raoul, you stay away from her. You know what I mean!"

"Yeh, just like you staying away from that bloody so called 'chef'," snapped Raoul with feeling, as Seb walked back into his office.

* * *

"Good Morning, is that the Penthouse? Is that Miss. Dubois?" said the voice on the end of the telephone.

"This is she," was the rather self important reply. Raoul laughed.

"This is Reception, Madam."

"Oh, Ra," she giggled recognising his voice. "I could get used to this. What's the problem?"

"How did you know there would be a problem?" Raoul questioned with a grin.

"Because they follow me around, darling!" she stated with an air of experience. "Don't tell me. Seb's got his knickers in a twist about me staying here."

"Correct! He's asked me to give you your marching orders," sighed Raoul apologetically.

"Tell him where to stick them!" she responded, resuming her arrogant attitude. "I'm a paying guest."

"But that's just it, I'm afraid, honey, you aren't. You haven't got a penny of that money yet, and who knows when, or if, you will," Raoul respectfully reminded his friend, getting straight to the point.

"Stall him for me, Ra, please," she whined seductively. "Give me a week to sort things out. Besides, I'm planning a soirée at the weekend. I want to show those cynics what style really is."

"O.k., I'll do my best to occupy him in some other way, but I can't promise," suggested Raoul as he mechanically put down the telephone, carefully contemplating his next move.

"Sorted it, or do I have to do it myself?" asked Sebastian as he burst back into Reception.

"Let's say, I've compromised. I've given her a week. And, before you start, she's already paid for that, and also intends to hold a 'do' at the weekend, so it's all good business. Who knows who will turn up and generate further bookings?"

Before Seb could object or consider the matter properly, Raoul casually chipped in with his trump card. "By the way, have you done those financial returns yet? You know they're urgent and have to be sent off when Elroy comes back."

It worked! Sebastian was very fussy about the finances of the hotel, and immediately headed back into the office looking worried and preoccupied.

* * *

"Whatever's this?" Sadie asked Harriett curiously. Both of them had been handed envelopes with their names on, by the hotel doorman, as they passed by on their morning walk along the beach with the dogs.

"I don't believe it! The woman's got the cheek of the Devil!" exploded Sadie on opening her sealed envelope. "Listen to this!"

she angrily nudged her dawdling friend who was too deep in thought to open hers.

"Miss. Della Dubois requests the pleasure of your company for a soirée of music, dancing and fun, at the Penthouse Suite of The Royal Palms Hotel, this Saturday from 8pm. A free buffet and bar will be provided. R.S.V.P."

"I'll give her bloody fun!" fumed Sadie. "And look, there's something handwritten on the bottom of mine. What's it say? 'You would be . . . advised to attend!' Open yours, Harriett!" she aggressively instructed.

"Oh dear! Yes. It's exactly the same. Oh no!" sighed Harriett in dismay. "I just couldn't stand to be in the same company as that dreadful woman again. Bloody hell," she whined. "I've got the handwritten bit too. Whatever is she thinking of?"

"Well, she's not intimidating me!" exclaimed Sadie belligerently. "If she wants me there, I'll be there. But she'll be sorry! My God will she be sorry!"

"Oh, do be careful, Sadie," warned Harriett anxiously. "The handwritten bit sounds ominously like a threat."

"Well, are you going then?" asked Sadie in a forceful tone which suggested Harriett really didn't have much option.

"Oh I suppose I shall have to, but I don't want to," whimpered her dog walking companion. "Perhaps we'll find out who her father is."

"Time to talk to the others, I think," concluded Sadie with conviction. "Let's turn it to our advantage and make her wish she'd never started all this nonsense in the first place."

* * *

Over the next few days, the same Islanders who had attended Olivia Van Leiden's funeral all received similar invitations. Reactions varied. Lady Laetitia contemptuously threw hers straight in the bin and warned her son that he had no say in the matter. He was simply not going. Luckily, Alistair had already surreptitiously managed to tear off a saucy handwritten message alluding to his night of passion on the beach, and the

75

consequences of it becoming common knowledge. The strange wording of the note had, however, sent arousing tingles down his spine . . . "I *saw* you . . . " implied that his sexual encounter had not been with the lover he thought he'd been with. Oh it was all still so hazy. Just whom had he shared those intimate moments with?

Lord and Lady Meadows became very tense and dubious, for obvious reasons, but Daphnee was determined to go all the same. Any reaction to the contrary might arouse unnecessary suspicion. Kittie couldn't wait, for this was obviously to be the source of more gossip, while dear Clarrissa thought it was lovely that she'd been asked to a party.

Father Antonio was initially uncharacteristically indecisive, but ultimately felt that he should attend, in case Harriett needed support. Elise Beauchamp's partner, Curtis, insisted they go, much against her wishes to the contrary, since it was a sin to miss a good party. "And boy, does this one sound as if it's gonna be one hell of a good party," he enthused.

Grace Elisabeth was not sure whether her invitation was in the capacity of work or pleasure. Sebastian reluctantly concluded that he and Raoul should be there, but only in their role as proprietors of the hotel, to keep an eye on things, and nothing more. Maggie Maynard and Dr. and Mrs. Tremaine sensed that it would be rude to decline, but the Colonel sent his apologies, fuelling more rumours, much to Maggie's annoyance, that it was indeed he who was the long lost father of the party's hostess.

* * *

That day, Raoul decided to spend his carefree early afternoon break on the private beach just in front of the hotel. Strolling aimlessly along the sandy pathway to the waterside, carrying his towel and trunks, his curiosity suddenly became aroused by a faint sobbing coming from one of the secluded grassy areas sheltered by a clump of lush green bushes; a favourite spot for nude sunbathing.

As he drew closer, he wondered why the lady standing with her back to the dunes, looking out to sea, seemed so upset. "D. D." he softly announced, using her pet name, as he gingerly approached, carefully wrestling with the overgrown shrubbery. "What's the matter?"

When the female turned around, recognising his voice, Raoul could see that he had been mistaken, and that it was Elise. "Are you o.k.?" he gestured sympathetically, holding out his hand. Much as she tried, Elise could not hide her tears. "Is it Curtis?" he hesitantly enquired, putting a reassuring arm around her.

"Oh, how did you guess, Ra! It's always bloody Curtis," she confirmed, puffing on her tobacco through quite a distinctive cigarette holder. "I don't know why I bother with him. All he ever does is give me heartache."

"Is there anything I can do to help?" Raoul asked awkwardly, consoling his tearful friend as best he could.

"Not really," she continued to sob. "It's his gambling again. He's been on one of the other islands and lost more than we can repay. It won't be long before we find him floating in the sea, considering the types he mixes with."

"I'm sure he'll sort it. He always does," comforted Raoul. "By the way, Elise, that's a classy cigarette holder you've got there. Is it new?"

"Yeh, it was an anniversary present from Curtis. Probably won it gambling, but I like it all the same." Raoul knew where he'd seen it before, but he didn't comment further.

"Come on, let's have a swim. Race you to the water," he unexpectedly challenged, trying to break the tension.

"Be with you in a minute, Ra. Let me just get myself together," responded his workmate more cheerfully, laughing at his boyish enthusiasm.

As she turned to gradually gather her things, a pre-occupied Elise sensed an unwelcome presence. The palms swayed unnaturally and the surrounding bushes then briefly shook, as if an animal had scuttled through them. The young woman suddenly experienced an eerie shiver. Still in a daze, she took no notice, but did vaguely wonder about what sounded like uneven footsteps fading away from the secluded spot.

Within seconds, the gentle swishing of the nearby waves in the strengthening breeze had confusingly masked whatever other intrusive noise there was and so, continuing to daydream about her problems, Elise slowly strolled towards the beach and thought no more about it.

* * *

"I never really realised what glamorous people Dr. and Mrs. Tremaine are," commented Clarrissa as the couple sauntered through the hotel lobby later that afternoon.

"Can't say I've noticed," mumbled Kittie with disinterest, as she sipped her ice tea. What better place for the twin sisters to 'people watch' and pick up gossip than a regular afternoon rendezvous in the Salon de Thé, situated right near the busy hotel Reception desk. "I suppose he scrubs up well. In fact, he's not bad looking for a doctor, that is. But she's nothing special," Kittie finally conceded.

"Afternoon, Raoul," greeted a chirpy Jimmy. "I'm booked in with Dimitri at three, for a massage. Alicia is going to relax in the spa. We've both been a bit tense lately and could do with some pampering."

"O.k. Jimmy, I'll just ring down and make sure he's ready for you. Alicia, if you'd like to go on through . . . ," advised their friend with a playful wink.

Raoul could receive no response by telephone, so becoming rather irritated that he had to exert himself, the duty receptionist had no alternative but to go down to the basement beauty salon himself and check that Dimitri had not forgotten the doctor's appointment.

Hastily entering through the swing doors of the massage parlour, Raoul found Dimitri, bare chested, clearly in a state of arousal, lying back on one of the beds in just his skimpy shorts, his eyes closed deep in ecstasy. "Why you stopped?" moaned the frustrated masseur, in a lazy whisper, unaware of the unexpected company.

"What the hell are you doing is more the question?" demanded his flustered boss, unable to remove his eyes from the young man's provocative pose. Dimitri jumped in surprise, covering his excitement with both hands. "You've got work to do! Remember, Dr. Tremaine, 3 o'clock, massage? Get your act together Dimitri. Guests don't like to be kept waiting!" The Greek hunk was about to excuse himself when Raoul intercepted. "Leave it. I've heard it all before! Just be grateful it's me and not Seb, or you'd be out on your ear." Dimitri lowered his eyes with a smug smirk of satisfaction. He knew the real reason his boss was so angry.

Before Raoul could leave, the changing room exit door clicked shut behind him, signalling that there had obviously been someone else in the Parlour, eager to leave without being seen. Raoul just scowled at Dimitri who was already preparing himself for his massage session, and ran back upstairs to invite Jimmy to his appointment, apologising for the slight tardiness.

Dr Tremaine lay on his stomach and Dimitri set to work. "You very tense, Doc. Muscle tension, too much stress. Too much work. You need more time with Dimitri," joked the masseur in a bid to lighten the mood. They continued to chat amicably and then Jimmy moved over onto his back, in a sleepy, relaxed, comfortable euphoria, while Dimitri continued to work his magic.

For all his sloppy ways, the young Greek was an acknowledged excellent masseur, and that was the main reason his services were retained. His popularity with the women, especially, made him slightly indispensable, and privately, certain men found his alluring ways irresistible too. Something he was all too ready to exploit!

As Jimmy was enjoying his post massage snooze, in just a small towel, which was all part of Dimitri's technique, the masseur went to fetch himself a drink from the bar, but quickly returned when he heard the sound of raised female voices. The fracas could clearly also be heard from Reception, so Raoul raced down to find an agitated Mrs. Tremaine, an embarrassed husband, a smiling Della Dubois and a sheepish Dimitri. "Please lower your voices," counselled Raoul as he took control of the situation. "Now, what's going on?"

An unusually angry Alicia tearfully blubbered, "I came in here to collect my husband and found HER pawing him all over."

"Darling, it's nothing like what . . . "

"Shut up, Jimmy!" yelled his normally placid wife, not allowing any opportunity for excuse or explanation.

"It's just a complete misunderstanding," insisted Della Dubois, calmly. "I came down to the Parlour for my 4pm massage appointment and could only find a sleeping Dr.Tremaine. I tried to rouse him . . . "

"More like AROUSE him!" interrupted Alicia, quite out of character.

"And then SHE comes in and starts hurling abuse at me," continued Della unapologetically. "I only wanted to know where Dimitri was."

Raoul was beginning to lose his patience and gave Dimitri the evil eye again. "And where were you exactly?"

"I go for drink upstairs. Massage, thirsty work. Leave client sleeping, quite normal procedure," he responded with arrogant confidence.

Raoul tried to persuade Alicia Tremaine that this was a plausible explanation, but she simply dismissed the affair as laughable, leaving the premises in a rage, completely losing her normally cool, meek and mild exterior. She warned both her husband and Della Dubois especially, that they had not heard the last of this, as Jimmy quickly started to dress himself and follow her out of the hotel, innocently pleading his case.

Aware of it or not, Della Dubois had just made another unforgivable blunder.

Chapter 10

*C*urtis Parker was casually taking a light breakfast, somewhat later than usual that morning, when he noticed that a sealed note had mysteriously been slipped under his apartment door. The envelope was white and clearly addressed to him in type written form.

Before opening the correspondence, he stared at it for a few seconds with some trepidation, thinking it might be a final 'request' for him to settle his gambling debts. Reluctantly summoning the courage to read the contents, Curtis roughly slit open the top of the envelope with his breakfast knife, still covered in jam, and unfolded a neatly typed letter.

"Dear Mr. Parker," it began. "We understand that you have accrued several gambling debts, and therefore owe a considerable amount of money to some very unpleasant people. We have the means to pay off these debts and also supply you with further funds.

We also acknowledge that you are the type of gentleman who could discreetly provide certain services and have no qualms about the outcome. If this is so, and you are interested in a little proposition, please be at the Church at 9pm tomorrow evening.

Please come alone, tell NO-ONE of this meeting, and go into the confessional box where you will be given further instructions.

If, however, you are not interested, please tear up this letter, dispose of its contents, and forget you ever received it." There was no signature or date.

Curtis was both excited and intrigued. Could this be his saviour, the answer to all his prayers, or was it a cunning trick by those to whom he owed money to get him alone and underhandedly settle the score, once and for all.

Though he was evidently a roughneck with gangster tendencies, Parker agonised for a while, perfecting his latest hair style in front of the mirror, as to what he should do. Should he discuss it with Elise? He instantly decided that she was jittery enough to be of any use. Should he go alone or get the support of some of his trusted cronies? But, then again, who could he really trust? Or, should he just simply forget the whole thing? Well, nothing ventured, nothing gained!

Decisions, decisions! Headstrong as usual, there was only one answer. Check it out. Go through with it as requested. What did he have to lose? His life was already being threatened. This would at least give him a fighting chance, if it was genuine. So, that's decided then.

It was a beautiful, balmy evening, after a day of almost intolerable heat which was now slowly becoming more bearable as night fell. Curtis decided a black T shirt and jeans would be sufficient to allow him to blend in with the fading light and approaching darkness. It slipped his mind completely that his striking bleached blond hair would somehow spoil the required camouflage effect and make him instantly recognisable.

As he left his small cabana apartment, he lit up a cigarette and slowly blew smoke rings into the air; something he often did when he was on edge. It was a quarter to nine. He had left sufficient time to amble through the complex before reaching the Church. Situated just off the main promenade, it perched proudly on a small, grassy hill, at the end of a gently sloping pathway.

The place of worship was an imposing building, constructed from old stone, and rather large for the present community, few of whom used it anyway. Many Islanders were wary of even going anywhere near it, believing in unsavoury tales from the past which painted it in a bad light.

Curtis approached with unusual caution, slowly wending his way through the pretty, little courtyard square adorned with colourful flowers and plants. It was so peaceful. The only sound was the trickling water from the small fountain in the centre of the gardens, which had often provided a well earned drink for animals and parishioners alike. He had a mind to linger and soak up the tranquillity, but there was no time.

It was just before 9pm. The American decided not to enter the Church immediately, but to conceal himself behind a nearby tree for a few minutes to try and establish just who had invited him there.

Apart from the gentle murmuring of the swaying palms in the very light evening breeze, there was no sign of life, so he resolved to follow his instructions, and shiftily slipped into the Church through an unlocked side door.

Once inside, Curtis experienced a cold, eerie feeling. He momentarily shivered in the candle lit shadows. In the musty air, there was a pervading fragrance he thought he recognised from somewhere. It beckoned him like a trail. What was it? Lavender perhaps?

The intruder had only been inside the building once before, briefly, for a wedding. Even then, for some inexplicable reason, the place felt unwelcoming. Uncomfortable and unfamiliar with the lay out, especially in the dim flickering light of only a handful of candles, it took Parker a while to get his bearings. Eventually, he established that the confessional boxes must be the old wooden partitioned compartments in one of the small Chapels off the central aisle.

Cautiously, he lifted the latch and gently pushed open the adjoining door on the left. Obviously not wishing to be disturbed, it gave a hostile creak and made the trespasser visibly jump. There was no-one inside, so who was he to speak to? On further inspection, he noticed something through the gauze in the middle panel which seemed to be sinisterly enticing him round to the other side of the confessional box, to the right hand door.

He couldn't back out now. He had a reputation to uphold. Besides, he was probably trapped anyway. His befuddled head began to pound as he fearfully edged his way into the opposite booth, completely unaware of what to expect inside. His heart was racing as he proceeded to work himself up into an uncharacteristic nervous sweat. Was it worth it?

Once inside, he sighed with relief. No apparent evil was lurking. Instead, on the small shelf in the middle of the wooden partition, there was a cassette player, wired with a pair of headphones. Even Curtis, with his limited brains and excess brawn, knew the task was to listen. The anticipated danger seemed to have passed and, once again, he felt more in control, confident he could cope.

Headphones on, he pressed 'play' and waited for a response. The distorted voice that greeted him was unrecognisable, and sounded neither male nor female. The recording had obviously been dubbed at a slower speed to mask the identity of the speaker.

"Good Evening, Mr Parker," it began. "It seems you were interested enough in our little proposition to take it a step further. Now listen carefully to the tape. Instructions cannot be repeated or replayed, since the tape will erase itself as it plays. Do NOT switch it off!" Curtis was still somewhat scared, but fascinated enough to continue to listen.

"We need your services to remove something from our Island. How, where and when, is up to you. We understand you have enough experience in these matters. Obviously, the task must be dealt with in such a way as to incite no suspicion whatsoever, and there can be no comeback. There is £50,000 in a white envelope taped beneath your seat. There will be another £100,000 on completion. You will be informed how to retrieve the balance when we are satisfied. These should be sufficient funds to pay off your debts and allow you further finance.

Should you fail to complete your side of the bargain, having taken the down payment, some of your rather more unpleasant acquaintances will ensure your disappearance, if you know what we mean. There will now be a pause on the tape. Either take the money to do the job, or go now!"

Curtis smiled to himself. He felt fairly confident. This will merely be drugs running, a piece of cake! The cassette tape continued to play silently for what seemed like an eternity. During this time he snatched the envelope from beneath the wooden bench and greedily sifted through the banknotes.

Two whole minutes later, the voice spoke again. "Good, Mr. Parker, you are still listening, and therefore must have examined your deposit and be willing to take on our request. Remember, you are now obligated. There is no going back. You must honour your commitment.

We wish you to *remove*, and interpret the word as you wish . . . " There was a long pause during which Curtis became fidgety and a little less sure of himself, but it was too late now for second thoughts. "We wish you to 'remove' . . . " it repeated . . . "Della Dubois!"

Parker was stunned. He couldn't believe his ears. Had he heard correctly? What a mess! He tried to replay the tape. It jammed. It would not replay. It had stopped.

"Drugs is one thing," he thought to himself. "But murder?" He had roughed up people before, but for all his bravado, he had never killed anyone.

The would-be gangster broke into a cold sweat and almost wet himself with anxiety. "Fuckin' hell! What a mess!" was all he could say, as he clumsily removed the headphones in a panic and fell against the swing door of the confessional, tumbling out. "I can't do that! I can't! Anything but that! Hello! Is there anybody there? Listen to me, I can't do that!" echoed through the rafters as he frantically ran around the Church, desperately searching for someone.

And then, realising that he was alone and committed to his fate, Curtis pushed his weight against the heavy wooden door leading to the courtyard and stumbled out. He had to get some air. The breeze of the night suddenly froze his fevered face. He just couldn't catch his breath.

"Fuckin' hell, I can't go back. It's her or me," he wheezed to himself, as the ghostly whispers of the swaying palms murmured confusingly in his ears. He had to get away from there, as fast as he could, back to some sort of reality, where he could think.

Fumbling and tumbling, he slid in an uncontrolled frenzy down the grassy alleyway, until he eventually reached the refuge of the complex. Here, he could once again hear the comforting noise of people. Here, he was, at last, no longer alone. But, the question was; could he go through with his mission?

Curtis had arranged to meet Elise in the hotel reception bar at 10 pm. It was now twenty past and, with an air of acceptance, she was just about to leave. She'd been stood up again. Why did she bother? As she walked through the sweet smelling front gardens of The Royal Palms towards the beach, she noticed a familiar blond haired figure coming unsteadily towards her. This time it was too late. She'd waited long enough. He could go to hell!

Elise attempted to blank her boyfriend and walk right by him, but as she got closer, his body language reflected that he was not his usual arrogant self. The wide swagger had been replaced by a hunched up meander without purpose. "Curtis. Is that you? Where have you been? What's up?"

Deep in thought, Parker raised his eyes unsurely from the sandy pathway he was following as he walked, "Oh, Leese, It's you!"

"Why, who were you expecting?" she demanded somewhat angrily.

"No-one," he responded with a blank look on his face.

"We had a date. Remember!" she forcefully reminded him.

"Oh, yeh, yeh, I was just comin' to meet you, but suddenly I didn't feel too good and . . . I must have . . . passed out. Yeh, that's right . . . passed out . . . on the beach."

Elise thought that she had heard all Parker's excuses, but this was a new one, and so crazy, it could even be true. She had to admit that he didn't look too good though. Even in the moonlight she could see that the colour had drained from his normally deeply tanned face. He was also dripping with sweat, unusual for such a cool guy. There was definitely something wrong.

"Let's go back to mine," suggested Elise, a little more sympathetically. "And I'll cook you something. You might feel better after a meal. I suppose you've been drinking and smoking and forgotten to eat again."

"Nah, that's o.k. I think I just want to go home to bed and sleep it off. Be on my own."

"Please yourself!" she replied in a huff, walking off. "I'll see you tomorrow . . . Maybe!" she added in a reluctant tone.

Tensely preoccupied, Curtis stumbled shakily towards his cabana apartment as though he were drunk. His careless lack of attention caused him to bump into several people on his way back, one of whom was Father Antonio, returning from the direction of Harriett Haversham's villa.

They met face to face in the shadow of a large palm tree. "I can't do it!" blurted out Curtis Parker. The priest, with the smell of alcohol on his breath, looked puzzled.

"Can't do what?" he slurred. Curtis just stared into the starlit sky, unsuccessfully tried to light a cigarette, and continued to repeat the same phrase, over and over again.

Father Antonio pulled himself together, stretched out his arms, putting one hand on each of the young man's shoulders, looked Parker in the eyes and said, "There are no problems, my son, only solutions. And you must do what you think best in the circumstances. I have every faith you'll make the right decision." He then gave him a knowing glance, clasped his hand supportively and continued on his way, walking with an uneven step, back to his Parish quarters. So, did the priest actually know anything, or was his advice merely pastoral?

Back at home, Curtis spent what seemed like hours agonising over how, or indeed whether, he could undertake such a dreadful deed as the one he faced. There was, however, one overriding driving force he couldn't ignore; the money. He needed it to survive. Realising this practicality, he began to consciously think more about the 'how' rather than the 'whether' and eventually, forgetting his guilt, drifted off to sleep, having come up with what appeared to be a foolproof plan.

Chapter 11

"Not there . . . ! There!" shouted the husky voice of Della Dubois, as she frantically tried to direct some of the hotel staff who had been delegated to help her to transform her Penthouse suite into the perfect party venue.

"Get rid of those yellow flowers. I prefer the red. No . . . ! Wait . . . ! Leave them! We'll have them all." Organised chaos reigned. Some of the younger staff were deliberately trying to provoke further agitation from the hostess, inciting an amusing backlash to compensate for the boredom of the task. It was only the stern glances from Senior Housekeeper, Grace Elisabeth Hickory, which kept them in check, and she was only doing her duty. She seethed to herself at the prospect of yet another intruder climbing the Island's social and financial ladder, just because of good fortune, and not because of hard work, as had been the case in her own life.

An original Islander, Grace still felt that she was not regarded as an equal, but still a servant, albeit a very respected one. She was firmly of the opinion that privilege was merely an accident of birth. Perhaps one day she really would have to make use of some of her specialised local knowledge to elevate herself properly within the community. If she wanted to, she could make real mischief. For as far as she knew, apart from Father Antonio, she was the only other person who had had sight of the original Parish records and the secrets therein, just before they conveniently disappeared a few years previously.

Exotic flowers and plants adorned the large marble pillars of the apartment. More comfortable chairs had been introduced, together with occasional tables and classy drapes. Several chaises longues had been cleverly positioned next to bowls of fruit and carafes of wine.

In fact, once the lighting requested by Miss. Dubois had been suited to her specifications, it was beginning to look rather more like a bordello than a Penthouse apartment, and ideally reflected the tastes of the good time party hostess.

"That's more like it!" Della Dubois complimented herself, as she admired her arrangement and dismissed the staff with barely a thank you. "And now it's MY turn!" She grabbed hold of the telephone and dialled the appropriate number.

"Good Afternoon. Beauty Salon," came the mechanical response.

"Elise?"

"Yes."

"Della Dubois, Penthouse Suite. I need you up here, now!"

"Have you got an appointment?" asked Elise, tongue in cheek.

"Never mind that! I want my make up, hair and nails done, plus a pedicure, for this evening," responded the hotel guest.

"I can fit you in with Sally, down here at 4pm," attempted Elise, trying to avoid such an ordeal.

"Forget it! I want YOU, up here, in my suite. Ten minutes." The 'phone was put down before the beautician could state otherwise.

"Who does that bitch think she is?" boiled Elise as she hung up. She'd have to go. It was her job.

Deliberately later than requested, Elise trudged up to the Penthouse suite, with all her equipment, in a mood to strangle, rather than beautify her client. This was going to take ages. And she had more important things to do. Unfortunately, she also had been invited to the party and mysteriously advised that it would not be in her interests to miss it. What was Della Dubois playing at?

To avoid an atmosphere, she was accompanied by Sally, her apprentice. A third party would hopefully dilute intimidation and get the job done quicker.

They rang the bell. Laughter came from inside and a male voice was clearly audible, but Elise couldn't quite place who it was. "You took your time!" was the sarcastic greeting.

"I do have other clients and they had made appointments," Elise pointed out.

"Who's she?"

"This is my assistant."

"She's not necessary."

"If she's not here to help, I can't do all the things you want," replied Elise in a curt, but professional manner, somewhat distracted by the silhouetted sight of a bare chested male leaving through the French windows. Steering clear of any possible discussion of who this was, Della Dubois swiftly instructed, "Come on then. Let's get on with it!"

As the polish was drying on both her nails and toes, Sally roughly gave Della's hair a good scrub, provoking all sorts of obscenities and aspersions about her lack of ability to do the job. The apprentice continued without batting an eyelid. She'd been warned by Elise to keep her mouth shut and do as she was told, to minimise any hassle.

The stylist then took over, and the "look" for the evening was agreed for Miss. Dubois' growing locks. Elise smiled to herself that the style requested would allow her uncoloured roots to be evident enough to make her client look cheap.

Almost in silence, the make up was then applied. Elise was in a dilemma. She wanted Della Dubois to look unattractive, but, as a professional, it would be her work that people would be judging, so she did her best.

After nearly two hours, Elise was dismissed with an insulting £5 for her trouble. Annoyed at the way she'd been made to feel, the beautician barged through Reception, bumping straight into Curtis. "Hey, you're not still in a mood with me, honey," he pleaded in an annoyingly charming manner. With indifference to her boyfriend, Elise made her feelings clear about her previous client treating her like lowlife. This, in turn, made Curtis feel better. He believed that his partner's boiling anger towards the target of his intended assignment could therefore, in some way, justify his actions after all. But he was still very uneasy about what he had to do.

* * *

"Oh God!" moaned a frustrated Harriett to Sadie, "I'm going to bloody hate this!" as they entered the hotel lobby, deciding to have a fortifying drink there first before their ordeal.

"Never mind! Every cloud has a silver lining," assured Sadie, in a strangely philosophical response.

"But this is ridiculous. Grown adults attending a so called 'soirée', just because they are afraid not to," continued to bleat Harriett, with a heavy sigh.

"Who's afraid? I'm not afraid!" rebuked Sadie. "I want to see her get what's coming to her."

"What do you mean?" asked Harriett, appearing naïve.

"Well," coughed Sadie, somewhat nervously. "It's going to be a disaster, isn't it."

"Oh yes, I see. I suppose it will be," whispered Harriett pensively to herself.

Neither of them had really pulled out the stops when it came to getting ready. Sadie wore slacks and a light grey blouse to compliment her silver hair, and Harriett had put on just a plain evening dress, by her standards, with hair, make-up and jewellery toned right down in comparison to her appearance at the much talked about 'Relaunch.'

"Evening Ladies," said a voice already at the bar. It was Dr. Tremaine and his wife. He was wearing a white cotton suit and she had a dark red cocktail dress on. "So you're also going to this fiasco," noted Mrs. Tremaine sympathetically, glaring at her husband. Thereafter, they both sipped their gin in silence.

"They're all sitting around the table looking as if they'd just been to a funeral," observed Clarrissa as she and her sister tottered into the lobby.

"Perhaps they wish they had. And we all know whose!" joked Kittie lamely.

"Ghastly woman! I still say this is absolutely preposterous," echoed a booming voice coming into the hotel. "She's so full of her own self importance, and in reality such people seldom have anything to truly feel important about!"

"Oh, just think of it as a night out, my dear," coaxed Lord Meadows. "You know you don't like to miss anything, and you do like to dress up. Though it doesn't look as if you've gone to too much trouble tonight, I must say."

"Don't be impertinent," she berated the Governor. "Some night out! Oh, do come along boy! For goodness sake, don't dawdle!" she impatiently instructed her son, who was reluctantly following behind with an equally under whelmed Daphnee Meadows.

"Alright, my dear?" spluttered Monty turning round to his wife and coughing on his pipe as usual.

"Oh, I'm fine," she replied in a cold, thoughtful manner. "In fact, I'm really looking forward to this," she sneered.

Father Antonio slowly limped in, minutes later, still wearing his cassock. "Can't stay long," he confided to the others. "Church business to attend to later."

"What at this time of night?" challenged Lady Laetitia, with a withering look of disdain.

"Time has no boundaries where God's work is concerned."

"Nor has a bottle of whisky," piped up Monty sarcastically.

"Come on, Curtis! You're not usually so averse to attending a party," moaned Elise, who also obviously wanted to be anywhere else but there. "It was you who insisted on coming in the first place, remember! If we've got to go, we might as well get it over with," she muttered, trying to encourage her boyfriend, who was still behaving oddly, to get into the lift. "The others are moving. Best if we all go in together."

Contrary to almost all the other females attending the soirée, Elise had made an effort, just to try and out do Della Dubois. She looked radiant with her hair up, shimmering gold evening dress and matching shawl. Her dangling earrings and necklace added to her stunning appearance. At least if she was going to be there, she'd make a lasting impact, she thought.

The reluctant guests seemed to all arrive together, as though planned, to forgo the opportunity of greeting the hostess individually in person. "How utterly vulgar!" commented Lady Laetitia loudly, as she set foot in the Penthouse suite for the first time, barging right past Della Dubois who stood in the doorway, smiling to receive her visitors.

"I believe they've just had it refurbished, especially for the party," said Clarrissa, whose eyes lit up like a child as she marvelled at the festive display in front of her.

"Who's footing the bill? That's what Id like to know," snarled Sadie to Harriett who, by now, was already beginning to look uncomfortable and forlorn at the prospect of a whole evening in the company of a woman she disliked intensely.

Elise and Curtis made their entrance a little later than the others, and couldn't avoid coming face to face with their hostess. The two women glared at each other. The unthinkable had happened. "Your hair!" blurted Elise, looking at almost a mirror image of her own style. "That's not how I did it!"

"No," responded Della Dubois adamantly. "After you left, I decided I didn't like it, so I called that apprentice girl."

"Oh yes, the one you said was incompetent," responded Elise indignantly.

"Well anyway, she came back and put it up for me. Did a good job too, don't you think? You should let her do more. She could teach you a thing or two!" bitched the bleach blonde. To make matters worse, both women were wearing stylish dresses which were almost alike with practically identical colours. To their embarrassment, people had already noticed the similarity, and tongues were wagging.

The atmosphere was initially almost unbearable, with low level conversation peppered with long, embarrassing silences. People just stood around like statues until Grace Elisabeth gave the nod to the staff to circulate the drinks in a bid to liven things up and lift the mood. "You must try the punch!" gushed the hostess. "I made it myself."

"Stay well clear of that then!" chipped in Daphnee Meadows to those in her immediate vicinity.

"Oh no! Please spare us. Anything but that," moaned Lady Lascelles as a steel band, which seemed to have appeared from nowhere, began to set up. "The woman has no sense of propriety whatsoever!"

By this time Sebastian and Raoul had joined the party, from separate directions, and Rory O'Rourke was busy serving up a tantalising buffet to guests eager to eat to provide some distraction. "Any fireworks yet?" chuckled Raoul to Jimmy Tremaine.

"Depends which kind you mean," replied the doctor mischievously. "No doubt there will be some before the night's out!"

The band began with some gentle Caribbean reggae songs, and even the most sterile guests found themselves inadvertently tapping their feet at least. Some even forgot themselves and started dancing, almost enjoying themselves, after a previously agreed pact of passive resistance.

Dimitri had by now appeared from one of the bedrooms, dressed only in a tight, white vest, emphasising his deep tan and muscular build, and matching clingy cotton shorts which left very little to the imagination, and commanded a great deal of lingering attention from several sources.

"Keep an eye on your husband," hissed the hostess at the Doctor's wife. "Wouldn't like him 'mauled' again," she tauntingly laughed. Alicia Tremaine seethed inside with anger, but maintained her dignity and composure, and just returned a sarcastic grin.

"Enjoying yourselves, you two," shouted an increasingly more inebriated Della Dubois across the room at Father Antonio and Harriett. "Don't do anything I wouldn't do. Oops, maybe you already have!" she added with a hiccup and a giggle. The two guests just quietly blended into the melee to avoid being targeted further.

"Managing alright, Sadie? Need a few quid to tide you over? Just let me know. Still, you've always got your nursing to provide you with an income, if you know what I mean," goaded the hostess with a loud belch.

"You bitch, I'll . . . " Before Sadie could get any further, Seb had grabbed her.

"Leave it. It's not worth it. Bide your time, Sadie."

Fearing they'd be next, Daphnee Meadows got in first. "Charming party, my dear. You must have gone to a lot of trouble," she praised with a smile.

"Good move, ol' girl," whispered Monty, patting his wife on the back.

"Yeh, I did, and I'm really enjoying myself!" burped a drunken response.

As time went by, people were becoming fidgety and expectant glances were being exchanged across the room. There was a feeling of anticipation that something would happen.

From his secluded seat in the corner, Alistair gazed up at the hostess, with lust and admiration. As she lurched forward, he stood up and she fell against him, grabbing his groin. "Whe . . . when ca . . . can we d . . . do it again?" he whispered.

"Alistair!" coquettishly replied the idol of his desires, with a wide grin. "I don't know what you mean."

" Y . . . you kn . . . know. The n . . . n . . . night on the bbbeach," the poor boy managed to eventually blurt out.

"How do you know that was me?" she teased, provocatively pouting her kissable lips. "Wasn't it pitch black? It could have been anyone," she suggested, waving across the room at Dimitri with a suggestive wink.

Alistair fell back into his chair and became increasingly more agitated as he gulped down a full glass of champagne. What had gone on that night? Everything was still such a puzzle. Why was she toying with his emotions? What was she insinuating?

Curtis Parker felt more and more restless. If he was going to put his plan into operation, he had to move, and move now. He agonised and agonised, and was gradually beginning to lose his nerve.

Pulling himself together, he eventually told Elise he was going to freshen up, and started to make his way through the crowd to the bathroom. As he did so, a strong waft of a familiar smell greeted his nostrils. It was the same fragrance he had experienced in the Church. His meal ticket was here, here in the same room, watching his every move. He couldn't bluff his way out of this one, even if he wanted to. He frantically looked about to try to identify the source of the lavender aroma. But by now it had drifted into the air around him and could not be pinned down.

Reluctant though he was, even allowing desperate last minute deliberations to race through his mind, Parker came to the inevitable conclusion that he simply had no choice. He had to see it through. He had to pluck up the courage to set the wheels in motion.

With renewed conviction, he unobtrusively placed a pre-written scribbled note underneath Della Dubois' half filled wine glass as she intimately danced with Raoul, just a few feet away. Looking carefully around, Curtis made sure that he had not been observed.

Keeping his nerve, he watched intently as she chatted and laughed, waiting patiently for her to return to her drink. It seemed like forever. Once or twice, she almost got there, but someone distracted her and, never refusing the chance of a dance, she returned to saucily strut her stuff.

Eventually, the hostess was too tired to continue, and left some male fishermen companions, who had gate crashed the 'do', to finally retrieve her much needed refreshment. Picking up the glass by its stem, Della Dubois couldn't fail to notice the conspicuous message clinging desperately to the bottom. She clumsily tugged it off. Her impish grin emphasised her keen curiosity to learn the contents. Some of the ink must have run, as she seemed to be awkwardly turning the scrap of paper to the light to try to read it properly. Seemingly unable to make sense of the scribble, her eyes squinted desperately to focus. It didn't help that she was already well on her way to alcoholic oblivion.

Della must have got the gist of the message, however, as she suddenly smiled and started to preen herself, making sure in a nearby mirror, that her hair was perfectly pinned up in place, and that she was still looking fabulous.

After all, she was about to meet a secret admirer, outside on the balcony!

Chapter 12

*C*urtis nervously scanned the room. The atmosphere had improved somewhat, in the sense that people were mingling in a more relaxed manner, but there was still an air of expectancy, as if everybody was waiting for something to happen. He looked over at Elise, who had by now resigned herself to the fact that her partner was obviously feeling more sociable and had found someone else to chat to. She too, had been way laid, by the twins who were twittering away to her, even though her glazed look of disinterest was obvious.

Minutes passed. Della Dubois had disappeared and was obviously waiting to be adored at the suggested rendezvous. Slowly, Parker edged his way through the party guests, his stomach knotted, sweat visibly glistening on his forehead. He almost jumped out of his skin at one point, when he was suddenly grabbed by the arm. "Alright, my son?" enquired Father Antonio softly, looking straight into his eyes. "All sorted after the other night?"

"Yeh. Fine, Father. Everythin's just fine." But just who was he trying to reassure?

Approaching the French doors which led from the Penthouse onto the balcony, he could see the dimly lit feminine shape of Della Dubois, looking out towards the sea, gently leaning on the wooden balustrade with her back towards him. Perfect, he thought. It's now or never.

Quickly checking from his vantage point, behind a pillar, that there was no-one else around, he crept a little nearer, his footsteps drowned out by the music, summoned up all his courage and, arms stretched out in front of him, lunged forward.

At the very second his strong hands delivered the final, fatal push, his blood ran cold, and unable to undo what he had done, he silently shouted, "No . . . !" into the night air, as the screaming body fell four floors and hit the ground below with an almighty thud.

What had he done? Oh God, what had he done? He had killed someone, but not just anyone. At that all important final moment, when there was no going back, the moonlight had revealed the tattoo of a scorpion at the base of the neck of the woman whose life he was ending. It was not Della Dubois. It was his own partner. It was Elise. He had just killed Elise.

Unable to pull himself together, Curtis just slumped into a crumpled mess behind a pillar on the poorly lit balcony, sobbing and shaking uncontrollably. His mind could not even start to contemplate the repercussions of what he had just done.

A few seconds later, he heard footsteps. By all accounts it was a woman. She was tottering unsteadily along the balcony, as if she were very tipsy. In fact, her body coordination seemed all over the place, and she tumbled a little and ended up just perching precariously against the next pillar to the hidden, huddled murderer.

After finally managing to unclip her purse, she clumsily rummaged through it, and took out something which she eventually succeeded in putting into her mouth.

To a camouflaged Curtis, it seemed like forever, but eventually the shuddering and shaking slowed down, and the disorientated woman became somewhat more steady and composed. She was still mumbling to herself, making very little sense and then, "Harriett, what are you doing out there? I've been looking for you everywhere," shouted an irritable Sadie Finch.

A wobbly and jaded looking Harriett came out of the shadows and softly answered. "I don't know. I really don't know."

"Well come back in here. I need to talk to you." Harriett pulled herself together and rejoined the party.

Suddenly, the Penthouse door swung open and a very, very flustered Duty Manager frantically gesticulated to catch Sebastian's eye. There was a swift whisper behind a guarded hand, and Sebastian's face turned white. Obviously in shock, he supported himself by leaning on a chair. He motioned to Raoul, who was dancing nearby with Alicia Tremaine, to come over.

Raoul was just in the mood to ignore his partner, but could tell from his look that this was not the time to play games. There was something wrong. He excused himself and made his way over to receive the chilling news. A body had been found on the steps outside the hotel, face down. It was thought to be the party hostess.

By now, several members of the gathering had realised that something was going on, and were beginning to look suspiciously uncomfortably at each other. After minutes of uncontrolled rumour, "Sebastian!" shouted a voice of authority. "What's going on?" Lady Laetitia's booming enquiry was enough to stop the music as well as the conversation and dancing.

"Well, em, this is em, most serious and em, embarrassing," laboured Sebastian.

"Spit it out then, young man!" she instructed, in an agitated tone which she did not usually use with the hotel proprietor. Seb pulled himself together, coughed, and prepared himself to make an announcement;

"Ladies and Gentlemen. It appears that there has been an unfortunate accident. Someone has fallen from the balcony. It is thought to be tonight's hostess. Dr. Tremaine is already in attendance. We will inform you of further news as we receive it."

At first there was silence. Sideways glances continued to surreptitiously circulate around the room, darting from one to another. Then, the brewing reactions exploded into a crescendo of noise, and the party started to disintegrate.

Supported by a shaking Father Antonio, Harriett had to sit down in a nearby armchair; her pale face and quivering lip registering the realisation of what had just happened. Sadie stared blankly, without any sign of emotion, straight into the thin air in front of her. Secretly she felt like jumping for joy, which would have been highly inappropriate and very incriminating.

Alicia Tremaine's face was cold and unflinching, as she apathetically prepared to leave to help her husband. Lord and Lady Meadows and Maggie Maynard remained composed with a stiff upper lip. More perceptive guests could see, however, that Monty was straining to conceal his emotions. Revealing how he really felt would have been a great mistake at this time, as the constant threatening glare of his wife reminded him.

Lady Laetitia and Alistair stood motionless, with their eyes lowered to the floor, while Kittie, already busily giving her views on the matter to her long suffering twin sister, made it plain that she had no sympathy, repeating, "You reap what you sow!" several times.

Sebastian and Raoul both seemed anxious, but for different reasons, and Grace Elisabeth, practical as ever, started to clear away some of the empty plates and glasses.

By this time, with only a cigarette for comfort, Curtis had composed himself, as best he could, and had slipped back into the party. The faint smell of lavender had already wafted under his nose, though again, he could not pinpoint the direct source. Under the pretext of returning from the lavatory, he innocently asked what had happened.

"That's what I'd like to know," echoed a husky voice approaching from the back balcony, followed by a smiling Dimitri, still fastening the zip on his shorts.

There she stood; large as life and in perfect working order. It was Della Dubois!! A stunned response greeted her from the remaining guests who couldn't believe their eyes.

Suddenly, everything changed. Harriett fainted, toppling from her chair, unable to bear the shock. A pre-occupied and unusually ham fisted Father Antonio, immediately endeavoured to tend to her. Sadie's face turned to thunder. Looking sternly around the room, she closely studied the responses of fellow guests. Everything from incredulity and guarded rage, to fright and downright despondency, depending on whom she observed, stared back at her. Though he did not outwardly show it, only Monty seemed somewhat relieved. After all, blood is thicker than water.

After several minutes of consternation, Alistair, of all people, broke the silence. "B,but . . . if . . . it w,w,was . . . n,not y,y,you . . . ,"

"Who the hell was it?" mused Raoul, completing his question. Immediately, there was a rush for the door, and when the lift was full, those left scurried down the stairs, leaving a very annoyed hostess, alone, in the middle of a party, wondering what exactly was going on.

As yet unaware of the real identity of the accident victim, Jimmy had been on the scene for some minutes. "Don't move her!" instructed the Doctor as other anxious guests began to crowd around him. The body was lying face down, awkwardly. "I need more light. Bring some lamps."

"Wait a minute," he continued hesitantly, after a swift initial examination. "There's a very, very faint pulse. Give me your make-up mirror, Alicia." With a deft movement of his left hand, Jimmy managed to slide the glass under a gap in the steps to the victim's nose. "She's, she's still breathing," he gasped. Curtis jolted and staggered back from the crowd to be physically sick, out of sight, in a nearby hedge.

Before Dr. Tremaine could proceed, the noise of helicopter propellers could be heard approaching from the distance. It was the air ambulance from one of the nearer, larger islands. Everyone stood back, covering their faces from swirling sand, as it smoothly landed on the hotel beach.

"You must have a sixth sense," Dr. Tremaine joked half heartedly to the medics on arrival. "I haven't got round to calling you yet," obviously trying to give the distinct impression that he hadn't been wasting time.

"We had a call ten minutes ago," was the response. "Some kind of accidental fall?" Thankfully, Curtis had had the presence of mind to immediately summon help on realising his life changing mistake.

"Do we have a name?" asked the medic, looking at the Doctor.

"Yes, yes, Della Dubois," he replied automatically.

There were gasps of horror. Purposely or otherwise, Jimmy had taken his time getting to the scene, and had not even been there long enough to realise his grave error.

"You wish!!" came a cry. "Oh dear, Doctor! We have got it wrong, haven't we?" sarcastically quipped the party hostess, who had by now followed everyone else downstairs. A look of horror transformed Jimmy's face to an ashen trembling mess.

Whom had he allowed to suffer and deteriorate through his unnecessary neglect?

Curtis could hold back no longer. "Do something for Christ's sake!" he shouted uncontrollably, shaking Jimmy Tremaine. "It's Elise! Look! The scorpion at the nape of her neck! It's Elise!" He then burst into floods of tears and had to be comforted by Raoul. Harriett fainted once again, while other sobbing bystanders spontaneously exchanged desperate looks of guilt and sorrow. The reality of the whole sorry mess was just beginning to sink in.

As Parker prepared to board the helicopter which was to rush Elise to life or death, he felt a tap on the shoulder. Still in a state of shock, he slowly turned around in a sedated haze. A hooded figure, face covered by a black veil masking its true identity, shimmered before him.

"You really must be more careful, Mr. Parker," whispered a muffled, unrecognisable voice. "May I suggest an eye test while you're at the hospital? We don't want any more mistakes, do we? After all, you still haven't successfully completed *your* side of the bargain."

Curtis lashed out in rage, but was immediately restrained by an inattentive Jimmy, who continued to administer a further sedative to calm him, unaware of what had just happened. A faint smell of lavender wafted through the air as the nearby swaying palms gently breathed a sigh of discomfort.

"And you won't be able to do that for much longer either, will you, 'Doctor'? Tut, tut, such incompetence! I shouldn't wonder if you were struck off. Or have you been already?" sniggered the distorted voice deftly disappearing into the darkness, leaving a confused and bewildered Jimmy Tremaine feeling completely vulnerable.

Chapter 13

"Well, have you sorted it out yet?" shouted a raucous Della Dubois, as she pushed by Lady Meadows and barged straight into the Governor's office, without knocking. Monty was puffing on his pipe, with his back to the door, staring out of the window at the calm, blue seas.

"Oh, Miss. Dubois," he greeted his unwanted guest. "Sorted what?"

"My money, of course! I want what's rightfully mine, my inheritance, and I want it now!"

Daphnee stood at the doorway, expecting an altercation as Monty fumblingly tried to explain.

"The lawyers . . . It takes time. Things have to be ratified on the main island." He had barely finished his sentence when the high backed armchair in front of the Governor's table slowly moved and a silver haired lady quietly stood up and turned around.

"I've beaten you to it," said Sadie, slowly and deliberately, as she looked her adversary straight in the eye. Monty's wife gradually began to edge her way between the two ladies in a bid to avoid an unsightly slanging match.

"Oh, I might have known you'd be sniffing around. What do you mean?"

"As Mrs. Van Leiden's carer, I have contested the Will, stating her not to be of sound mind when she compiled it. I've even got Dr. Tremaine's backing," smiled Sadie sardonically.

"Well you're bloody liars. You know that's not true," interrupted Della Dubois with a distinct air of exasperation.

"And you know different? How many times did you come and see her? How many times did you even speak to her? Ay? How many times did you even acknowledge her? I was with her all day, every day," continued Sadie, with a heavy note of resentment. "I cooked, I cleaned, I waited on her hand and foot, tended to her when she was ill. And where were you? Some daughter!"

"You know I never knew she was my mother. How could I have . . . ?"

"Ladies, Ladies, please!" coughed an increasingly flustered Monty. "Let's let the lawyers sort it out."

"Let's face it," beamed Sadie. "You've been trying to get your greedy little hands on your so called 'mother's' money for ages, by trying to blackmail me."

"Yes, and if things don't go in my favour, I might have to try a little harder. I'm sure the Governor would like to know all about your grubby past and just what kind of a responsible *'nurse'* you have been."

"Get your facts right next time, lady!" spat Sadie. "Use a reliable source. The information you have, or think you have, relates to someone else. You see, Kittie and Clarrie aren't the only identical twins in the world! And I'm not the only nurse!"

"You're bluffing," screamed Della Dubois, almost out of control.

"Try me!" threatened Sadie. "There'll be no more money from me now, one way or the other, so go and peddle your trash elsewhere, and see where it gets you."

"You two are witnesses," screeched Della Dubois, obviously on somewhat shaky ground. "She's called me a 'blackmailer' and threatened me. You wait. When I bloody find out who my father is, you'll wish you'd never crossed me!"

"Now who's threatening who?" grinned Sadie. "Do you really think he's going to admit to it, having YOU as a daughter?"

With a self assured, sideways look at Monty, Sadie then gently, but firmly, pushed the younger lady out of her way and left.

An air of uneasy tension filled Lord Meadows' office and, before the inevitable question was asked, Daphnee quickly excused the Governor. "You'll have to come back. My husband's been under a lot of strain recently. He needs to rest now."

"Oh, I'll be back alright," reaffirmed the feisty female. "And when I do, you'd better have some answers!"

Monty gently eased into his favourite chair, and sat with his head in his hands. "Where's it going to end? Where is it all going to end?" he sniffled, looking up helplessly at his wife.

"I really don't know," she said thoughtfully. "But you're not to worry. I'll deal with that little minx, daughter or no daughter."

* * *

Della Dubois was considerably annoyed, to say the least, at having been dismissed from the Governor's office in such a way and, as she kicked her way belligerently down the pebbly pathway toward the beach, she caught sight of Harriett Haversham aimlessly walking her dog. She made a bee line in her direction, and waited patiently under a shady palm until Harriett, wilting in the sun, was within striking distance.

"Pleased with yourself?" she aggressively whispered into Harriett's face, as she barred her path. Harriett nearly jumped out of her skin.

"I, I don't know what you mean," replied the older lady, nervously. "What on earth are you talking about? You frightened me, leaping out like that."

"Yes, and you have good cause to be frightened, haven't you?" replied a devious Della. Harriett just stared at her in bewilderment. "I told you that you'd do something you'd regret one day when you had one of your turns. And now you have."

"Oh, come along now, do make some sense. I've no idea what you're talking about," struggled a befuddled Harriett.

"Let me give you a clue," teased the temptress. "My soirée, the balcony; you flailing uncontrollably around. Elise Beauchamp's 'accident'. Ring any bells?"

"You're surely not suggesting that I . . . " began Harriett indignantly.

"Can you prove otherwise? Can you?" interrupted her interrogator. "Where were you when it happened? You certainly weren't in my apartment, were you?"

Harriett blanched and began to feel sick in the stomach. Parts of that night had been a complete blur, but she wouldn't have . . . she couldn't have . . .

"Attempted murder is a serious offence," continued the scheming sex siren in a semi mocking, semi officious manner. "But don't worry, I may still need you, so I'm not going to grass you up just yet," she smiled sarcastically. "Just don't leave the Island, as the Police would say."

With that, Della Dubois turned on her heels and, with a very smug look on her face, started to head back to the complex. "That was a stroke of luck!" she said to herself. "I feel much better now!"

Initially, Harriett just froze, motionless, and then, when the confrontation had eventually sunk in, she began to shudder. "I can't remember. I just can't bloody remember!" she spat forcefully, shaking herself in frustration, fists clenched, angry at the possible implications of her partial amnesia that night. "Could she be right? Could that bloody bitch possibly be right . . . ? I was on the balcony . . . I didn't feel well . . . but I couldn't have . . . surely not . . . ! Oh God help me!"

As Harriett stared out to sea, deep in thought, desperately trying to piece together in her own mind the events of that fateful night, she heard a familiar greeting pass her by. "Good Morning! Nice day."

"Morning," she mechanically responded, without turning around. It wasn't, however, until minutes later that the chance acknowledgement actually dawned on her. Who was that? Who had been that close by, and what had they overheard? Oh God, she couldn't recollect that either!

* * *

"I, I d,d,do h,hope the b,baby's alright," Alistair suddenly looked up and announced during the regular morning refreshment ritual with his mother in the hotel lobby.

"Baby? What baby? What the deuce are you talking about boy?" she responded, irritated at such an inane comment.

"The b,b,baby," he persevered, flicking through his note-book. "E, El, Elise's baby."

Lady Laetitia shook her head and looked at her son in abject dismay. It would be like pulling teeth to try and extract an explanation from him. She paused. Then she had a brainwave. "Have you written it down?" she asked, clinically and loudly. He nodded. "Then give me your notebook."

"It, it's p,pr private," he argued insecurely, knowing he would be no match for his mother.

"Stuff and nonsense," she retorted, snatching the booklet, seemingly open at the relevant page. She lingeringly perused her son's notes with careful regard. "You have beautiful hand-writing, Alistair," she complimented "You should put it to better use!" What she read, however, perplexed her.

"Having haircut. Still waiting for Elise, now on the tele-phone! Appears worried. "How did you know I was pregnant? You dare tell Curtis, you bitch. O.k. so you know who the father is. Nobody will believe you. Keep your nose out. I don't respond to blackmail. I'll get even with you yet!" Elise tearful. Gone to bathroom. Seems exceedingly upset," was the entry.

"How did you discover this?" asked Lady Laetitia in a softer tone. "Surely Elise didn't let you overhear such a private conversation?" Alistair pointed to a mirror, and then to his lips. "You were lip reading, through the glass," she confirmed. He nodded. "If this information is true, you may have stumbled on something unfortunate, personal and private, and it must be kept so. Say nothing about this to anyone, Alistair. The well being of others could be at stake."

Laetitia's manner was unusually gentle and comforting, as she clasped her offspring's hand and warmly gazed, straight into his eyes. The hairs on the back of Alistair's neck stood up, and he felt a modest tingle of pride envelope his whole body. This was one of the very few occasions he could remember when his mother had neither shouted at him nor belittled him. Instead, she had confided in him, like an adult. She had treated him like her son, not merely an unnecessary embarrassment.

* * *

"And another thing . . . ," continued Kittie to her long suffering sister, while they sipped their ice tea at a shaded table on the terrace. Clarrissa had no alternative but to patiently listen while her gossipy twin droned on and on like a gattling gun that would never stop. "Where's that French woman, nowadays? I haven't seen her for ages. I wonder what's happened to her. Perhaps I should visit, find out what's going on? . . . She was always parading around in those different colour turban hats . . . And just you try stopping her from crooning away at evening functions . . . ! Never did really know much about her, though. Now she seems to have . . . well . . . , vanished."

"Perhaps she's left the Island, gone on holiday," suggested Clarrie reflectively, when she could get a word in.

"I can't see how. She never left on that little aeroplane with Elroy, and there have been no boats coming or going lately, well, not since that yacht, and that never came in to the harbour. Come to mention it, we didn't ever get to the bottom of that either, did we? There are some funny things going on at the moment on this Island and . . . "

"You're worried you don't know what they are, dear?" interrupted her sister cheekily.

"I'm just taking a neighbourly interest, Clarrissa, that's all, just a neighbourly interest!" was the instant rebuke.

Clarrissa had boldly risked enough impertinence for one day, so she let her sister continue to waffle on and make mischief, without further hindrance, while she happily daydreamed and contemplated the merits of living on such a beautiful, relatively unspoilt island, in such glorious weather, in such a secluded part of the world.

* * *

"Is that the lot?" Dr. Tremaine asked his wife hopefully, as he peered out of his Consulting Room ten minutes after morning surgery had begun. Actually, it wasn't really a Consulting Room;

it was one of the downstairs reception rooms converted for the purpose in their comparatively modest home. And 'Morning Surgery' had only consisted of a tourist with an insect bite, and the rebandaging of one of the fishermen's hands, after he caught his right index finger in a rusty hook.

"Yes, that's it. You're really pushed aren't you?" she added scornfully.

"Oh darling, you're not still in a mood with me over that Della Dubois business, are you?" Jimmy whined, kissing his wife's cheek.

"Maybe I am," she said playfully, but then her mood instantly darkened. "I think they're on to us, Jimmy, and I've rather grown accustomed to our lifestyle here. I wouldn't want to give it up now."

"Yes, come to think of it, someone made a snide comment, which I chose to ignore, when I was treating Curtis. I didn't recognise the voice, and whoever it was quickly disappeared, but seemed to be intimating that they meant business."

"Oh, I think we both know who we're talking about," replied Alicia with a sardonic sigh. "And if nobody else is going to sort it, we may have to." The doctor looked rather perplexed. "Well, Jimmy," continued his wife, deep in contemplation. "Think of the alternative. Wouldn't that be too impossible to bear? Raoul's given us one lifeline already, we wouldn't be so lucky again."

"Yes, I suppose you're right. It's the survival of the fittest. We'll just have to be strong. Keep your eyes and ears open, and we'll act if necessary."

"I'm afraid it will be a case of 'when' not 'if', the way things are going at the moment," sighed Alicia pensively.

Turning her back on her husband, the doctor's wife then slowly made her way outside and sat on the wooden steps at the front of their home. Gazing deeply into the softly breathing palms, she desperately searched for some kind of much needed inspiration.

Chapter 14

"Haven't had a chance to hang them yet then?" enquired Maggie Maynard, with an air of anticipation, as she passed through Reception on her way to the hotel bistro for lunch. Sebastian looked up from the desk and just blankly stared, raising his eyebrows, indicating that he didn't understand what the Colonel's wife was talking about. "My paintings!" she laughed.

"Oh, well no, yes," replied Seb almost apologetically. "Had a few disagreements deciding just where to place them. Must get it right for our celebrated local artist."

"Oh, you flatter me, young sir," she mimicked preciously, and smiled proudly as she made her way to her usual table.

"That's a point," Seb mumbled to himself, thoughtfully. "I'd forgotten all about that . . . Raoul? Raoul!"

"What now?" came a somewhat aggravated response as Raoul threw down his magazine, took his feet off the office desk, and marched into Reception. "Can't I even have a bloody break without you bothering me?" he whinged, leaning lazily against a supporting wall.

"Where's Dimitri?"

"How the hell should I know? I'm not his keeper!"

"No," asserted Seb calmly yet deliberately. "But you are in charge of staff. Therefore, I'd appreciate it if you'd change your tone, lower your voice, look at the rota, go and find him, and ask him what he did with Maggie Maynard's paintings. And if he's up there with Della Dubois again, sack him!"

"Take it easy. Remember we may need him," replied Raoul, carefully checking who was around.

"Don't you think there are more important things to sort out than a few bloody drawings," he argued in a forcefully loud whisper.

"We'll do that later, in private."

"Don't worry, I ain't listenin'," piped up Grace Elisabeth, as she polished the nearby lounge tables. The two men just looked at each other and laughed. Grace Elisabeth was part of the furnishing. They'd always conducted their business in front of her, personal or otherwise, without thinking.

"No, Grace, of course not!" chuckled Raoul as he went off on his mission.

* * *

By lunchtime, Raoul had tired of trying to find Dimitri. If the odd job, masseur, swimming pool attendant didn't want to be found, then Raoul knew that there was no way on earth he would find him. He'd turn up with a plausible excuse sooner or later, and all would be fine again. Best to waste no more time looking. He would reprimand Dimitri and placate Seb with some story later. It wouldn't be the first time, or the last!

Meanwhile, the temperature outside was also steadily rising, and the blue sky above looked flawless, as a gentle breeze from the clear sea brought its fragrances in land, and completed the perfect atmosphere of a day given.

Taking off his shirt, Raoul once again felt drawn to the nooks and crannies of the hotel's private beach. He desired tranquillity and solitude; somewhere to freshen up his tan and relax in the sizzling sun for half an hour before he had to return to his gruelling schedule of duties.

Almost in a trance, he strolled along the sandy pathway towards the sea, but became abruptly more alert when he imagined he heard sobbing. Raoul couldn't quite locate the direction of this barely audible emotion, but eventually found himself standing in a familiar setting.

In the small, secluded, grassy area, surrounded by gently swaying bushes, he once again saw the silhouette of a woman, with her back to him, looking out to sea. She was quietly weeping to herself.

A shiver went through Raoul's body. He stood motionless, rooted to the terrain. Déjà vu! It couldn't be . . . ! "Elise?" he whispered unsurely, developing a sudden cold sweat. "Elise, is that you?"

"I thought that poor cow was dead," was the sniffling, but defiant response, as Della Dubois turned around and made herself known.

"Oh, DD, it's you. For a moment, I . . . Are you o.k.? I thought I heard crying."

"Me? Crying? What have I got to cry about?" she answered, with her tough as nails glare.

"Nothing, I suppose," shrugged Raoul. "But you're human, like the rest of us and . . . Well, you probably want to be on your own, so I'll . . . "

"No!" she quickly responded, in her gravel toned voice. "No, stay and chat for a while, I'd like that."

Raoul could see that his friend was putting on a brave front, but acted as if he hadn't noticed. "I suppose life's been a bit of a whirlwind for you lately," he began, as they both sat down on a patch of sandy grass.

"Sure has!" she exclaimed thoughtfully, eyes fixed firmly on the gently rolling waves. "First I've got no parents. Then I have. Then my estranged mother dies, without even ever speaking to me, and my father hasn't got the balls to openly identify himself. One minute I'm poor, the next I'm a wealthy heiress . . . Though it remains to be seen if I'll ever lay my hands on the money," she sighed, somewhat resolved that she wouldn't.

"You know, Ra, all my life I've had to fight, fight for what was mine. Struggle, struggle to be accepted, and sometimes it gets a little tiring, a little bit . . . " she almost began to break, but instantly controlled herself and continued, " a little bit . . . tiring," she repeated.

"I expect it will all sort itself out," reassured Raoul. "These things have a way of . . . well . . . sorting themselves out."

They both looked at each other. "Not very good liars, are we?" consoled Raoul, with a feeble chuckle and a friendly cuddle. DD just slowly shook her head and smiled.

"No, we've known each other long enough, and intimately enough, to realise that I'm putting on a brave face, and you're feeling awkward with a vulnerable female to console."

"I am interested though," confirmed Raoul, clearing his throat.

"In what?" asked Della, somewhat surprised.

"In you. Your past. I know nothing about you really."

"What's to know?" she laughed. "What you see is what you get! That's why people don't like me."

"Yeh, I know that, but how did you end up here, on this island? Give me the censored version if you like," he giggled, now more at ease, "but tell me something."

"Well, I ain't givin' away any dark secrets, cos we've all got skeletons in the cupboard, but I will tell you . . . the story so far, shall we say."

Raoul listened intently as Della Dubois began to delve back into her childhood. She meandered through her memory and related how she had been given up by her mother at a very early age, 'because of circumstances', and had never had a father; how she had grown up through a succession of foster homes, some good, some bad, until she was old enough to make her own way in the world. She had been used by men, so she had decided to use them back. She was a tough little cookie, and soon learnt how to look out for number one with no difficulty.

At 17, she gave a false age and details, and joined a Caribbean cruise ship, skivvying. Her penchant for gambling led her to the ship's Casino in her spare time, where she regularly lost all she earned. The Manager noticed, however, that she was a skilled player and, in return for obvious favours, offered to train her as a croupier. 'My big break!' she laughed. As the punters played the tables, so she played them, until she had put enough money aside to one day get off the ship at a bustling port and never return.

Island hopping, she avoided bills and commitment, and ended up working in the Café-bar in our own little secluded community. When the old man who owned it died, she took over the business, and it just became hers. No-one else wanted it. There was no Will or anything. It just happened. One day she had a Café-bar, just like that! She had often wondered about the lack of red tape at the time, and supposed the whole affair had simply been ignored, or that someone had put in a good word for her. But who?

"Come to think of it, it was all too easy. Wait a minute . . . , I don't suppose . . . old Joe . . . he couldn't have been my father, could he?" she mused. "He certainly treated me . . . well . . . properly. Perhaps my own father was right under my nose . . . ? No! Too much of a coincidence, and I couldn't see him and Mrs. Van Leid . . . , my mother, together. No, I'm clutching at straws, or am I?"

Raoul noticed that Della Dubois seemed to come alive when talking about her sense of 'belonging', and that she was desperate to find out the information which eluded her. He didn't want to spoil things by mentioning that, at her mother's funeral, the impression was given that her father was still very much alive.

"Ra, do you think there's a record on the Island, of all the inhabitants and their ancestry or something?"

"I suppose the nearest you'd get would be the Parish Records," Raoul suggested with a shrug. "And the story goes that they're incomplete because most of them have disappeared."

"Where would I find out about them?" asked DD excitedly.

"Either from the Governor or Father Antonio, I shouldn't wonder."

"Then that's where I'll start, first thing tomorrow. I'll do my own detective work!" concluded a newly spirited Della Dubois.

Enough had been said, so they both lay lazily back in the comforting seclusion of the grassy, sandy slope, and contemplated the deep blue sky above. Then, while the heiress, full of renewed energy, made plans out loud, Raoul began to immerse himself in a sense of warmth and well being. Perhaps he was now just a little closer to understanding what made Della tick, after all.

Yes, her outrageous exhibitionist tendencies were sometimes embarrassing, but weren't they just a front for her inner sense of insecurity? Deep down, he had always thought so. She did seem to invite people to dislike her though. He felt heartened he could now see beyond that.

The two comrades cosily relaxed in the reassuring heat of the sensual sun, but inevitably, after a short while, soon began to lose themselves in moments of intimate tenderness. Fleetingly, Raoul's conscience was beginning to trouble him. Was delicious Della just a convenience, or a habit he just couldn't break?

* * *

An hour later, Raoul sauntered back into the hotel, with the prospect of his dreary afternoon shift on Reception in front of him. He got the usual glare from Seb, who never did like his lunchtime disappearing acts, but on this occasion there was nothing to reproach his partner for, so the handover was quite amicable, after Raoul had showered and changed into some suitable clothes, of course.

"Been anywhere nice?"

"Just down to the beach, for a swim, to cool off." He didn't like lying, but what he said was true in some respect. "Any problems here?" he asked in a mechanical tone; though it was obvious he wasn't really interested.

"No. Quiet as the grave, so to speak. Did you find Dimitri?"

"Who want me now?" came the response, as the young Greek, sleepily emerging from a nearby store room, heard his name.

"Nobody!" shouted Raoul swiftly. "Just remember what we discussed." Dimitri merely stared back with a puzzled look, but guessed that Raoul had covered for him yet again, so he silently nodded.

Seb was not convinced, but said nothing. Why did he keep bailing him out? What were his motives? Or did Dimitri have the upper hand in some way? One day he'd have to get to the bottom of it all, but at the moment he had other fish to fry.

Partway through the afternoon, as he snoozed behind the desk with his feet up, Raoul was startlingly awoken by the reception bell. He looked up to find Grace Elisabeth grinning gleefully at him. "Oh, Grace, you just woke me from a great dream," sighed the receptionist blissfully.

"Anyone I know, Mr. Raoul?" she teasingly giggled.

"That would be telling! Anyway, since you've rescued me from my slumbers, I'll have a nice cup of ice tea, please." Grace gave him her 'I ain't your servant look,' but willingly catered to his needs all the same.

"I don't do this for everyone," she reminded, attempting a semi serious glare.

"I know you don't," conceded Raoul, blowing her a kiss, "but you know I appreciate it all the same. By the way, Grace, can I pick your brains?"

"I ain't sure there's much to pick, but you can try," she laughed. Raoul became slightly more earnest. "You've lived here all your life, haven't you, Grace?"

"Sure have!" she proudly replied.

"So you'd know if there are any records of the inhabitants of the Island? You know; births, marriages, deaths and all that sort of thing."

Grace Elisabeth's face darkened, and she seemed to be considering her answer carefully. "Mr. Raoul, people come and people go. What's the point of writin' it all down?" Raoul obviously wasn't getting anywhere, so he probed further.

"Sure. But there must be some kind of details, somewhere." Grace seemed reluctant to converse further on the subject, but didn't wish to appear unhelpful.

"It's best to leave all that sort of thing to the ones whose jobs it is," she concluded after some deliberation.

"And who may that be?" Grace could see that Raoul plainly wished to pursue the matter, and wouldn't give up, so she decided to pass on what she knew.

"Father Antonio has kept records, as long as I can remember, of most things that have happened on the Island since he took over the Parish, but it's more like a diary than an official document. It's personal and private, and I ain't sure he'd let you see it anyway. Besides, some years ago, part of his work went missing. Man, was he vexed!" she emphasised.

"I heard something to that effect. But what do you mean, they were stolen or something?" enquired Raoul with deepening interest.

"Let's just say, they was removed from their resting place, sir, and they ain't been seen since."

"This all sounds very intriguing. Where was their 'resting place'?"

"You don' wanna go near there. Stay away!"

"Grace, you're not making any sense. What's all the mystery?" demanded Raoul, standing up. The housekeeper lowered her eyes.

"There's a curse on that place. I'm just trying to protect you, that's all."

"Don't worry. You know I'm just inquisitive. I only want to improve my knowledge of the Island. Don't get annoyed."

Grace realised that she'd given too much away already and beat a diplomatic retreat, berating her boss for stopping her work. Curiously, it wasn't long after, that Raoul spotted her sneakily slipping out via a side entrance, scurrying off, definitely with something on her mind.

Apart from when he had to deal with the trivia of unwanted guests, Raoul spent the rest of his time on duty that afternoon pondering about his conversation with Grace. What had he stumbled on? He made up his mind to visit Father Antonio, as soon he was able, but meantime, thought he'd glean some more information from other locals.

"Good Afternoon, Miss Kittie, Miss Clarrie. Enjoying afternoon tea?" Kittie immediately looked suspicious. She guessed Raoul wanted something. He wasn't one to fraternise with the guests voluntarily.

"Oh hello, Mr. Raoul," gushed Clarrie, "I expect you're fed up sitting behind that boring reception desk all afternoon when you could be enjoying yourself." Clarrie had a way of stating the obvious, but in such a sweet manner that you had to forgive her.

"Yes, just passing the time chatting to Grace about the curse actually," stated Raoul nonchalantly, looking for a reaction.

"That's nice," smiled Clarrie.

"Curse, what curse?" asked Kittie in a businesslike fashion.

"Oh, you know, the one about the Parish records. Where was it they were stored again?"

"I'm sure neither of them knows what on earth you're alluding to Raoul, and nor would anyone else. It's all a load of piffle anyway!" interrupted a passing Lady Laetitia before Kittie could even open her mouth.

"What is, Lady Laetitia?"

"Beg pardon?" she bellowed.

"What is? What's a load of piffle?"

"Nothing!" she immediately responded with a glare.

"But you just said . . . "

"Come along, Alistair!" she beckoned to her bewildered son. "We haven't got time to stand here all day twaddling."

"B . . . but, m,m,mama, w, we, h,ha,haven't h'haven't . . . "

"Haven't what?" she boomed, seemingly agitated.

"Haven't . . . had . . . tea . . . yet," he managed to get out in one sentence.

"Nor shall we," she concluded. "Not today!"

As they left, Alistair turned shiftily around with a knowing glance, which intentionally caught Raoul's eye.

What was it? What on earth was it that he was being excluded from? The frustrated young man began to seriously question himself. He was on friendly terms with everyone. They all liked him for his outward sense of humour and fun, didn't they? So what did they want to hide from him . . . and why?

Perhaps Seb had been idly gossiping about Raoul's candid and acrimonious views on the regulars, usually voiced out of ear-shot, and they were now wary of him? But his partner wouldn't do that. He was too loyal, and besides, he didn't engage in idle chit chat.

There was certainly a jigsaw to piece together here, and Raoul intended to waste no time dodging the beckoning puzzle. But who could he really trust?

Chapter 15

Unable to sleep, Raoul got up next day before the crack of dawn. Seb was still dozing peacefully beside him, so he silently slipped on the first pair of shorts and T shirt he could find and, without his normal ablutions, went downstairs where some of the early morning staff were already preparing breakfast.

Stealthily creeping through the front lobby, hoping not to be seen, he walked straight into a disconcertingly chirpy Grace Elisabeth who was just arriving for work. "My, my, Mr. Raoul, can't you sleep?" she teased, drawing unwanted attention to the fact. She was well aware that Raoul was known for not being at his best in the morning, usually avoiding company and conversation like the plague.

"No, I didn't sleep very well last night actually, so I thought that an early morning swim might do me good," he lied. He sensed that Grace didn't believe a word of it, but continued obliviously on his way. After all, he wasn't answerable to her, was he?

Raoul excitedly made his way up the sandy pathway to the Church, but did occasionally linger to appreciate the unique and beautiful atmosphere of this early part of the day. The tranquillity of the morning was broken only by the gentle wash of the waves on the beach and the birds greeting the new sunrise. A light breeze wafted up from the shore, bringing the delightful senses of the sea. Raoul soaked up this exhilarating new experience and resolved to get up early again sometime, simply to enjoy this, as yet, unfamiliar pleasure.

Reaching the pretty Church courtyard, the young man decided to catch his breath for a few minutes, on a bench under a shady tree, and work out what he was actually going to do. He needn't have bothered to deliberate since, as luck would have it, he had no time or opportunity to formulate a plan. Seconds after he had perched pensively on the seat, he felt a presence behind him. Strangely, he was neither startled nor afraid, for he sensed his company to be friendly.

"Is something troubling you, my son?" Father Antonio softly asked as he awkwardly sat down beside him, obviously in some pain.

"No, Father, not at all, but you seem to be struggling. Why do you ask?"

"Oh, I'm fine. Just wear and tear on an ageing body, but it is truly a rare, yet pleasing, sight to see you in my Churchyard, especially this early in the morning. I would wager it's not just chance that has brought you here," reasoned the canny priest, with a twinkle in his eye.

Thinking on his feet, Raoul decided that he would courageously cut straight to the chase and see the reaction, a reaction he had totally not bargained for. Expecting to be fobbed off, he began to openly quiz the priest. "I'm interested in finding out about past history on the Island and thought I'd look at the Parish records. Do you keep any?"

"It's too early in the morning to play games Raoul, you've come to explore some of the Island's darker secrets, haven't you?"

"Well, yes, perhaps I have, I suppose. You see, everyone clammed up when I innocently asked if anyone kept details of those who live or used to live here. I got the impression that there was some kind of mystery, and I'm rather partial to mysteries. Then I discovered that you kept a journal, and that what was in it disappeared. That intrigued me even more. There was also mention of a curse."

At that point, he looked Father Antonio hard in the face, waiting for a response which would warn him off, as the others had done. He was surprised, therefore, when the priest candidly volunteered the information he was seeking without so much as a hesitant thought.

"Well, it's like this," began the cleric, with a sigh. "Some years ago, there was a beautiful, young native Island girl who stood out from the crowd. Not content to just fit in like all the rest, she wanted to make a name for herself, and rise above the ranks as it were. The story goes that she intentionally aggravated the Island's female population by openly flirting with their husbands, sons and lovers. She made mischief and, it is said, that she secretly gave sexual favours to some of the more influential males. This inevitably caused all sorts of problems, and the peace and tranquillity of our little community suffered as a result.

I kept note of this in my journal, merely as hearsay. Anyway, after considerable provocation, the ladies of the Island got together and shunned the native beauty, made her life a living hell in any way they could.

One night there was an almighty storm. Everyone feared for their own safety. For some reason, the native girl had been made homeless by then, and was caught out in the open, in the middle of this terrible raging tempest.

Despite impassioned pleas, everyone refused her shelter, some even watching her struggle for life. Eventually, pitifully weak and bedraggled, she managed to make her way to the Church crypt which had, by chance, been left open. I knew nothing of this. I had been ill for some days, and was laid up in bed in my quarters. My gout was playing me up quite badly at that time, you see.

Well, anyway, it appears that the Island girl took shelter inside. However, during the storm, the heavy wooden door slammed and somehow wedged itself shut, blocked by falling rubble from the outside. She was trapped within.

Some say this had been done deliberately, either by the angry elements or by other 'scheming forces'. There was no way out. Only one entrance to the underground crypt exists, the way the poor creature went in. The mighty door is situated at the side of the oldest part of the Church, and leads below by a precarious set of stone steps. I, myself, rarely go down there for fear of slipping, but it is where the records were, and are, still kept.

After the storm had died down and things got back to normal, there was no mention of the girl and I, well, I blame myself. I never went down to the crypt for about a month as I was still unsteady on my feet. When I did, I needed some of the Islanders to help me remove the debris piled up in front of the old door and prize it open.

On eventually gaining access, we cautiously descended the steps, armed with a handful of candles for light. There was no-one there. Nothing unusual. If the girl had been in there, she had disappeared. There was no body, nothing untoward, that is until one of my helpers noticed the journal. It was flapping open on the very page of the fateful day of the storm. There were names of certain 'gentlemen', scribbled crudely in blood, right across the double pages of the heavy leather bound book, a book too heavy for anyone to carry away without help.

It was concluded that these names, some in a sort of code, beneath the large, scrawled heading, 'REVELATIONS', were the names of the males whom she had pleasured, unbeknown to their wives. There were also curious clues to scandalous secrets belonging to some of the other Islanders, contained in verse, all written in blood!

We were too tired to continue that day, so we resolved to return and solve the spine chilling riddle the following morning. We made a makeshift lock to secure the crypt and laboured home, uneasy, stunned and exhausted.

Early next day, I secretly went alone to retrieve these emotive pages of my journal, for fear that they may have caused strife on the Island. When I arrived, the heavy wooden door was open and, on further investigation, I discovered that the offending pages written in blood had been ripped out. Ominously, however, there was another message, also written in blood, but not in the same hand, on the next clear page. It read;

'Whoever ventures into this crypt,

Will find themselves in blood dipped.'

This was clearly meant as a deterrent towards subsequent investigation. I personally took all this with a pinch of salt, but ever since, I have been extremely wary about going into the crypt of my own Church, and do so only when necessary.

Time has turned this episode into rather an exaggerated tale on the Island, but the natives refer to it as 'The Curse of the Fallen Woman' and many see the whole area as taboo, even though it is on consecrated ground. The more educated among us feel the entire thing was a masquerade, and believe it's an old wives' tale. However, I was there. I know what I saw."

The priest was about to finally rest his dry throat when he seemed to recollect something else. "And one other thing, I'm not sure if it's relevant, in fact it's probably sheer coincidence, but there has been a candle of remembrance burning in a side chapel of the Church ever since that fateful episode. It never goes out. It is always replaced and rekindled. Try as I might, I've never been able to discover who keeps it alive or who it's for."

Raoul was enthralled by the story of the so called 'curse', and so astonished that Father Antonio had shared it with him, that he didn't interrupt him once, neither for question nor for comment, but he was itching to ask one vital two part question. "Who were the other Islanders with you on the day you first discovered the pages in blood and do they still live within the community today?" So he did.

Father Antonio looked him straight in the eye at that juncture and softly, but firmly replied, "Such a question, I knew you would ask, my son. But the answer to it will go with me to my grave, believe me!"

With that, he politely wished Raoul 'Good Morning!' and suggested that they both go their separate ways for breakfast.

Raoul pondered for a while as he slowly trudged back along the familiar pathway to the hotel. What an astonishing story! Was it true or was it myth embroidered in the passing of time? How come Father Antonio was so frank with him about the affair when other Islanders refused to discuss it? It must have had some substance, he concluded, since the priest had recounted his own part in the tale. He could have been lying, of course. Do priests lie?

Chapter 16

Embroiled in his thoughts, Raoul searched in the pouches of his shorts for a handkerchief to wipe the trickling sweat off his brow; sweat no doubt produced by the rising heat of the early morning and the excitement of the day so far. Fiddling idly in his left pocket, he managed to locate what felt like a cotton tissue and, as he withdrew it, something quite heavy nestling inside fell out and landed on the grassy verge beside him. He instantly bent down and picked up the shimmering article, a silvery round piece of metal. It was a watch, quite an expensive one at that. "How did that get in there?" he murmured to himself. "It doesn't belong to me."

Probing to ensure there was nothing else in the pocket, Raoul realised, on closer examination, that the shorts he had slipped on in haste, in the early hours of that morning, weren't actually his. They belonged to Seb. He and his partner were approximately the same size in the waist, and sometimes did borrow each other's casual clothes, either by design or, as in this case, in error. Even so, he was certain the watch didn't belong to Sebastian either, so now there was another minor mystery to solve. Whose was it and why was a personal item belonging to someone else concealed in his partner's pocket?

Working on a vague hunch, Raoul racked his brains to try and remember where he had seen such a time-piece before. He dimly recollected previously mentioning to somebody that their wristwatch was far too good for work, and that no responsibility would be taken by the management for loss or damage. Following this train of thought, he soon realised who the owner of the article was, and his mood darkened as he became uncontrollably enveloped in mounting anger.

Raoul quickened his step and steadfastly continued his route, almost marching in frustrated rage back to the hotel and right into the lobby, forcefully swinging doors open and knocking furniture out of his way on arrival. Grace Elisabeth was busy serving breakfast, but hastily made her excuses to the guests and headed directly towards Raoul, looking extremely perplexed.

"Everythin' alright?" she asked nervously.

"Yes, of course. Why shouldn't it be?" her boss barked back.

"Well there's no need to bite my head off. I'm just a little concerned about you today. Gettin' up early. Then comin' back here like a ragin' bull. It ain't like you. Thas all."

Grace's soothing words and motherly concern jolted Raoul to his senses, and he began to calm down. After all, he needed to carefully consider his next step, and Grace was taking more than a passing interest.

"Yes, yes, you're right. Sorry, Grace, I'm all hyped up. That swim got my adrenalin going and I haven't worked it all off yet."

"But you ain't got no swimmin' gear," she observed pragmatically.

"No exactly!" he responded with a smile, leaving Grace somewhat bewildered and none the wiser.

"Where have you been?" asked Seb anxiously, as Raoul quietly entered their first floor suite.

"Out!"

"What this early?"

"Maybe I've been out all night. Would you have noticed or even cared?"

"Come on, less of that! Could say the same about you," sighed Sebastian putting his hand on Raoul's shoulder as they both stood motionless at the window, looking out to sea. "Let's not argue. It's my day off. Let's spend it together."

Raoul slowly turned round and they gently hugged, each one placing his head on the other's shoulder. Raoul stared into space. He had too much on his mind, and wanted to be alone today, but he didn't really want to upset Seb. He had to think on his feet. How was he going to get out of this one?

"Let's see. What's the time?" mused Raoul looking at the newly found chronometer, now on his left arm. As he did so, he deliberately waited for some kind of reaction or comment about the watch from Seb, but none was forthcoming. Not a flicker, not a word! Either he didn't recognise it or he was playing his cards very close to his chest.

At that very moment, either by luck or by misfortune, the telephone rang. It was the internal line. The men both looked at each other and laughed. The tension had been broken; the interruption was right on cue, as usual. After about a dozen rings, Seb regretfully decided that he could ignore it no longer and prepared to answer the call. Obvious persistence indicated it was important.

"O.k.," he nodded. "I'll be down straight away. I was expecting it."

"Who was that?" asked Raoul with a forced lack of enthusiasm, after it became obvious his partner was not in the mood to discuss the matter voluntarily.

"Reception," seethed Seb, putting on his jacket.

"They're bloody useless! What can't they manage this time? We might as well do everything ourselves!"

"Can't leave this to them. There's some rumpus down there with Della Dubois, no doubt providing a floor show for the other guests. I'll have to go and sort it out myself. Looks like you're off the hook again," he shrugged with an acceptant smile.

"Well, I'll go if you like," half heartedly offered Raoul, obviously not really wishing to be involved.

"No! I'll do it. It's your fault she's still here anyway. I told you to kick her out. Time is slowly running out for that little Madam!"

"Oh, here come the heavies," mocked Della Dubois in her loudest fishwife bellow, as Sebastian appeared in Reception moments later and nodded to the grateful young receptionist, indicating that he would relieve her of the unpleasant task ahead. "This, this 'woman' will not . . . hick . . . let me in to my . . . hick . . . suite," she slurred straight into Seb's face, barely able to stand without wobbling, and stinking of alcohol. Her flimsy clothing barely covered her assets. She'd obviously been out all night drinking, and was much the worse for wear.

"My key's not walk . . . work . . . ing and I need a pa . . . asss key."

"That won't be necessary," softly replied the hotel pro-prietor.

"Good!" she nodded in full agreement. Then, "wat . . . da . . . ya . . . mean, won't be nec . . . cess . . . ess . . . ary?" shaking her head in befuddled bewilderment.

"You're not staying here any more."

"Wadda ya mean, . . . 'not stay . . . ing here'?" she mim-icked, lurching from side to side.

"Exactly what I said! You have not paid your bill, and it is the policy of this hotel NOT to accommodate guests for free."

"But..but, I'm a bloody . . . bloody mill . . . million . . . nil-lionairess," she argued unsteadily, in a drunken, husky drawl.

"Madam, if you are a 'millionairess', then settle your bill. Until you do so, you are not welcome here. Even then, I'd have to think twice," continued Seb, calmly and firmly. "Now, I have taken the liberty of putting your personal belongings in the lobby, so I suggest you leave. Dimitri will escort you off the premises." The young pool attendant, waiting in the shadows, had to now decide where his loyalties lay.

"What? Whaaaat?" Della Dubois just glared, eyes wide open, in disbelief. She could not comprehend what was going on. Well, she was in no fit state to! "You . . . yoooou haven't heard the lazzt of this. I'll show you! I'll sh..show you all," was her parting shot, waving her fist, as an embarrassed and angry Dimitri thought discretion to be the better part of valour, and roughly began to manhandle his lady friend out of the hotel, for her own good.

Fortunately, few people were around, but there were two ladies, deep in conversation, apparently watching every move. They were in the nearby bistro, being served breakfast; crois-sants with strong freshly ground coffee, and a glass of water.

The unlikely alliance of Lady Daphnee and Alicia Tremaine seemed to be observing the chain of events with great interest, and it appeared that they had come into the hotel shortly after

Della Dubois. Two pairs of steely eyes coldly and carefully monitored her every movement as she falteringly tottered in her high heels towards the exit supported by her young, Greek friend.

Noticing she seemed to be the object of ridicule, Della Dubois could not contain herself, and broke free from her escort, making a bee line for the ladies' breakfast table. "What are you bitches bloody staring at?" she reproached in a threatening tone, hoping the challenge would provoke a confrontational response she could seize upon to vent more of her pent up anger.

"It looks as if you could do with a glass of water, my dear," Daphnee Meadows softly suggested.

"You think so? Well in that case . . . I'll have yours!" spat the lush, knocking into the table and grabbing the tall glass, by now containing an almost unnoticeable cloudier liquid, suitably placed within arm's reach. She greedily gulped the contents, banged the empty container down on the table, and continued to make her way outside, reeling like a fish on a line.

On reaching the terrace, Della Dubois suddenly stood dead still, clutched her throat with both hands and, after gyrating violently, vomited all over the front steps of the hotel, before passing out into unconsciousness.

The two women glanced at each other uncomfortably and, as if scripted for an audience, to exonerate herself from the mishap, the Doctor's wife innocently, but rather loudly, announced, "Oh dear, that glass had my medication in it, and if the mixture comes into contact with alcohol, the results could be very dangerous. Very dangerous indeed!"

Sebastian had been purposely hovering in the background and had witnessed the whole affair. With an unobtrusive grin, he couldn't help but wonder if the women's presence, and the subsequent events, were coincidental, or if Della Dubois had just fallen into a very well planned and carefully executed trap?

Chapter 17

"Oh dear, I suppose I'd better fetch my husband," sighed Alicia reluctantly, as she got to her feet somewhat unsteadily, obviously appearing to be suffering from shock. "Miss Dubois seems rather unwell. I do hope it's nothing serious!"

By this time, other guests had gathered and were surrounding the unfortunate reveller, now slumped precariously onto the handrail of the hotel steps, supported by a nervous looking Dimitri. "That's it. Put her arm around your neck. Try to get her moving!" shouted a voice, as Raoul rushed downstairs, having just caught the tail end of the debacle. "Get some coffee. Let's try to sober her up!"

Alicia had barely had time to reach the terrace before her husband came striding up the pathway to the hotel. "What's all this?" he asked. "Alicia, I've been looking for you everywhere. Why didn't you tell me if you were going out early? I've been worried sick."

"Well, I'm hardly going to get lost on this Island, am I?" she reasoned, shrugging her shoulders.

"It's Della Dubois. She's had a night on the tiles and passed out!" interrupted Raoul. The Doctor hesitated. All eyes were now on him. He had to consider whether personal feelings or professional duty should take precedence. It didn't take him long to make up his mind. He instinctively began to gently slap his patient around the face and tried to rouse her. No response.

"I fear this may be more serious than at first thought, darling," simpered Alicia, approaching her husband and gripping his arm as she stumbled.

"What do you mean?" he asked with a puzzled look.

"Well, she needed some water, and before we, that's Lady Meadows and I, could stop her, she seized the glass from our table, the one with my medicine in it, and drank the lot."

"What medicine?" curtly asked the Doctor, now under real pressure to do something.

"You know, that concoction you made up, especially for me, yesterday, to settle my nerves. Well, I'd mixed it into a full glass of water and just had my dose; it's all been so stressful lately and . . . "

Before she could gabble on any further, Jimmy interrupted. "Well, that wouldn't do her any harm, but . . . " The Doctor then suddenly swung round and just managed to knock the coffee out of Raoul's hands as he put it to Della Dubois' lips.

"What the hell are you doing, Jimmy? I'm trying to help!" growled a startled Raoul, squaring up to his friend.

"Well, if she has swallowed that stuff," the Doctor defended himself, "it shouldn't be directly mixed with coffee or anything else containing caffeine There's a chance she could have an allergic reaction, and it could kill her."

Alicia's face lost its colour. "But . . . you said . . . one . . . shouldn't . . . " The Doctor's wife tightly grasped her husband's arm again, as she began to feel woozy and unsteady on her feet. "One shouldn't . . . drink . . . alcohol, yes, alcohol . . . with it!" she insisted, slurring her words. Jimmy froze.

"But, I said that to get you off the sauce, darling. You've been hitting the bottle a bit lately. I didn't think I had to remind you about . . . Oh no! Don't tell me you . . . But, you never drink coffee or tea, never! You know caffeine doesn't agree with you. That's why I used . . . " frantically pleaded the Doctor, displaying a mixture of fear and guilt. "For the love of God, woman, you knew the ingredients I blended. You knew I used monoamine oxidase inhibitors, they help depression. You're a bloody trained pharmacist, for Christ's sake."

"But, today I just was . . . wasn't . . . think . . . ing straight," Alicia slowly tried to explain. "I didn't . . . , I didn't suppose . . . just one cup of coffee would do any harm . . . just for a ch . . . change," she whined, massaging her stomach before, too weak to stand any more, she keeled over into her husband's arms.

Jimmy didn't know what to do. He couldn't cope. He was shaking like a leaf. All that training, all that experience, and now when it came to the crunch, he had seized up. He had two women to tend to at once, and one was his wife, clutching on for dear life. He really had to pull himself together and do his job.

He put a mirror to Alicia's mouth. She was still breathing faintly, and he'd already checked that Della Dubois still had a pulse.

"Concentrate on your wife!" finally echoed a reluctant instruction from one of the onlookers. "And I'll see to this one!"

It was Sadie Finch who had taken charge of the situation. Having cut short her early morning walk on the beach to see what all the commotion was about, she had left her dogs with Harriett, trailing behind as ever, to see if she could be of service. When she discovered what had happened, she couldn't lose face, and had to remember her professional ethics. After all, people were watching, and she couldn't be seen to be belligerent if she wanted everyone to finally get their just deserts.

"Oh, goodness!" muttered Harriett breathlessly, as she wearily caught up, desperately trying to control three unruly barking dogs. "The Island's female population seems to be dropping like flies. What in heaven's name is going on?"

Just as Sadie began to slap Della Dubois round the face, and she could have been a little more gentle, the good time girl regained consciousness and started to splutter and cough. She then lunged forward and began to retaliate, punching and kicking.

"Get off me, you bloody bitch! She's trying to kill me!" she bawled to her captive audience, as the pushing and shoving was getting out of hand. "She wants my money, and she'll do anything to get it. Stop her somebody! Stop her!"

"That's rich coming from you," barked Sadie, trying to restrain her. "I was trying to help, but if that's your attitude you can . . . "

At that point, Della Dubois stopped struggling, stood upright and motionless, and then bent forward and vomited once again. This time, all over Sadie's famous beige walking suit.

The former nurse was beside herself with rage. Her fuming eyes slowly looked down at her ruined clothing but, despite her greatest impulse to the contrary, she maintained her dignity, deciding there was a time and a place for everything. That time and that place were fast approaching, but not here, and not now, and definitely not in front of witnesses!

The scene was soon beginning to resemble the January sales; shouting, shoving, crying, comforting. Somebody had to restore order and, as usual, authority came in the form of Lady Laetitia Lascelles, approaching the hotel with hapless Alistair twenty yards behind her, both anticipating some calm, leisurely morning refreshment.

"Stop all this nonsense now!" she commanded in her inimitable voice. "I don't know what's going on, but this is no way to proceed." Those who were able almost stood to attention at the sound of her instruction. Then, gradually, everyone came to their senses and jumped to.

Dimitri dragged Della Dubois, moaning and groaning, back to her former abode, the modest quarters of her beach front café. She was obviously just going to have to sleep it off. He unceremoniously banged open her bedroom door, formerly a place for fun and frolic, deposited her on the unmade bed, ensured she was reasonably comfortable, and made a quick exit as she snored and burped her way into oblivion, in her typical unladylike fashion. The odd job man then predictably made himself unavailable for the rest of the day. There had already been enough excitement for him.

Alicia Tremaine was showing few signs of immediate recovery, so Sebastian took it upon himself to relieve Jimmy of the responsibility of his wife, and telephoned the main island for assistance. The Doctor reconciled himself to the fact that his wife needed more medical attention than he could give. He dutifully, though reluctantly, prepared to accompany her to hospital in the hovering helicopter. Strangely, he vowed not to be long. The community needed a medic, especially in the light of present circumstances. But why was Jimmy's intended, swift return obviously such an urgent priority? Just what were his real motives?

Everything had happened so quickly and in such confusion. No-one noticed that, on arrival, a passenger had shiftily alighted from the air ambulance and disappeared, without fuss, into the bustling throng.

Chapter 18

That day, Lady Laetitia presided over morning coffee in the hotel bistro. After making it abundantly clear to both the proprietors that the unsatisfactory behaviour prevalent on the Island at present displeased her greatly, she pressed on to let her feelings be known to everyone else; from Kittie and Clarrie to Harriett and Father Antonio. Then, she made it her business to pay Monty Meadows an official visit.

Fortunately, Lady Daphnee had had time to reach her husband's office and recount her version of the morning's events, so the Governor was already prepared for yet another bout with his long term sparring partner.

"I sympathise with you Lottie," he began, puffing on his pipe, as he typically broke into a nervous sweat after hearing her catalogue of complaints. "But there's not a lot I can do. People are people and they behave unpredictably. Until it's against the law, I cannot act."

"Don't be ridiculous, Monty!" argued Lady Laetitia. "You're losing your touch. I don't want your sympathy, I want action! It never used to be like this on the Island. Or is history repeating itself?"

At that chilling suggestion, Monty coughed tensely and seemed ill at ease. Daphnee Meadows took the sound of his continued spluttering as her cue to make an entrance. "Morning again, Laetitia! Quite an unfortunate chain of events earlier on."

"There's nothing unfortunate about it, Daphnee, dear. There's one person at the centre of all the unnecessary nonsense on this Island, and I'm still waiting for someone to take the bull by the horns and do something."

"Perhaps someone was trying to," Lady Meadows suggested coyly, staring meaningfully straight into Lady Laetitia's eyes as she slowly left the room.

"That's as may be. But it clearly didn't work, did it?" she seethed. "Monty, think on!" she threatened, making her way out of the office and pacing down the corridor. "I've got contacts, you know, and I shall use them if need be!"

The Governor continued to puff irregularly on his pipe, and once more turned, deep in thought, towards the beautiful sea view from his window. His eyes welled up. He was growing so tired of all this bickering and seemed to be searching for a way out.

* * *

Raoul, too, had had enough drama for one day, so he took advantage of an early relief from his shift on Reception, to take his customary stroll along the less well trodden tracks of the Island.

As he reached Edith's abandoned villa, he stood by the gate at the end of her path, and allowed himself to wallow in fond memories of their times together. The garden looked beautiful and had been tended, probably still by her former gardener. He recollected the fun they had had in each other's company, and then grew sad as he wondered whether he would ever see his French friend again. He missed their chats, her accent, his opportunity to use his mother's native language, her unintentional humour in the use of English. The place was not the same without some jazz number blasting out for all to hear.

Raoul scratched his head, deep in thought. What had become of Edith? Was she still recuperating on the main island? Had she moved on? There had been no news. He visualised her looking out of the window at him. She was smiling. Petite and immaculate, her brightly coloured turban hat made her feminine form unmistakeable.

A gentle breeze then shook Raoul out of his reverie, and momentarily reawakened him. He blinked to adjust his eyes, streaming in the sunlight. Then he shivered. There *was* someone there; a figure standing in the window. It wasn't a dream or his imagination! It was her! Edith was there!

135

Raoul excitedly ran up the path towards the front door and tried the handle. It was locked. Why had Edith locked herself in? Maybe she was jittery about security after the unfortunate episode of the 'accident'? Perhaps she was still uneasy about strangers! He banged on the door. "Edith, Edith, c'est moi!" There was no response. Somewhat frustrated, Raoul fiddled to find the spare key, usually located under a large plant beside the porch. The pot was unusually heavy and refused to budge at first. It seemed it hadn't been moved for some time. Slowly, the visitor eventually managed to painstakingly wedge a nearby broken brick underneath, and niftily fiddled for the key. It was still there! He gradually eased out the rusty, iron implement, put it in the lock and turned it.

"Edith, Edith, où es- tu?" Raoul excitedly enquired. Again, there was no answer. He proceeded to look around the kitchen, then the lounge. Everything was just the same. No-one had cleared up. The wine, the glasses, the glossy fashion magazines; just where they had been abandoned on the day Edith left the Island under a cloud. But he had just seen her. She was there. Why didn't she make herself known? It didn't make sense. He was her friend. There was no threat.

Raoul, now more half heartedly, continued his search upstairs. The bed was not made. Some books in French and two pairs of spectacles lay on the dresser. The bathroom tap was still dripping. Nothing had been moved. Had his vision just been wishful thinking? Had he deluded himself? What was going on?

Everything was just as it was. It did occur to him, however, that one thing was missing; the blood stains on the settee and carpet. They had vanished. Someone had been in, but who? And why had their work been so specific?

Disappointed by his futile search, and beginning to doubt his own eyes, Raoul pulled shut the old, wooden front door. Despondently, he securely locked the premises, leaving them just as he had found them, and carefully hid the misshapen key back under the plant pot.

Wandering back through the front garden, he decided to explore the grounds, just out of curiosity. Edith's comfy chair, where she used to sit with a glass of her favourite wine, still nestled under the shade of a welcome palm, and the pages of her magazines, untouched, rustled in the gentle breeze. Even her old reading glasses were still on the rickety, wooden table where they had often played cards. "Happy memories!" thought Raoul to himself, as he dejectedly made his way back down to the beach.

With the sun directly in his eyes, and still immersed in confusing thought, the inattentive daydreamer almost tripped over a wandering dog unexpectedly appearing from behind an overgrown bush. She seemed to recognise him and playfully started to sniff his legs. Her owner was nowhere to be seen, and it was unusual for a pooch to be wandering alone. "Where's your Mummy, girl?" Raoul whispered, as he tickled her under the chin, half expecting her to answer, of course.

By and by, the muffled sound of hushed voices, coming from the other side of the clump of bushes, soon interrupted the little encounter, and enticed the dog to turn tail and retrace her own tracks. Raoul was not one to shy away from prying further, so he peered through a convenient gap in the hedge.

In a small, secluded, grassy dune, a curious rendezvous was taking place. Sadie, Harriett, Maggie Maynard and Daphnee Meadows were sitting in a circle earnestly chatting. The sound of the waves and the slight wind made it impossible for Raoul to hear what they were saying. Sadie was quite animated. Harriett looked forlorn, as usual, fiddling with her beads, a sure sign of discomfort, and Maggie and Daphnee listened intently.

Unfortunately, Sadie's other dog had come searching for her companion, and started to bark as she stumbled on the snooping intruder. In mid conversation, the ladies swiftly stood up, and Sadie came striding towards Raoul's vantage point. He reacted quickly, stepping back as if he were still walking. "Oh, hello, Sadie! Thought I recognised the dog. Rather late for your constitutional, isn't it?" he beamed, as though taken by surprise.

"Yes, I suppose it is. But with all that kafuffle this morning, they didn't get a proper walk, and neither did I. By the time I'd changed my clothes and cleaned myself up . . . . Well, the less said about that, the better! It's probably time to go back now though. The sun is beginning to burn. The dogs will need some shade and a drink. Are you heading that way? I'll walk with you."

Sadie's invitation was more like an instruction, as she ushered Raoul back in the direction of the hotel. She clearly wanted him out of the way. The minute he had the merest opportunity, he artfully looked over his shoulder to see if the others were following, but they had dispersed in different directions. Not the most sensible of moves, since it was not unusual to see them all walking together, except for Daphnee Meadows, that is. She didn't have a dog. They were undoubtedly up to something, but what? He could only surmise it was private, and annoyingly, not for the attention of others.

As Raoul entered the hotel lobby, he could see Sebastian on the telephone in Reception. He waved to announce his arrival, and to appear punctual he looked at his watch, or rather the watch he had found in Seb's shorts. He was still openly wearing it, but no-one had yet remarked on the distinctive time-piece.

He expected the usual fuss because he was late, but Seb was thankfully deep in conversation and continued talking. Raoul was reasonably dressed so he took over, without a word.

"That was Jimmy," Seb volunteered, putting down the receiver. He'll be back in a couple of days. Apparently, Alicia did have a reaction to something or other, but it's nothing serious. She just needs rest and observation."

"That's good," replied Raoul mechanically, still confused by his strange adventure.

"Do you know, I've just had the weirdest experience," he tried to confide, but Seb continued regardless, showing complete disinterest.

"He mentioned Elise too. She's still in a coma, and it seems she was pregnant."

"Was or is?" asked Raoul with great concern. "And what about Curtis?"

"Don't know. Didn't really get to the bottom of it. Anyway, it doesn't look too good." Raoul's thoughts now drifted to another dear female friend who had left his life, albeit temporarily, he hoped.

Their conversation was interrupted by the arrival of Ryan O'Rourke, who came to seek Sebastian's approval for the following week's dinner menus. The uneasy tension between Raoul and the Head Chef continued, but he wasn't about to make a scene. Instead he flaunted the watch on his wrist in full view. There was a slight sign of recognition from O'Rourke. Raoul could tell from his eyes. He continually glanced in its direction.

Raoul now felt ready for a confrontation. "Like it?" he taunted. "Very distinctive, isn't it?"

"Oh, I don't know" replied Ryan nonchalantly. "I used to have one just like it. But I lost it!"

"I bet you did!" seethed Raoul with feeling, as the chef made his way back into the kitchen. He then turned on Sebastian who seemed to be holding his breath in anticipation of trouble. "What's up with you?"

"Nothing! Don't forget to enter those reservations in the Diary. I've listed them for you on the note pad."

"Yes Sir, Mr. Torrington-Chambers!" responded Raoul sarcastically, with a salute, as was his habit when Seb gave him an unwanted instruction.

During his late afternoon stint in the hotel, Raoul had relatively little to do, so he could once again indulge in his thoughts. He just wasn't able to reconcile the fact that things appeared to be happening to his friends on the Island, without any rhyme or reason.

He resolved to be more active and supportive in his friendships, and his first stop would be a call on Della Dubois, when she was ready to receive visitors. After all, she had a right to know what he had discovered about the existence of records, sketchy though they may be, relating to the Island's inhabitants, and the possibility, therefore, of an opportunity to identify her father.

Chapter 19

For all his good intentions and resolve, Raoul was sidetracked the following day. It was his plan to visit Della Dubois as soon as he could during his afternoon break, but the duty receptionist had a migraine and Raoul had to do a double shift. Despite his pleas to Seb to cover for him, they both knew that he'd already had his fair share of time off, so he didn't argue the point, and reluctantly accepted his responsibility.

It wasn't therefore, until early evening that Raoul was actually granted some free time. He was quite tired by then, so he grabbed a quick snack in the bistro, and went upstairs to change and shower. The next thing he knew, he lazily awoke from an unintended nap to hear voices in the private lounge of their apartment.

It was Seb, and he'd brought a visitor. The door was ajar and he overheard the tail end of plans being made. "So that's a date then? You think you can handle it?" enquired Seb with a chuckle.

"Oh, I can handle anything on offer," was the confident response. "Don't you worry. You won't be disappointed."

Raoul heard the door shut and the guest left. He knew the voice, but decided not to react. Instead, he pretended to be still snoozing when Sebastian came into the bedroom. "Hey, Raoul, wake up!" He was gently roused with a peck on the cheek. "You know you won't sleep tonight, and then you'll be grumpy in the morning if you relax now," his partner whispered.

"Oh God, I must have dozed off, and I should have been somewhere two hours ago."

"But I thought we could spend some time together. It's not often we're off at the same time."

"Sorry, Seb, I thought you were doing the late shift, and I've arranged to see Father Antonio about the orphans' party."

"What orphans' party?"

"Well, that's just it. Wouldn't it be nice if they had one, here, at the hotel," enthused Raoul, hastily buttoning his light cotton shirt. "I won't be long, promise, and if you're still up when I get back . . . ." He was already out of their suite and on his way downstairs.

Outside there seemed to be a change in the air. The night sky was peppered with an abundance of small, fast moving, wispy, white clouds. In places, they seemed to join together for company, at times completely covering the moon and masking its much needed light. Raoul studied the peculiar patterns above him with interest, whistling as he briskly walked down to the beach café and the home of Della Dubois.

The café was closed and the area was deserted, but he could see through a small slit in the shutters that the lights in the back room were on. He assumed, therefore, that his friend was in. Now all he had to do was establish whether she was in a fit state to receive visitors.

Raoul knocked, and announced his arrival as he turned the door handle and went in. Nothing was ever locked. The rooms inside showed no signs of life. Dirty glasses and plates littered the kitchen table, and the remains of a light meal stood on the draining board. The cushions on the lounge sofa were in care-less disarray, and the radio was still on. The unmade bed gave the impression that someone had left in a hurry. All in all, everything was normal in the home of Della Dubois. But she was not there!

Deciding to wait, the unscheduled caller went back into the kitchen and, so as to not completely waste his visit, thought he'd do some tidying up. Della Dubois probably wouldn't notice or appreciate it, but it would occupy him until she returned.

As Raoul ploughed his way through the mountain of unwashed dishes, he piled them on the draining board to dry, and began to clear the table. Beneath one barely sipped glass of red wine with a lipstick mark on the rim, there was a screwed up scrap of writing paper. Raoul didn't hesitate. He unfolded it with the clear intention of finding out the contents.

It was neatly hand written, in ink which had been smudged with red wine, making it difficult to decipher. As far as he could make out, it was some sort of challenge; "If you want to know who your father is, wait for the answer tonight at ten, on the old seat by the Wishing Well at Fallow Falls. Come alone, or you'll be disappointed." It was signed, 'M'.

There was no indication of a day or a date, so when it was written was anybody's guess. And who was 'M'? A puzzled Raoul went through all the 'M's he could imagine; Meadows. Maynard, Moreau, Montgomery, Maggie, and wasn't Kittie and Clarrie's surname Mallory-Morrison? It could have been anybody really. Perhaps that was the reason for the café owner's absence. Perhaps tonight was the night!

Raoul pondered for a while. Was it worth the bother to go up to the Falls, just on the off chance that something might be going on that very evening? Should he even get involved? It was really nothing to do with him after all. Predictably, it didn't take long for his sense of adventure to get the better of him. It was preferable to aimlessly hanging around, waiting.

Anyway, by now, he was fed up doing someone else's house-work. After all, he didn't do any at home. He flatly refused to help out with such chores in the hotel. It wasn't that he saw himself as too good for domestic tasks; he just genuinely found them boring and too much like hard work. It was even up to Grace Elisabeth to clean and tidy their apartment. Seb didn't have the time, and he didn't have the inclination. By any standards, Grace did a better job and you could trust her, even with the personal and private items often left lying around.

Raoul was soon out of the door and, though he didn't really know why, steadily making his way up to the suggested secret rendezvous. Being at the highest point on the Island, Fallow Falls boasted the best views. You could just about see everything. It was a bit of a trek; up past the Churchyard and along a cliff path, but the effort was well worth it, even at night. Perhaps, especially at night!

There were numerous stories about the commanding peak. Apparently, many years ago, there had been a gently trickling stream, with its source just below the cliff top at the edge of the Island. Its clear, running water gradually grew into a fountain as it descended, and eventually, before escaping to the sea, provided a beautiful refreshing shower, said to bring luck to those who experienced it. As time passed, this natural gift had dried up, and now all that existed were the raw and rocky remains of its route. The Falls were now fallow, hence the name.

The fearless and more adventurous in the community sometimes used the now parched ascent as a cliff climb from the beach, but frankly, it was a dangerous way to reach the top, and had already claimed some lives. Following that route wasn't even an option. Besides, the tide was coming in fast and the sea looked strangely ominous. Raoul would take the scenic path.

It was actually a lot further than he remembered, and the intrepid adventurer was becoming embarrassingly breathless as he reached the end of the track leading to the lush, green picnic area at the top. While carefully negotiating his way through some interesting bushes, Raoul unexpectedly heard screams. Unmistakable screams, coming from a female. With renewed energy, he quickened his step and shouted. "Who's there? What's the matter? It's Raoul. I'm on my way!"

Eventually reaching the clearing, he could just make out the shape of a woman, frantically running towards him and waving her arms about. She was still some way away, on the grassy bank, and difficult to distinguish. Luckily, the fleeting clouds momentarily allowed the moon to shine through and visibility was clearer. "I saw it . . . ! I saw it all!" she shouted. "I was there!" It was, unmistakably, an extremely animated Della Dubois. "Thank God, it's you! We need help! You've got to save her. She was going to tell me . . . "

Raoul raced towards his friend, stumbling on the uneven surface as he approached. Della Dubois could just about speak. She gripped Raoul's arm and tried breathlessly to explain. "It's Maggie, Maggie Maynard . . . She's hanging . . . hanging off the edge . . . of the cliff."

Incredulous as to how this came about, Raoul didn't have time to think. He skilfully slid down the bank behind the old iron bench, almost tripping over a collapsed easel as he did so, to the safest possible point, and then lay flat on the ground. He cautiously crawled forward, and manoeuvred so he could manage to peer down over the edge.

Sure enough, there she was; a petrified Maggie Maynard clinging to a flimsy branch of a rotting tree, on a narrow ledge, about fifteen feet below. He could see the whites of her stunned eyes. She wasn't shouting. She wasn't shaking. She was too scared to even move. She just held on to her precious branch as it creaked, then cracked, then sent her rolling helplessly, without even a cry, down the slippery slope to her doom.

Chapter 20

"Come on!" urged Raoul. "There's nothing we can do up here. We'll have to head for the hotel and telephone the coast guard." While they hastily clambered down the cliff path, Della, somewhat out of breath, recounted the chain of events which had led to the tragedy.

"I found this . . . this note under my door," she began in her husky voice. "Whoever wrote it . . . said they would tell me . . . , tell me who my father was . . . if I met them, up here, . . . tonight. I had a glass of . . . wine and deliberated about what to do . . . "

They quickened their pace, as much as they were able. "Of course, I had to check it out. I . . . I knew it could have been a hoax, but . . . Anyhow . . . , I was just labouring up . . . up the pathway when I," she stopped to catch her breath, "when I saw someone . . . standing in front of the old bench, by the wishing well.

As I got closer, I could see it was a woman . . . at an easel . . . painting. I couldn't actually identify her, but I guessed it was Maggie Maynard. She's the only painter I know, and the message had been signed with the letter 'M'. It seemed to fit. Obviously, she's the only one prepared to give me the information I'm searching for," she continued, shrugging her shoulders in dismay. "I don't know why though . . . . I don't really even know the woman."

"Hell!" she suddenly cried, as she stubbed her toe on a boulder. Raoul just looked at her flimsy footwear and rolled his eyes in disbelief. "Anyway . . . , when I approached, she saw me and waved, and then stood back to admire her work. I suppose she must have stepped back too far, and jolted herself onto the bench. As she knocked into it, she seemed to lose her balance, and ended up sitting down with a bump. The thud caused the back of the seat to split from the base . . . I heard it crack!" she confirmed. "Then, she went head over heels, backwards down the slope, rolling over the edge."

Della Dubois panted uncontrollably, once again fighting for breath, as they neared the Church cemetery. "There was nothing I could do!" she exclaimed, shaking her head, still with a fixed gaze down at the pathway in front of her. "There was just nothing I could do! So I screamed, and before I had time to investigate, you came along. Boy was I glad to see you!"

"Hang on," interrupted Raoul. "That bench has been there for years. It's wrought iron. It wouldn't just break like that, unless . . . "

"Yes! Exactly! Unless someone . . . , someone had tampered with it. And WHO was that meant for?" she demanded rhetorically.

"More to the point, who would do such a thing?" Raoul questioned. "Surely, if it had been Maggie, she wouldn't have fallen into her own trap now, would she?"

Suddenly, Della Dubois stopped dead and turned around. "I'm going back!" she shouted abruptly.

"Why? Why on earth would you want to go back?" asked Raoul, not quite believing his ears.

"We can't do anything up there . . . We're so close to getting help." He was now himself wheezing uncomfortably from over exertion. His stomach felt tight.

"The painting!" shrieked Della excitedly. "That's it! She was painting my father."

"No! No point! It doesn't make sense. Maggie isn't that type of artist. She only paints what she actually sees, in front of her, at the time, she's told me. Come on, you're exhausted. You won't make it back up the track. I'll go with you tomorrow. First thing. It'll still be there. We must get proper help now. We must!"

"You go on then. I'll follow," assured Della. Raoul looked at her for confirmation. "I will! I will!" she nodded. "I just can't go any further now . . . Not without a rest." He wasn't sure that his friend would keep to her word; she could be very single minded. But he had to trust her. He had no choice. There were more pressing priorities.

Raoul finally reached the Church. It was in darkness. He banged loudly on the door of Father Antonio's quarters and called out for help. There was no answer. He couldn't waste any more time. The priest was probably in an intoxicated sleep. From past experience, he knew he wouldn't be able to rouse him. He had to reach the hotel. It was his only chance of getting some real assistance.

It must have been about twenty minutes since Maggie had fallen. It was touch and go whether it was land or sea that would have claimed her. Raoul felt helpless. All his efforts would probably be in vain, but that was no reason to give up.

The hotel Reception area was deserted. There wasn't even anyone on night duty. Only the ticking of the magnificent antique clock in the foyer, and the breathing of the air conditioning fans, broke the silence.

Raoul was angry at being abandoned at a time like this, but his anger would have to wait. He grabbed the telephone and flicked through the papers on the desk to find the number for the local coast guard. Still panting, he dialled and waited.

A preoccupied voice finally responded. Raoul briskly began to explain the details of the incident, but was almost immediately interrupted and asked for the name of the victim. He gave it and heard the voice shout it back into the office. The coast guard then calmed the caller, explaining that a fishing boat had picked someone up just off the Island and was taking them to the nearest hospital.

The description Raoul gave fitted. The official had no details of the condition of the casualty, but asked Raoul if he would be able to sensitively alert next of kin. If the authorities had to come to the Island, it would cost them valuable time; time which could be usefully spent liaising with the fishermen.

The hotelier explained who he was, and then assured the coast guard that he would take on the onerous task, with the necessary compassion. He had never met the elusive Colonel, but now was his chance, albeit in sad circumstances.

Without stopping to recover, or even think what he was going to say, Raoul hastened towards the Maynard residence.

He'd never been there before, and wasn't really quite sure exactly where it was, especially in the dark. He vaguely knew the direction, so he followed the old lane out of the complex, and hoped for the best.

In no time at all, he came across a rambling, secluded, old building, situated in well kept gardens, surrounded by trees and bushes. It wasn't the type of place you would find unless you were actually looking for it.

There was a light on in the porch way, and as Raoul ventured through the gate and up the gravel path, a dog began to bark loudly and incessantly. Another light went on. "All right, all right, old girl. It's probably just your mother. Forgotten her key again, I suppose. Damn nuisance. I've told her about going out this late." The voice was gruff and sounded irritated.

There was a creaking sound of a key being turned, and the front door began to open as Raoul reached the front step. "Hello!" he shouted, trying not to cause alarm, but the door immediately banged shut. He could hear the sound of a bolt being hastily pushed. "Don't be concerned, Colonel. I'm a friend of your wife," the young man announced reassuringly.

"Well, she's not here," was the abrupt reply.

"I know. That's why I'm here."

"Explain yourself, Sir. What are you doing on my premises at this time of night?" responded the agitated voice. The dog began to bark again and was promptly silenced.

"I'm afraid there's been an accident. Your wife, she's had a fall. She's going to the hospital on the main island. I'm from the hotel. They asked me to inform you."

There was a long, still pause. It seemed as if the Colonel was agonising over his response. Then, finally, after what seemed like an eternity. "How did she do that? Is she all right? She's a tough old girl, you know. She'll pull through. She's always been accident prone."

"No, you don't understand," pleaded Raoul.

"I'm sorry. There's nothing I can do," was the curt response. "I'm housebound. I'm sure she'll get in touch. Good Night!" barked the Colonel discourteously, and both the inside and the porch light were switched off, leaving Raoul in complete darkness.

He stood there in disbelief. What had just happened? He had come all this way on an errand of mercy, and had been treated like an unwelcome intruder. The whole affair seemed strange. And it was the voice inside that bothered him most. There was something curious about the voice. He just couldn't put his finger on it. It was very distinctive. He thought he'd heard it somewhere before, but couldn't place where. Even if the Colonel was a recluse, surely he would react to such news with more anguish. And hadn't Seb met the chap, when he went to buy Maggie's paintings?

Raoul's blood ran cold. There was nothing further he could do. He had tried his best, and done what had been asked of him. He reluctantly consoled himself. He could do no more.

Chapter 21

Raoul wearily returned to his hotel suite feeling distinctly perturbed and frustrated. He wanted to talk, to interrogate Sebastian and come to terms with what he saw as a failed performance on his part, but his partner was fast asleep. In any case, there would be no point in trying to have a coherent conversation with him at that time of the morning. Things would seem clearer in the cold light of day.

Though wound up like an alarm clock, Raoul resolved to trouble himself no further, so he swallowed a handful of the tablets Jimmy had prescribed for him, lounged pensively on the balcony sofa and was soon dead to the world. How did he get involved in this mess anyway?

The clatter of breakfast dishes suddenly encouraged the night owl out of his blissful sleep. He had a throbbing headache, and was initially decidedly disorientated. Why hadn't Seb woken him? Probably, because it was more than his life was worth to disturb his partner's slumber! And the pills always made Raoul drowsy, bad tempered and argumentative when they eventually wore off. Little wonder Sebastian was nowhere to be seen!

After pouring himself several cups of strong coffee from the bubbling percolator, Raoul leaned over the veranda, looking out to sea, and cast his mind back to the previous night, trying to piece the jigsaw together. It crossed his mind he'd arranged to meet Della Dubois at some point, to escort her back up to Fallow Falls and investigate matters further. But there was no need to look for her. She was already furtively loitering in the hotel garden, beckoning him to come down.

Raoul slipped out through the back kitchen, or at least tried to, until Ryan O'Rourke spotted him, and loudly announced that Seb was looking for him. He gestured to the chef to mind his own business and continued on his way.

"Ready then?" he asked Della, motioning to the peak.

"Waste of bloody time! I've already been," she fumed.

"You don't hang about, do you?"

"No, I was up at the crack of dawn, and there's no sign of her painting anywhere. All that for nothing!"

"And what about the bench?" he eagerly enquired. "Did you examine it?"

"Badly perished on the back rest, or that's what it looked like to me. Just needed some weight on it to force a clean break. But it could have had some help, I suppose. Looks like it was an accident though. We'll never know, will we?"

* * *

With all the events of the past few days, it had almost slipped Raoul's mind to pass on the information he had gleaned from Father Antonio about the Island's Parish records.

Without building up her hopes, he suggested that he and Della go for a walk along the beach, away from prying eyes and ears. She was somewhat reluctant at first, still angry and disappointed from the last fiasco. But when Raoul reassured her that he had discovered a line of enquiry which might be more fruitful, she bounced back to her normal bubbly self and was once again full of optimism.

Raoul truly felt for his female friend. He appreciated her desperate need to belong, and didn't for one second question her motives. Indeed, he found it all the more uplifting that he might, in some way, be instrumental in changing her life and bringing her much needed piece of mind.

As they strolled along the soft, white sands, Della Dubois heard all about the old wives' tales, the so called 'Curse of the Fallen Woman', and the possibility that what she was after lay in the bowels of the Church crypt. She found the stories most amusing, and didn't take them seriously for one minute. In fact, she thought the accounts to be so hilarious that her witty derision caused the ambling pair to eventually end up in fits of laughter, embellishing the original anecdotes with more ridiculous details, and attributing the roles of certain Islanders to the key parts.

By the time they had finished, the two of them were behaving like children in hysterics; kicking sand at each other and splashing into the welcoming waves to cool down from their playful exploits. There was now, of course, only one way for them to finish off such seductive antics. Nestling down into a secluded sand dune, they once more, with the wash of the waves and the heat of the sun providing just the right atmosphere, experienced the sensual intimacy of each other until they felt truly fulfilled.

Once again, casual intimacy had triumphed over complex commitment. There were never any recriminations, no feelings of guilt. Both of them knew it was just pure lust; another means of releasing the different tensions that had grown around each of them. Their feelings were physical, not emotional. It was friendship, not love. Wasn't it?

Trudging back to the hotel, Raoul became very quiet, lost in his own thoughts. Della Dubois had other things on her mind. Even though she had initially treated the improbable yarn with complete contempt, she strangely decided it could have some substance after all.

Raoul had stopped listening by now. He thought Della was clutching at straws. She, on the other hand, was already openly and excitedly making plans to begin her quest when the couple spotted Sadie and Harriett, coming towards them on their daily constitutional with their faithful hounds.

"Oh, Sadie, I do like your new outfit. How colourful! It's very you!" teased Della, as they all came face to face.

"Thanks, you did me a favour," she replied with a sardonic smile, admiring her own terracotta slacks and top. "I wanted some bright new gear, and you seem to have provided just the push that I've needed for a long time, in more ways than one!"

"We'll definitely see you coming in that," quipped Della, pushing her luck.

"Make sure you do!" threatened Sadie, now in a more sinister tone. "Take a good look. When I get what's rightfully mine, I'll have a new outfit for every day of the week. But if things don't go in my favour, you'll need to keep looking over your shoulder until your neck aches."

Raoul could see that the chance meeting was likely to disintegrate into a slanging match, so he quickly intervened and nudged Della's arm to go. "I haven't finished yet," snapped Sadie, barring their path. "There's talk of an accident involving our friend Maggie. You always know what's going on. Is it true?"

Before Della Dubois could give her version of events, Raoul pushed his way in first. "Yes, yes it's true. Apparently, she was up at Fallow Falls painting, late last evening. She lost her footing and, well, she's in hospital on the main island." Harriett fiddled anxiously with her beads, and gasped in horror. Then she and Sadie gave each other uncomfortable sideways glances before slowly turning to move off.

As Harriett lagged painfully behind, Della Dubois broke free from Raoul's grasp and caught up with her. "Another one of your little misdemeanours gone wrong?" she whispered forcefully into her ear. "We'll add that to the list, shall we? Remember my party? Poor Elise, she's still in a coma you know."

"Leave me alone, you dreadful, dreadful woman," pleaded the former celebrity, waving her arms about as though she was shaking off a fly.

Harriett was a far easier target to bully than Sadie. She rarely stood up for herself. Father Antonio had always said, 'Some people enjoy life, and some people endure it.' Unfortunately, Harriett Haversham would now have to place herself in the latter category.

Snatching herself away from her tormentor's clutches, Harriett inwardly resolved that enough was enough. "And tell your old man I'll be giving him a visit soon. I want a guided tour of his Church," Della Dubois instructed, as she slowly distanced herself. Harriett merely shook her head in despair and quickened her step to catch up with Sadie.

"What was she on about?" demanded Sadie. "Your 'old man'? Who's she talking about?"

"I really don't know," answered her forlorn walking companion, shrugging her shoulders. "Just another of her pathetic attempts to try and manipulate people and stir up trouble, I suppose."

"Well tell her where to get off!" barked Sadie, shaking her head, scoffing at Harriett's apparent lack of backbone. In her own way, the silver haired spinster was, at times, becoming as much a bully towards Harriett as Della Dubois herself.

Raoul became uneasy. He had just witnessed Della's performance at first hand. A strange mixture of feelings welled up inside him. How could a woman who had just been so tender, change so quickly into a woman who could also be so harsh and so vindictive?

* * *

It was now early afternoon, and as Raoul wandered aimlessly back into the hotel, he once again witnessed Sebastian and Rory O'Rourke huddled together in Reception. Noticing his arrival, the Chef scuttled off with a piece of paper in his hand, and Sebastian picked up the telephone. Raoul was too emotionally exhausted for a row, so he showed a deliberate and distinct lack of interest in his partner's behaviour.

When Sebastian put down the receiver, he looked sheepishly at his other half. "Don't seem to see much of each other nowadays, do we?" he sighed, with a knowing glance.

"Like you care," was the response. Raoul couldn't look him in the eye.

"Believe it or not, I do," continued his partner. "But then, I've not got a guilty conscience."

"Well, it depends what there is to feel guilty about, doesn't it?" reasoned Raoul irritably. "Things aren't always what they seem, are they?"

Before another senseless circular argument could develop, Seb diffused the situation. "By the way, I took a telephone call for you from the coast guard. He said to tell you that the patient's doing better than expected, but will be staying in hospital for convalescence. Are you going to tell me what that's all about, or is that a secret too?"

Raoul recounted the events of the previous night and the early morning in detail, well almost, offering his sense of community service as explanation for his absence. Seb's reaction to yet another accident on the Island seemed to mirror that of many others. He instantly transmitted a nervous, uncomfortable tension.

"One thing," Raoul asked inquisitively. "You met the Colonel when you went over to Maggie's to buy the paintings, didn't you? I'm curious. What's he like?"

"I didn't say I met him, I said he was there. But I never actually saw him. Come to think of it, I did get the impression there was more going on there than meets the eye. But, there could be quite a simple explanation, of course. He's known as a bit of a recluse. Probably he's just shy. Has anyone ever seen him?"

"Not to my knowledge, except perhaps Maggie, of course . . . maybe," he quipped, as they both began to laugh and made eye contact.

How could they both feel so awkwardly embarrassed in each other's company? They'd been together for years. One thing was for sure. The love was still there.

* * *

"Isn't it awful!" commented Kittie, as she sipped her afternoon tea.

"What, dear?" enquired her sister, with an air of distraction.

"Another accident! Oh, you haven't been listening again, have you Clarrie?"

"Oh, yes. Yes, I have, dear. Poor Maggie!"

"Poor Colonel is more like it," coughed her twin, as her tea went down the wrong way. "I wonder how he's managing. Shall we pay him a visit?"

"Perhaps not, dear. Best not to interfere. Not there anyway," persuaded Clarrie, giving her sister a knowing look.

"For once, I suppose you're right," conceded Kittie pensively. The two ladies continued to contemplate their surroundings, waiting patiently for something else to happen which Kittie could offer her opinion about, and Clarrie could passively accept with as little effort as possible.

The telephone rang in Reception, producing a welcome air of anticipation to break the boredom. There was no-one at the desk, so the ringing continued, unanswered. "Oh I do wish they'd answer the damn thing," shouted Kittie in the hope that her raised voice would command more response than the sound of the telephone. "That's it! I'm going to answer it myself," she decided, in a tone of self importance.

"Do you think you should, dear?" asked Clarrie innocently.

"Well nobody else is going to, and it sounds urgent," shrugged Kittie as she got up from her seat. Clarrie tittered to herself, trying to imagine the difference between a telephone sounding urgent and not urgent.

"The Royal Palms Hotel . . . ." Kittie had just put on her best telephone voice when the receiver was gently taken from her hand.

"Thank-you, Miss Kittie, but I believe thas my job." Grace Elisabeth politely took over with a reassuring smile, and Kittie returned to her tea, somewhat annoyed that she had missed her chance.

The caller was obviously, either not prepared to speak to the Housekeeper, or had given up, because the line went dead by the time Grace began to apologise for the delay. "Can't be that urgent," said Grace shaking her head. Clarrie sniggered to herself. Her sister must have been wrong for once!

Frustrated by her eluded opportunity, Kittie seized upon the chance to aggravate Alistair, who had been quietly writing away in the corner of the lobby for the past half hour. "That book of yours must be nearly finished by now, all the time you spend on it," she caustically observed with ulterior interest.

"You're r..r..right," beamed the young man unexpectedly, closing his note pad. "Time f.f.for a swim." With that, he inclined his head forward in a respectful goodbye, and briskly headed for the exit.

"Nothing ever seems to happen here," sighed Kittie, shrugging her shoulders once again, with a distinct air of frustration and boredom.

Chapter 22

As the sun gradually came up and introduced another God given day, Father Antonio heaved back the creaking Church door with some difficulty. Supported by a cane, he limped his way to the Altar, apologised to God for not being able to kneel at the Cross, and uncomfortably sat down to pray. His gout was getting worse. He hadn't been bothering to take his daily tablet to combat his condition, and he was suffering as a result. He wearily tugged at the old bell, and it wasn't long before a scattering of parishioners joined him in the pews. At eight o'clock precisely, he began early morning Mass.

Harriett was a little late, but she never missed an opportunity to show her devotion to the man she loved, and faithfully sat through the thirty minute Latin service, which the priest, clearly in pain, struggled to conduct. She clasped her Rosary beads tightly in one hand, and held the Bible in the other. Today, she felt unusually sensitive, and tears trickled slowly down her face as she lovingly looked at the pedestal of her affection and adoration.

Her mind often used to drift longingly back to the wonderful times they had enjoyed together all those years ago in Italy. They were so young, so free. They could laugh and dance, hold hands and embrace in public. No-one else mattered. How happy they were!

Now, circumstances and external pressures had brought them here, to an Island, where snatched, intimate moments had to be secret, and nervously hidden from ever watchful eyes. Sometimes, she felt they were getting too old for all this subterfuge. Didn't they now owe it to themselves to enjoy their twilight years in peace and tranquillity, together? But admirably, Antonio's vocation and loyalty to the Island were so strong, that she already knew the answer. They'd have to manage as best they could, as they had been doing for almost half their lives.

She did worry about his health, however, and his regular penchant for a tipple. Perhaps it would be better to simply call Della Dubois' bluff. Let her tell the world what she knew, or thought she knew. To hell with it! Take the consequences. But she couldn't do that to her beloved Antonio. He had pleaded with her to keep up appearances, and she had to abide by his wishes. More's the pity!

And all that business with Elise; she really didn't try to kill her, did she? It was all such a blur. She just couldn't remember. That played on her mind too. Could she cope with it all? She had to! At least love gave her strength.

As the Mass at last came to its conclusion, the few Church-goers there were, scuttled out to enjoy the rest of the day. No-one had noticed the petite, well dressed lady who had been praying, head bowed, at the back of the Church. Inconspicuous, in a dark suit and a veil, she had already made a quick exit, before anyone else had had the chance to turn around to leave.

Father Antonio bid his followers 'Good Day' from the Altar. He was unable to labour his way to the door to undertake his usual, personal farewell. The increasing anguish was taking its toll and could clearly be seen in his tired face. Harriett remained in the front pew, and stood to escort the unsteady priest into the vestry.

They had no sooner reached the side entrance, when a strong gust of wind indicated that the front door had blown open again. Harriett went to close it, but came face to face with Della Dubois.

"Have you come to pray, my child?" Father Antonio asked, before either woman had chance to speak.

"No, I've come for some answers, actually. And by the way, I'm not *your* child," she smirked. "Otherwise that would make HER my mother, wouldn't it?"

Harriett nobly stood between the priest and his visitor as Della advanced, making it quite clear she meant business. "Oh, don't fret, I'm only here for information!" she sneered. "Anyway, don't you think you've shielded him long enough?"

Della Dubois looked Father Antonio straight in the eyes. "Do you know who my father is?" She asked in such a direct manner, it almost caught him off his guard.

"I'm sure that your father will make himself known to you when he is ready," he softly answered.

"Is that the only response you're prepared to give?" she challenged. The priest stood his ground and remained silent, head bowed.

"Why should he help you anyway, even if he does know?" bleated Harriett. "You're prepared to make our lives a misery, why shouldn't we do the same to you."

"Oh, I haven't even started yet, so watch your backs!" she threatened, becoming a little more volatile. "Anyway, he's a man of the cloth. It's his job to help others."

"STOP! In the name of God, stop this bickering . . . , both of you." Father Antonio had had enough. He was in agony. "Please remember where you are. This is not the place for altercation. Now Miss. Dubois, will there be anything else?"

"I thought you, especially, would understand the plight of someone wanting to find their father," Della softened. "My anger is born from frustration. You of all people must understand that. Both of you . . . must understand that."

Harriett and Antonio looked at each other. For the first time, they felt a pang of sorrow for the brazen madam. "It works both ways," gently reasoned the cleric. "The father must also want to find the child. There are no doubt other lives involved in all this; other lives which could be shattered by such a disclosure. And one must, therefore, consider the motives of both parties."

"I didn't come here for a bloody lecture," interrupted Della Dubois, quickly back to her normal shameless self. "The least you can do is give me a tour of your crypt. I know the answer's there."

"Whether it is or it isn't, I can't do that."

Della lunged forward. Antonio held up his hand in defence.

"Not because I'm not willing to, but because I am unable to." She stopped dead.

"What do you mean?"

"I am unable to manage the steep steps in my condition."

"What condition?" she spat in disbelief. He pointed to his right foot which was swollen like a football. He wasn't even able to wear his sandal. Reluctantly, Della Dubois conceded. "So be it! Then I'll go on my own!" she decided, with a nod of unyielding conviction.

"I must advise against that," counselled the priest. "It's not somewhere a person should go alone, least of all a woman. The place has . . . let's just say, unwelcoming forces."

"Oh, I've heard all that baloney. I'm not afraid of old wives' tales," laughed Della dismissively.

"You must be accompanied, for your own sake," insisted the Father.

"Well, I'll take Dimitri. No-one would tangle with him. Satisfied?" Father Antonio shrugged his shoulders in powerless frustration. "Just make sure it's unlocked," ordered Della, as she turned her back on the couple and barged her way out of the Church. "I'll be going sometime tomorrow."

Harriett and Antonio were both somewhat shaken, lost for words after such a disagreeable episode. They felt the need to sit silently, beside the Altar, to try to contemplate fully what had just happened. Neither of them paid any attention to the creaking door of the confessional box gently opening and closing, as a shadowy figure silently slipped out.

* * *

Monty slowly slurped his coffee and toyed idly with his breakfast, simply stirring the fruit in his cereals round and round the milky bowl. The early morning sun shone brightly through the old, stained glass, terrace roof, enticing leafy silhouettes to dance mischievously on the antique oak table below. But, instead of appreciating the dawn of another beautiful day and enjoying his first light meal since getting up two hours earlier, the Governor seemed troubled.

His thoughts were focussing on the right thing to do. Should he come clean and put Della Dubois out of her misery? Or should he let things lie? He couldn't tell her anything about her past anyway; he was as ignorant about it as she was and, after all this time, would it make any difference? The past was the past. He had always had a soft spot for her, it's true, but the recent revelation hadn't inspired him to want to build a close father and daughter bond with someone for whom he had no paternal feelings whatsoever. He felt indifferent.

After all, he hadn't watched her grow up, witnessed her walk or talk for the first time, or done any of the special things that fathers do with their children to enrich their lives and bring them closer together. It certainly would be a bit late to start now.

Then he had to examine her motives for being so desperate in her quest. Was she really looking for a true father and all the emotional baggage that would follow, or merely the key to some financial jackpot? On the evidence so far, the answer to that seemed pretty clear.

His pompous side was telling him that he also had to consider his position, and the possible repercussions of any action he might take. He wasn't just anybody. He was the Governor of the Island. He had a reputation to protect and a position to uphold. A scandal could jeopardise everything, his whole way of life. Why should something which innocently happened over thirty years ago come back to haunt him now? It just wasn't cricket!

And then there was Daphnee. The couple had their own private secrets from the world, like everyone else, but they'd muddled along, and together they had carved out a nice little niche for themselves. She wouldn't tolerate any change in lifestyle now, unless it was for the better, and for them, this was really about as good as it gets; a luxury home on a paradise island, status, money and, until now, piece of mind.

The sound of high heels coming down the marble hallway brought Monty out of his reverie and back to his breakfast. He was trying to put on a brave face, but as soon as Daphnee opened the door, he clumsily knocked over his cup of coffee with his elbow, scattering pieces of their best china all over the floor.

"You really are going to have to pull yourself together, my dear," advised Lady Meadows, in a very matter of fact manner. "I told you things would be sorted, and they will be, soon. Just put the whole thing out of your mind and leave things to me. I'm not about to let some little gold digger spoil our idyllic way of life, now am I?" she self-confidently reassured her husband. There was a cold, calculating tone to her voice, and it reminded Monty just what she could be capable of. Daphnee certainly hadn't got where she was today by luck!

He resolved to do as his wife had suggested; take the line of least resistance, and say nothing. The more he thought about it, the more he convinced himself it was the right thing to do. No point in stirring up a hornet's nest. After all, Livvy could have been lying. There was no proof. She seemed plausible at the time, but perhaps she was bluffing. Anyway, he had done as she had asked, to the letter, so really he was off the hook. Besides, like everything else, it would all probably die down soon. Storm in a tea cup!

It was the old story. If Monty concentrated on his version of the truth long enough, he would probably end up believing it. Sometimes, he even forgot that he and Daphnee weren't actually legally married! But, who was he kidding?

* * *

Della Dubois wasted no time in planning her next move. She hastily made her way to the hotel to seek out Dimitri. As she peered into the lobby, she saw Raoul and Sebastian, both on duty at Reception. Luckily, they hadn't spotted her. She didn't want to antagonise Seb any more, she just wanted to get Raoul on his own. She felt it best not to publicise her intentions to all and sundry. In fact, the fewer people who knew, the better.

Mingling with a small bunch of guests, Della slipped in at an appropriate moment, and then sat unobtrusively in the wicker chair in the corner, shielding herself with a large newspaper.

Every so often, she glanced to the side of her reading matter to see if Seb had left. No such luck! They seemed to both be engrossed in lengthy tasks.

"M . . . M . . . Morning D . . . Della!" acknowledged a voice rather too loud for comfort. A beaming Alistair stood there, no doubt intending to engage the object of his desires in conversation.

"Sshh!" responded Della, irately putting her fingers to her lips. Alistair recoiled like an embarrassed schoolboy. He looked so crestfallen that Della Dubois silently beckoned him back, and motioned for him to sit down next to her.

"I want to speak to Raoul," she mouthed, knowing his ability to lip read. "But I don't want Seb to know. Get him to meet me outside on the terrace, on his own, in ten minutes." Alistair just sat there nervously, fixed to the spot. He was experiencing a mixture of sensations. On the one hand, he was elated that the woman he was infatuated with wanted him to do her a favour, but on the other, he was disappointed that it was Raoul she wanted to be with, and not him.

"Go on then!" she ordered somewhat irritably, waving him away with her hand, at the risk of dropping her newspaper. There was still only a stunned, clueless reaction from Alistair, so Della had to resort to another more personal approach. She leaned forward revealing her ample cleavage. "Pleeeeease. Just for me. I'm sure you'll think of something," she whispered reassuringly, blowing Alistair a little kiss and pouting her lips provocatively. This had the desired effect.

Alistair stood up, boldly walked up to Reception, and coughed to signal his presence. "Alistair, Good Morning! How can we help?" enquired Sebastian with a welcoming smile. Raoul just kept his head down to hide the fact that he was reading a magazine and probably, therefore, not entering the bookings into the diary as Seb thought. Alistair had to think quickly, on his feet. He had attracted the attention of the wrong man.

"I've, I've l..l..ost my p..pen on the t..t.terrace," he announced.

"Well, if we find it, we'll let you know," smiled Seb, continuing indifferently with his work.

"B..b..but it's mamma's!" he insisted, banging his fist on the desk. Such a forceful reaction was quite unusual for Alistair, and prompted Seb to instruct Raoul to see if he could help the guest to find the pen.

Raoul looked up, and was about to tell his partner to do it himself, when he noticed Alistair winking and motioning erratically with his head for him to follow. "Oh God, the poor lad's got another affliction now," he sighed to himself as he reluctantly did as he was bid.

On reaching the terrace, Raoul's arm was unexpectedly grabbed by Della Dubois, and he was promptly hoisted out of sight. It was like something out of a French farce. Alistair just stood there as Della, once again, waved him off with a seductive smile.

Talk about mixed messages! Alistair felt cheated and therefore determined that his inquisitiveness should get the better of him. He wanted to know what was going on, so he wended his way inconspicuously into some nearby bushes bordering the hotel lawn, and sat himself on a wall in the sun, well within earshot of the mystery that was about to unfold.

"What the hell's going on?" Raoul asked incredulously.

"I'm looking for Dimitri," Della announced, as though it were obvious.

"So am I. He's never around when you want him!" complained his boss. "Why all the cloak and dagger?"

Della Dubois explained her intentions of visiting the Church crypt, and the fact that she needed an escort. With Dimitri proving to be so unreliable, she then pressed Raoul to accompany her. She stressed that she needed someone she could trust, in the wake of recent mishaps on the Island.

Raoul didn't see any reason why he shouldn't take part in his friend's adventure. After all, he had paved the way in the first place by acquiring the vital information from the priest. In fact, a bit of excitement could be just what he needed.

"Find it?" asked Sebastian, as Raoul returned unsurely to Reception.

"Find what?" he answered with a puzzled look.

"The pen!" exclaimed Seb, shaking his head in disbelief. "That's what you went out for, wasn't it?" This brought Raoul back to the task in hand.

"Oh, yes. Yes, we found it. It had rolled under . . . someone's seat."

"Thank God for that! The last thing we want today is Laetitia fussing around up here. Right, I'll leave it to you now. I'm off to lunch," announced Seb, as he made his way into the kitchen.

Raoul watched his partner head into the chef's domain before he sneakily left the desk. He then tip-toed across and stood at the swing door, pushed it slightly open, and once again saw the two of them huddled in a corner, laughing and whispering.

Raoul's every impulse was to face it out now. He'd had enough, and was just in the mood to kick open the door, pick up the nearest saucepan, and start wielding it about in rage. But something stopped him. Why should he give them the satisfaction? Surely he could be more inventive. There was more than one way to skin a cat. After all, O'Rourke was only still there by the skin of his teeth!

One of the bell boys owed his boss a favour. Raoul knew that the young man had a crush on him so, in much the same way as Della Dubois used her puppy dog, Alistair, he put his charms to good use and persuaded the employee to do a double shift on Reception. He had to get away from it all. He desperately needed to think.

* * *

Whistling his way up the sandy, palm lined promenade, Raoul began to cheer up as soon as he left the hotel. The wind was a little stronger than usual, but the heat of the sizzling sun lifted his spirits and put him in a better frame of mind. He headed for the tranquillity of the cemetery. He liked to relax on the inviting bench, under the gently swaying, shady palms, and have a peaceful doze, away from everyone and everything.

No sooner had he found his usual spot and made himself comfortable, than had he drifted off into a sensual slumber. The tranquillizers Jimmy had given him helped bring him the restfulness he craved.

Not long after, Raoul woke with a start, and instinctively rose to a sitting position. His drug induced dream had been so life-like that he was thankful to be where he was when he stirred. He couldn't remember details of what had happened, but the experience had been so real, it was emotionally draining. He racked his brain for clues of his stupor, but just couldn't recollect a thing, except that it hadn't been pleasant. He put it all down to his previous mood trickling its way through his sub conscious thoughts, and pulled himself together, touching the bench and the tree to make sure he had returned to reality.

As he slowly regained his senses, Raoul imagined he heard a gentle sobbing coming from behind the hedge. He became increasingly annoyed with himself. Surely he was hallucinating. He had to get a grip. But could he just let it pass? Perhaps it was real!

Stealthily he climbed on top of the bench and peered prudently over. There *was* someone there. A woman, some way away, dressed all in black, with her back to him. Head bowed, she was staring at the grave in front of her, and speaking softly in between sniffles. The wind carried her tears and, at one point, she became so overwhelmed that she broke down completely. She had obviously lost someone very dear to her, and sought comfort in the closeness the cemetery offered her and her departed loved one.

Feeling ashamed at the unintentional intrusion on her grief, Raoul was beginning to lower himself back to ground level when the woman tearfully turned round. He caught a glimpse of her face. His mouth opened in disbelief. He was stunned into immobility. He could do nothing but remain perched precariously, like a statue, so as not to be discovered. What was this all about? Why in heaven's name was SHE there? And more to the point, whom was she grieving for?

He had known her all this time. Why had he no inkling whatsoever, that she was concealing such profound sorrow deep in her heart?

Chapter 23

When the coast was clear, Raoul silently eased back down onto his favourite bench, and just sat for a while, in contemplation. Should he mention what he had inadvertently seen to anybody? Should he approach the lady herself and offer support? No! She had chosen a private moment to express her sadness. She hadn't entrusted him with her pain, so it wasn't really his business, was it?

One thing though; he couldn't leave without discovering whom she was pining for. He would have to climb over the hedge and look at the headstone. It was going to be somewhat difficult to pinpoint the actual grave she had been tending, but Raoul had a rough idea, and made his way to the spot.

As he approached, his heart sank. All the plots looked the same. So, which one was it? Utterly confused, Raoul scratched his head in deliberation. There were no real clues; no names he knew or recognised, no fresh flowers, no recently trodden grass or footprints.

Frustrated and about to give up, Raoul cannily concluded that the grave he was looking for must have been the one which was unmarked, perhaps for a reason, but certainly not through neglect. He was no further on in his uninvited quest, but he couldn't let the matter rest. All the way back to the hotel, he considered the best way to find the answer he was looking for. The direct approach was not an option. But surely Father Antonio would know who was buried in his cemetery! When he had the chance, he'd find out.

Sebastian looked distinctly annoyed as he managed a busy Reception single handed. The mere fact that he was raising his voice to those staff going about their business showed he wasn't in the best of moods. He hadn't been himself lately, and it was beginning to show. Normally, he coped without a whinge, but recently he had changed. What was troubling him? As if Raoul didn't know, deep down inside!

"Take a break. I'll take over," offered Raoul helpfully, as he reached the desk.

"You don't even do your own shifts half the time, let alone mine," griped Seb sarcastically.

"But . . . , I have got a bit of a headache. Yes. Why not? You can do my shift, Raoul. I'm going to lie down. Don't disturb me."

Raoul regretted his proposition as soon as he had made it. He was used to Seb saying 'no', and that he'd rather do things himself because they would be done properly. Nevertheless, it was his own fault. That would teach him. He was now stuck with the boring task until evening, and there wasn't even anyone around in the lobby to entertain him.

* * *

Next morning, an exhausted Raoul was gently woken with a kiss on the cheek and breakfast in bed. There was a bouquet of red roses on Sebastian's side of the bed. "A bit over the top for covering one shift, isn't it?" joked a baffled Raoul. "And it's not my birthday."

"No," agreed Seb seriously, gently rubbing Raoul's prickly crop. "It's not your birthday, but it is our anniversary!"

"Oops!" blushed Raoul.

"It's o.k. I didn't expect you to remember," confessed Seb with a grin, calming his embarrassed partner. "But it doesn't mean we can't celebrate, does it! We're having a day out. And before you can think of an excuse, I've hired a very expensive yacht and we're going to sail the sea, in luxury. It's all laid on."

"What just the two of us?" gushed Raoul like an excited child, astonishing himself by his unexpected spontaneous reaction.

"No, Ryan's coming." Pre-empting his partner's explosive reaction, Sebastian quickly added his trump card. "And so is

Dimitri." Raoul's face was a picture. "Well, we won't have to do a thing with one at the helm and one catering to our every culinary desire. It'll be a perfect day of relaxation; a chance for some quality time for us, and an opportunity to appreciate our beautiful surroundings. Something we rarely do!"

Raoul couldn't argue with that and held out his hand in friendship, giving Seb a peck on the cheek as he pulled him out of bed.

"What about this place? Who's going to look after it?" Raoul half-heartedly questioned.

"All taken care of," he was reassured. "Now come on, get yourself together. We set sail in twenty minutes. Tally Ho!" Seb left the room triumphantly, and a dazed Raoul started getting ready. Perhaps it wasn't such a bad idea after all!

* * *

An hour later, Della Dubois peered round the marble pillar at the entrance to the hotel lobby. Not recognising the receptionist at the desk, she thought she'd waste no further time loitering and confidently went in. "I'd like to see Dimitri," she boldly announced. The young bell boy just shook his head. "Well, Raoul, then," she impatiently added. "I am expected."

"I'm sorry, Madam, they're both out," he answered apologetically.

"But they can't be! One of them must be here. Either will do. I will see whoever is available, immediately!" she instructed, by now more than somewhat vexed.

"Both Dimitri and Mr. Raoul will be away all day, Madam. They've gone out on a yacht. A celebration of some sort, I believe," confided the male employee, unable to resist raising his eyebrows in insinuation.

A cold shiver went down Della Dubois' spine. What was going on? Her closest friends had abandoned her. And why were they together? She had always suspected there might be something going on between those two. The love hate thing was a little too convenient. All sorts of possibilities flicked through

171

her thoughts. Above all, she felt that she'd been both betrayed and double-crossed in her hour of need. Who else could she turn to now?

Barging her way briskly out of the hotel, Della came swiftly to the conclusion that she would now have to go right to the top, the Governor of the Island. Relations between them hadn't always been that special, but she'd use her womanly whiles, if necessary. She knew he had a soft spot for her, and if she couldn't trust him in his position, who could she trust?

Lord Montgomery was deep in paperwork when Della Dubois, wearing a short, flimsy, red polka dot dress and pink high heels, flounced in and, without a by your leave, proceeded to fling open his office door. She hadn't even had the courtesy to acknowledge the Governor's inattentive wife, responsible for vetting the entrance of visitors, daydreaming at a desk outside. Such blatant rudeness provoked Daphnee to rise angrily to her feet and chase after the intruder. "Miss Dubois, you really can't force your way in here like this without an appointment. My husband's busy. There's protocol to be observed."

Della continued to ignore Lady Meadows and, in her normal pushy manner, perched herself on the arm of the chair in front of a bemused Monty. "I want someone to go with me into the Church crypt," she brashly blurted out. Monty stared at her in bewilderment.

"And how exactly does this concern me? I should have thought Father Antonio was the one to ask," he reasoned.

"Never mind all that. No-one's that keen to go with me. I need someone reliable; someone who will verify the name of my father when I find the information in the Parish records."

Monty almost choked on his pipe, and broke into a nervous coughing fit at this revelation. "You ought to give that up!" Della advised knowledgably. "It's not doing you any good, is it? You always seem to react like that every time I'm here. Anyway, I've picked you because you're supposed to be sorting out my inheritance, and you're taking a bloody long time about it too, if you ask me! Perhaps finding out who my father is will speed things up!"

The answer to Monty's previous agonising moral dilemma had just been decided by Della Dubois' very own words. Finding her father was a means to an end. Nothing more.

The Governor felt a combination of sadness and anger. He was melancholy because, secretly, he had rather liked the idea of a long lost daughter, desperate to find him, and ready to bring some love back into his life. Above all, however, he was fuming for having wasted time and emotion giving Della Dubois the benefit of the doubt. She was running true to form after all.

Assessing the situation quickly, Daphnee seized her chance and changed her approach. "As you can see, my husband is very busy and not in good health," she began, throwing Monty a knowing look to leave the matter to her. "But I'm sure that I could help," she offered with confident reassurance.

"Since when have you ever wanted to help me?" spat Della dismissively.

"Since I realised that you were so determined to discover who your father is, my dear. We all need to find our roots, and I can sympathise with your yearning for family values. I really do respect your principles and admire your perseverance."

Della preened herself, but Monty could contain himself no longer and made his excuses to get a drink for his irritating cough.

"How do I know I can trust you?" hesitated Della, in a more softening tone.

"You don't!" replied the Governor's wife, tenderly touching the younger woman's arm in false friendship. "But it looks like I'm your only hope, and nothing untoward will happen to you while I'm with you, will it? After all, I am the First Lady of the Island." Daphnee winced at her own pompous words, but they were sufficient to convince Della Dubois. She was beginning to warm to a new ally whom she may have hastily previously misjudged.

After arranging to meet Lady Daphnee later that day, Della Dubois made her way out of the Governor's office, feeling pleased and positive that she was one step nearer to achieving her goal. She failed to notice that Lord Meadows hadn't even returned, and excitedly rushed home to find some suitable footwear.

Minutes later, Monty shuffled back into his office, and was greeted by a very smug, smiling Daphnee. "I hope you know what you're doing, ol' girl. Have you thought it through?"

"Not yet, but don't panic. This is the chance I've been waiting for! Don't forget, she came to us."

"Could be dangerous," he warned. "And what if she finds what she's looking for, or for that matter, something worse. It could be dynamite in her hands. Who knows what's lurking down there. Even Antonio is reluctant to penetrate too deeply into the bowels of his own Church. It's nothing more than a cave really, you know."

"I've told you. Don't concern yourself. Leave it to me. I know what's at stake. She won't get very far. I'll see to that."

At that point, an unusually strong gust of wind blew through the open window and rearranged some of Monty's carefully classified papers. "Weather's on the turn, by the look of it," he announced.

"Perfect!" answered his wife, as she looked to the sky for inspiration.

* * *

"Wow! This is what I call luxury," enthused an exhilarated Raoul, as he inspected the fabulous yacht hired by his partner. The interior was finished in walnut, with brass fittings, and offered all conceivable mod cons. The galley looked well stocked with food and drink, and Rory O'Rourke seemed in his element preparing something which smelt and looked delicious. There was also a small, well appointed, private sitting room which led to a cosy, intimate bedroom. All in all, the vessel was the epitome of opulence, and glided smoothly across the waves at an effortless speed.

"Well, I thought I'd push the boat out, pardon the pun, for our anniversary," proudly announced Seb.

"It really means that much to you?" questioned Raoul, looking Sebastian straight in the eye.

"Yes. Yes, as a matter of fact, it does, actually. We've had our ups and downs, but we're still here, together."

"Wish we were on our own though," Raoul suggested quietly.

"Yes, but I told you, we're here to relax. Let them do all the work. After all, we pay them enough."

"Suppose you're right," reluctantly admitted Raoul, relaxing on a comfortable lounger on the original teak sun deck.

With a wide smile that said it all, Seb settled in to his deck-chair, after ordering a gin for himself and an ice cool lemonade for his partner. He looked every inch the man of means in his worldly Panama hat, coloured, cotton shirt and cargo pants. Raoul, meanwhile, had already discarded his clothes in favour of some rather revealing swimming trunks. His toned torso was glistening with sun oil, as he stretched to catch the rays. He wanted to take the opportunity to top up his all over body tan, and couldn't help but notice O'Rourke's furtive, lingering glances as he came out on deck to serve the drinks.

"Hope there's ice and lemon in mine," he reminded the chef, who just scowled as he placed the glasses on the table, obviously also feeling that the company was not as palatable as it could have been. Doubtless he was there solely under duress. Raoul was all the more determined, therefore, to give him a rough ride, and the looks they exchanged made it clear that it wasn't all going to be plain sailing. Sebastian seemed oblivious to the atmosphere, still basking in the pleasure he was giving his partner.

Within minutes, the warmth of the soothing sun on his body, and the gentle rocking of the boat in the wandering waves, eventually lulled Raoul into a deep sleep. For a while, at least, everything was peaceful and perfect.

In what seemed like no time at all, the sun worshipper's sense of serenity was soon to be spoilt. An increasingly agitated sea, created by a thunderstorm brewing on the horizon, forced the yacht to react adversely, struggling against the angry currents. The clouds in the sky were announcing a change in the weather, as they turned from wispy white to a bruised black. Booming claps of thunder echoed through the air, and flashes of lightning appeared to be dancing on the choppy, distant waves.

Still groggy from his nap, Raoul realised that he was now alone on deck. There was an eerie feeling of solitude as, for a moment, he felt abandoned. He steadied himself by grabbing the nearest rail and then slowly made his way into the galley. His timing was perfect. The noise of the approaching storm masked his movement, and he was able to peer through the kitchen porthole for a good few moments before an angry wave jolted him through the hatch. What he had seen both startled and surprised him as, for once, it was not what he expected.

Looking unbearably uncomfortable, the scowling helmsman and the shamefaced chef sheepishly separated and immediately went about their business. Raoul smirked with derision. He now had an ace card. Their intimate secret had been discovered!

* * *

Wiping sand, blown by the strengthening wind, from her face, Della Dubois could not contain her excitement as she watched Lady Meadows ambling up to the Churchyard at the agreed time. She waved enthusiastically, and received a smile and nod of response from her new, well connected friend. She'd purposely arrived a little earlier to have a quick exploration of her own and, above all, to make sure that her journey would not be wasted.

Della had already established, from her initial inspection, that the heavy, outer wooden portal was slightly ajar, and that Father Antonio had, therefore, kept his promise. She knew, however, only too well, that help would still be needed to successfully gain access into the old, unwelcoming entrance to the cellar of the Church, and that she would indeed be grateful for the support of the Governor's wife.

Both suitably dressed for such an escapade, in head scarves, casual clothes and sturdy shoes, like spirited schoolgirls, the two women began their adventure. After initial greetings, conversation was kept to a minimum, merely pleasantries.

Their means of entry hid in the wall on the neglected side of the Church. Overgrown shrubs, bushes and brambles seemed to form an inhospitable barrier, warning would-be visitors to keep out. Undeterred, Della and Daphnee squeezed through the narrow gap left by the priest, unable to ease the sturdy door open much further. The females smiled triumphantly at each other after overcoming their first hurdle. Little did they know that each one was about to undertake a mission with a completely different personal agenda.

A dark, winding passage, illuminated only by the natural daylight filtering through from the entrance, meandered into yet another smaller, but equally forbidding door. This one had a long handled, rusty, iron key visibly protruding from the lock. Della Dubois led the way. She recklessly bolted forward to use the opening device without delay, almost as if it was about to disappear before her eyes if she didn't reach it in time.

They both breathed a sigh of relief. The lock was unexpectedly manageable and the door creaked open with little fuss. What followed, however, was not anticipated; a steep, stone staircase with a sharp descent. A fatal fall could have easily awaited, had Della not been so uncharacteristically cautious in her approach. She had felt Daphnee's breath on the back of her neck. Something had told her to be careful.

"Oh shit!" cursed Della, pushing back her elbows as if she had the reins of a horse. Daphnee was still behind, as close as a shadow.

"What?" the older woman enquired solemnly.

"There's no bloody light down here."

"Well, I expect it was constructed well before the arrival of electricity," Daphnee mumbled to herself, somewhat sarcastically. Then, remembering her supposedly sunny disposition, smiled in support. "Oh, I was prepared for that. Here, take a candle. Hold on! I have to find a match."

"Don't worry, I've got my lighter," remembered Della, taking the opportunity to spark up a much needed cigarette at the same time as she lit the candles.

"No thanks. I don't!" responded Daphnee, turning away in disgust as she declined the offer.

Della Dubois blew smoke rings into the stale, stuffy air as both women stood at the top of the staircase, peering studiously down into the dingy crypt. It was a party trick she had picked up from Curtis, for comfort, during times of stress. Daphnee coughed in disapproval, then added with an icy shiver; "This is a bit daunting, don't you think?"

"Oh, surely you're not afraid of the dark," taunted Della insensitively. Daphnee's glare was hidden in the half light. The friction between the two was in danger of surfacing, and neither wanted that to be apparent, so they both giggled nervously to break the growing tension.

"Be careful and follow me!" instructed Della forcefully. She slowly and warily began to descend the narrow, stone steps, tightly clutching a rail of rotten rope, fastened through links into the wall. There must have been at least twenty uneven slabs of slate to negotiate.

As they shakily proceeded, Della religiously lit the large, thick candles conveniently placed at regular intervals in iron holders. Gradually, their gloomy destination began to reveal itself. The musty atmosphere eerily enveloped the two ladies, while uninvited gusts of wind fanned the flickering flames of light and distorted the sultry shadows.

Suddenly, just as the explorers reached the few remaining steps at the bottom, there was a blood curdling shriek which echoed sinisterly through the cavern. Daphnee had lost her footing and slipped on a loose stone. She was unsteadily sliding her way down on her back, past Della Dubois, eventually hitting the cold hard terrain with a dull thud.

"Are you o.k.?" asked Della somewhat unsympathetically, showing greater interest in the secrets she was about to uncover in the murky underground grotto which extended before her.

"No, no, not really," sobbed Daphnee, trying to be strong and keep a stiff upper lip. "I think I may have broken my ankle. It's really painful." Della Dubois raised her eyebrows in contempt.

"Well, I'll just have to go on alone then, won't I!" she stomped, a little more true to form.

"Oh well, thanks for your concern," fumed Lady Meadows. "What about me?" Della fumbled in her bag.

"Take these. Go on! They're painkillers," she reassured, offering her accomplice a crumpled packet. Daphnee just stared in abject disbelief. Her facial expression said it all.

"What? You're just going to leave me here?" she questioned, shaking her head incredulously.

"Look, I came here for a purpose and well, you're hardly going anywhere, are you? Just rest there a while. I'll pick you up on the way back. I won't be long! Trust me."

Before Monty's wife could reply and bemoan her abandonment, Della Dubois had disappeared further into the crypt. Something told Daphnee Meadows that she would long regret her double crossing offer of help, and that Della Dubois' last parting words would be a chilling irony.

Chapter 24

Without fear or further thought for her accomplice, Della Dubois zealously continued her exploration into the main body of the crypt. Tightly clinging to her candle, she began to illuminate the sanctuary of secrets. The smell of damp from the moist walls almost made her heave, but undeterred, Della began rummaging through the old artefacts and papers, eagerly hoping to find the answers to her uncertainties.

As she roughly rifled through some old scrolls, written in Latin, Della's heel unintentionally nudged against an oblong canvass leaning carelessly against the side of a sturdy wooden table. It just missed her ankle as it toppled unsteadily forward. Stepping lithely aside, she aggressively grabbed what appeared to be a useless old painting, and lifted it up to the waning candle for closer scrutiny.

Blowing off a fine layer of dust, Della instantly recognised the distinctive style of the artist. It was unmistakably the work of Maggie Maynard. Though still battling with rather dim light, the investigator began to smile in triumph. It wasn't what she was after, but it was further ammunition should she need it. It didn't take a genius to work out who the intimate couple were canoodling at Cuddlers' Cove!

It crossed Della's mind that the painting looked neither worn nor old, and it hadn't really been competently concealed either. Presumably, it had just been clumsily left in haste. Perhaps there had been more recent visitors to the venue than she had been led to believe.

An unexpected gust of air suddenly made the lights flicker as the trembling candles blew. Della Dubois momentarily froze, but thought no more about it. Irreverently, she continued to rearrange the carefully classified documents, becoming increasingly short tempered as she found nothing of any value to her.

Patience was not one of Della's virtues, and the little restraint she had left was rapidly running out. She wanted answers and she wanted them now!

In an unbridled fit of pique, the unsuccessful forager belligerently kicked the antiquated table guilty of cradling nothing but worthless, theological doctrines and deeds. Such a disrespectful disturbance was apparently unappreciated. In unexpected retaliation, a hostile chunk of wood, clumsily sculpted into the side corner of the desk, forcefully dislodged itself and slumped wilfully onto its tormentor's toes with an equally angry thud. "Ooh! Ouch! Bloody hell!" cried Della, spontaneously lashing out again with her other foot in antagonised spite. But then, in the blink of an eye, her mood abruptly softened as her changing fortune began to dawn on her.

"Well, well, what have we here?" she jubilantly beamed, closely examining the amateurishly sealed hollow compartment which the irritated piece of furniture had conveniently revealed. "Oh very original! Just like in the films!" Her mild twinge of physical discomfort instantly disappeared as, rubbing her hands in optimistic anticipation, the intruder soon realised that she had stumbled on something. Something she certainly wasn't meant to!

In semi darkness, kneeling down on a grimy rag, Della fearlessly proceeded to gradually insert her slender arm into the long, narrow opening. Carefully easing her right hand further and further in, avoiding cobwebs and insects, her fingers eventually touched what appeared to be the smooth binding of a book, standing upright, and wedged to one side. She retrieved her candle from the inkwell she had placed it in, and shone the light more clearly into the direction of her discovery. Sure enough, there was a tall, bulky ledger staring ominously back at her.

Della Dubois' arm was just not long enough to reach her target, and she became so frustrated at grasping unsuccessfully, that she cut her wrist on a splinter of wood. Not being at all squeamish, Della allowed the blood to trickle down her hand, unchecked. But, she did stop . . . to think. Retrieving the reading matter needed more careful consideration. Perhaps her usual 'bull at a gate' approach required some refining.

Withdrawing her blood soaked arm, Della unceremoniously wrenched off her headscarf and, using her teeth to steady the operation, tied it in a knot around the open cut. "There, that'll do!" she announced convincingly. "Now, think girl, think!"

Without venturing further, Della waved her candle around the crevices of the dingy cavern. She was at a loss. How could she reach what she wanted? The answer was staring her right in the face. A long brass pole, with a bell shaped dome on the end, lay on the table in front of her. She had moved it off the documents before she had started sifting through them. It had been acting as a paperweight. "Of course! The candle extinguisher! That will do." By voicing her encouraging thoughts out loud, she was subconsciously willing them to automatically succeed.

Della eagerly picked up the snuffer, which was suitably heavy, and pushed it deftly into position. It reached! And . . . , if she could just get . . . the protruding bell shaped bit . . . over the corner of the ledger, . . . she could jam it in behind and gently, . . . and carefully, . . . ease out the bound set of documents . . . with just a final, forceful tug . . . . Like that! What a stroke of luck! It worked! She'd done it!

The tormented chronicle had yielded itself, albeit somewhat unwillingly, and toppled turbulently out of its secret hiding place with a bad tempered thump; its pages flailing helplessly on the grubby stone floor.

Like a hungry child snatching food, Della greedily grabbed her prize and placed it facing her, in a closed position, on the tired table. She shrieked with delight as she read the title in bold, but old fashioned, handwriting; "Parish Records." Inside would be the answer to her future and her fortune.

Not wishing to miss a clue, Della Dubois flicked laboriously through the first few pages with utmost care. Names were listed, dates of births and deaths of the Island's inhabitants, together with footnotes relating to personal details such as children and marriage. The handwriting was the same throughout, sometimes smudged, sometimes shaky, sometimes barely legible, but the same throughout.

It was by no means the best light to scrutinise the information, and the candles were slowly diminishing in size. Some had blown out. It wasn't worth lighting them again. Dare she disobey Father Antonio's last, but firm, instruction and remove the book? Best not!

Several pages in, a paper pouch seemed to have been painstakingly inserted. Two sheets had been unobtrusively stuck together, on the sides and in the corners, unnoticeable unless someone was being particularly meticulous. Such a pocket could only mean one thing. Secrets! At last! Could this be it? Della Dubois was more than keen to find out. She turned the well thumbed journal on its side, and lightly shook it. Some tattered photographs bashfully fell out. They were the original sepia kind, and evidently very old.

Single minded as ever, Della was disappointed when she realised that the snap shots were of absolutely no relevance to her. But they did take her fancy all the same. Even she marvelled at the inherited, smouldering, Latin looks of the young male in the dark suit. He hadn't changed much. He was still a fine figure of a man, even now. And the lady by his side? Yes, she too, looked positively beautiful; radiant in her long, white gown. The years had been good to her as she had gracefully grown older. They made a fine couple, standing there, so gloriously happy, hand in hand.

Della Dubois felt a slight tinge of sentimental sadness, and perhaps even a pang of remorse? After all, she had just had the rare privilege of casting her own personal eye over Father Antonio and Harriett Haversham's illicit, but blissful, wedding photographs. A treasure few others would ever glimpse.

Suitably coming to her senses, Della's first thought was to remove the photos from their home and take them with her. Wouldn't they be dynamite? But the emotion of the moment had even touched her heart. She wasn't made of stone. Deep down, even she had feelings. So, she carefully placed them back in the folder and turned the page. Some things were sacrosanct, even to her. She had seen them. That was enough.

Flicking further through the records, Della's lack of patience predictably returned. She had, as yet, found nothing to her advantage. A cold draught blew around her feet, swirling up the dust on the cold stone floor, and causing the candles to waver once more. She was rapidly losing her cool.

Unaware her scarf was working its way loose, Della once again became mercilessly rougher with the book, and nicked her open wound with a paper cut from the sharp edge of one of the defiant pages. She cursed out loud. It was almost as if the ledger had given her a warning to stop . . . . And there was the reason why! The Records were open at the very page she wanted. At last she had found it!

At the very moment she peered purposely forward to read the required details, a heavy bang echoed through the cavern. A wind tunnel, created by a slamming door, had eerily blown out every single candle.

What had happened? Della Dubois sensed the worst. She stood helpless and vulnerable, in utter darkness. A cold shiver went down her spine. "Hello! Daphnee! What's going on?" she shouted frantically. Hearing the familiar creak of a key being turned in a lock, she knew right away what had happened! She had been double-crossed!

"Open the door you bitch!" she yelled in frantic desperation. But her futile command merely resonated around the cave, ringing endlessly in her ears. "You won't get away with this! I knew I couldn't trust you. They'll be looking for me soon, and then watch out!" Della Dubois was panic stricken and blindly fumbled for her bag, and her lighter, to put a flame to the candle.

To her relief, the first spark immediately allowed a small amount of visibility. But before she could reach the wick of the nearest candle, it had extinguished itself. Della hysterically flicked the spark, again and again. It would not ignite. It just would not ignite.

There she was, in an unfriendly, unfamiliar place, in total darkness; without food, without water. She couldn't even move without the possibility of endangering herself. Disheartened and doubtless defeated, she slowly slumped sobbing onto the table.

She was done for! Just how long would it be before anyone would find her? Would they even bother? Was this their ultimate master stroke? Had they finally won??

Chapter 25

"Don't worry," said Sebastian, coming out of the lounge area, as the luxury yacht continued to bob up and down in the increasingly agitated waves. "It probably won't reach us. We'll just get the tail end of it."

"What?" asked Raoul, still looking somewhat perturbed about what he had just witnessed.

"The storm!" laughed Seb. "I could organise everything else, but I couldn't control the weather."

"Oh, yes. It'll soon pass, I expect," murmured Raoul, with his mind clearly on other things.

The sun was fortunately managing to dodge the thickening clouds, so Sebastian encouraged Raoul to go back out on deck and make the most of the special day. A gusty, but warm wind excited the sails into a deafening flap. Concentration would be impossible, so Raoul did not even contemplate reading the book he had brought. He decided to just relax again on the sun lounger, and watch nature take its course.

It hadn't really occurred to him to wonder why Sebastian had not followed his own suggestion and joined him. He took it for granted that his partner had limited tolerance towards the sun, and that he'd stayed inside to read the newspaper, or even catch up on some work. He wasn't the type to just sit and do nothing for long.

Dimitri seemed deep in his own thoughts as he stood moodily at the helm, but, from time to time, he caught Raoul's eye and then instinctively looked away again. You never could work out what was going on behind those smouldering, dark, Greek eyes, but it was even more difficult today as they were shielded from the sun by an expensive pair of designer sunglasses. His facial expression was fixed, but he occasionally gave a taunting smirk as he postured wearing just his tight shorts, and a bandana to control his flowing, dark hair. Raoul showed a distinct disinterest. The young employee was wasting his time. Realising this, he scoffed with a grimace of contempt at the lack of anticipated adulation. He wasn't used to being ignored, and he didn't like it.

The claps of thunder and the lightening flashes were becoming more regular and eventually, after two hours at sea, Dimitri displayed some difficulty in controlling the yacht. At the first opportunity, he beckoned to Seb, who was watching from the lounge, to come out on deck. Together they surveyed the weather and decided to replot their route, since their original destination was now taking them right into the storm.

"Looks like we're going to have to make for Mystique and stay overnight," accepted a disappointed Seb, as the boat rocked unsteadily from side to side.

"Then why the long face?" shouted Raoul over the deafening sound of the sea. "We haven't been to the main Island for months. Stroke of luck I'd say."

"But it spoils my plans for a candlelit dinner for two in a secluded little bay I've found," bellowed Seb. "Ryan and I have been working together for weeks, to get just the right menu organised. He was going to prepare all your favourites. I did so want to make it a night to remember."

Most of what was said was lost in the wind. The discussion seemed to take second place as fountains of water suddenly splashed heavily over the starboard side when the boat encountered a particularly vicious wave. Everyone grabbed the nearest nailed down object aboard to steady themselves. A blinding flash of lightning swiftly followed a tumultuous boom. The giant thunder clouds were slowly advancing.

Raoul sensed Sebastian's deep disappointment, and slowly realised that he may have misread the situation. Perhaps, the intended surprise explained all the secretive huddling in corners with the chef he disliked so much.

"And so it shall be!" enthused Raoul, trying to retrieve some enthusiasm, while their vessel dipped and dived with the rhythm of the sea. "Let's stay in somebody else's luxury hotel for a change," he suggested keenly. "There are several to choose from. We'll have the Penthouse and a meal in a first class restaurant."

"It won't be the same, though, will it?" continued Sebastian, still crestfallen.

"Oh, come on! We can order room service, if you like. It'll be just as much fun," pleaded Raoul, desperately trying to save the situation.

By now, Dimitri and Rory were doing their best to control the wayward sail, but as no-one on board had any real sailing experience, their efforts were haphazard and fruitless. The yacht obviously had a mind of its own. The noise of the sea slapping against the craft now made it impossible to converse further on deck, so at a relatively calmer moment, Seb signalled for every-one to convene below.

Dripping wet, Sebastian explained the new plan to the crew. "And when we arrive, you two can have the night off," declared Raoul. "I dare say you'll find something to occupy yourselves," he sarcastically quipped, looking Dimitri in the eye. They both nodded in silence.

"Anyway, it doesn't look as if we've got much choice, does it?" conceded Seb. "The storm's getting worse. At this rate we'll be lucky to make it anywhere in one piece."

On leaving the safety of the cabin to go back up on deck, Raoul purposely ushered Seb and Rory ahead and roughly grabbed Dimitri by the arm. "Keep your tacky little habits to yourself," he warned with a snarl. "Leave us out of it! Transport your trash in your own time. We don't want to be implicated."

"If you were no my boss . . . " Dimitri began, wrenching his arm away and squaring up to Raoul.

"Well I am!" he confirmed, equally aggressively. "So, don't bite the hand that feeds you!"

Dimitri backed off. Under normal circumstances, it would have been no contest, but this time he was wary. He had never seen Raoul so angry. "Come on you two. We need your help. What are you doing down there?" demanded a harassed sound-ing Sebastian. The call came at just the right time. They had disengaged, but there was something physically arousing about their intensely close encounter that lingered within each of them.

* * *

Monty looked distinctly worried as he sat in his office, puffing noisily on his pipe. Daphnee's bed hadn't been slept in again last night. He remembered the last time she did that. It was after some 'do' or other. She said she needed some 'space', whatever that meant. Was it a repeat performance, or was it too early to be unduly worried?

Why on earth did she volunteer to help Della Dubois? It was this which made him feel uneasy. What if they had found something! The game could be up. Surely there was nothing to find. They were on a fool's errand. Perhaps he should casually pay the young lady a visit and find out what had happened. Or would that make his concern too obvious?

With a deep sigh, Monty Meadows got up from his chair, put on his white, cotton jacket and Panama hat, and made his way to the door. He collected his walking stick on the way out.

No sooner had he left the premises, than he bumped into Sadie and Harriett walking their dogs. "Morning, ladies!" he said somewhat distractedly, as he tried to pass them without further conversation.

"I was just coming to see you," launched Sadie in a manner that meant business. "I want you to ring the mainland and find out about the progress of my claim. It's been weeks now. Something should have been decided." Harriett raised her eyebrows at the mention of the issue. Her friend had become completely obsessed by it.

Poor Monty couldn't face such an encounter so early in the morning, so he fielded the question with one of his own. "Have either of you seen my wife?" he nonchalantly asked. Harriett shook her head woefully.

"Should we have?" Sadie asked, sensing the seriousness which lay behind the Governor's question.

"No, no, not at all!" responded Monty with a wave of his hand. "She went out for a walk and I was going to catch her up, that's all."

"Well, she's not on the beach. We've just come that way. She can't be far. Perhaps she's up at the hotel," suggested Sadie. "Anyway, what are we going to do about my telephone call?"

"No need, ma dear," bluffed Monty, thinking on his feet. "Someone rang yesterday, as a matter of fact. It's all in hand. You know these legal things take time. We wouldn't want them to rush it and come to the wrong conclusion now, would we?"

"I suppose not," accepted Sadie. "But there is only one conclusion, isn't there?" she added vehemently.

"Quite!" smiled the Governor, as he lifted his hat and slowly ambled away from the two women.

Monty hated walking on the sand. It was uneven and he often stumbled. This time it was necessary, however, to reach Della Dubois' waterfront café.

He looked at his watch. Most unusual! There was no sign of life. The bar shutters were down. There was no music. The wicker tables and chairs outside were in disarray. Umbrellas had been toppled over, probably in yesterday's unusually strong winds. For all intents and purposes, it all looked quite neglected, though it had been some time since he was last there.

Two fishermen, walking by, acknowledged the Governor with a nod, pointed to the café and shook their heads, as if to indicate that it wasn't open. Monty smiled in thanks and turned to go. "I should have thought that was patently obvious!" he commented ungratefully under his breath.

As a parting shot, Lord Meadows thought he would inspect the back of the premises. Same thing; shutters down, looked deserted. After tapping several times on the door with his stick, Monty gave up and started to trudge back home. Daphnee would probably be there waiting for him by now.

"Daphnee? Daphnee! I'm back. Where are you, ol' girl?" Monty called out expectantly as he entered the main door of his residence, some fifteen minutes later. There was no response. He looked in the breakfast room. Everything was as he had left it. "Damn inconvenient having to make one's own breakfast," he mumbled to himself, as he searched for signs of his wife through the rest of the building.

Montgomery scratched his head in bewilderment. Though likeable, he was a bumbling sort of chap and, therefore, sometimes most irritating. In fact, many of those in the upper strata of the Island's community often wondered how he got the position of Governor in the first place. No-one really knew. He had probably been a high flyer in his youth, during his diplomatic career, and was still trading on his past record. Behind every great man there was usually a woman. Unfortunately, at the moment she wasn't there! "Have a cup of tea and wait, I suppose," he decided, after anguished deliberation.

The clock ticked and ticked, and Monty watched the hands go round until he was mesmerised. It was the telephone which eventually brought him out of his almost hypnotic state. It had been ringing for some moments before he realised. "That'll be her! Knew the old girl would get in touch sooner or later. Hello, Daphnee. Where are you, girl?"

The mystified female caller took several moments to convince the Governor that she wasn't called Daphnee and was, in fact, the secretary of a diplomat, telephoning on official business which needed Lord Meadows' urgent attention.

"Bloody bureaucracy; it'll be the death of me," sighed Monty, as he sifted through some relevant documents relating to population percentages. "Tedious twaddle, if you ask me," he muttered, noisily slurping his tea. "Oh where's Daphnee when you need her? She deals with all that kind of thing."

Heavily preoccupied, Montgomery was totally unable to concentrate. "There's only one thing for it," he announced, picking up his stick and putting back on his hat.

* * *

"Good Heavens!" bellowed a stupefied Lady Lascelles as her servant announced the arrival of the Governor at her home. "Send him in, girl," she instructed immediately. "What on earth's

191

the matter, Monty?" was her forthright greeting. "Last time you came here, it was . . . " she stopped in her tracks. "Well, let's just say, it was a long time ago, wasn't it?"

She quickly lightened the mood. "Did your chauffeur drive you?" she chuckled sarcastically.

"This is not a matter for levity, Lottie," was his instant rebuke. Laetitia could see by the look on his face that her unusual attempt at humour had been misplaced. "Take a seat, ol' chap. Have a cup of tea! Tell me why you're here," she softened.

"I can't find Daphnee," he blurted, as soon as he could get a word in.

"What do you mean? You've misplaced her?" Lady Lascelles was not known for her tact or sensitivity.

"No, don't be ridiculous. She's been out all night. She hasn't been home since yesterday afternoon."

"Marital troubles, I suppose, and pretty serious too, I expect, if you've resorted to coming to me to sort them out!"

"Will you . . . " The look on Laetitia's face told Monty his behaviour was inappropriate. He was shouting. "Will you just listen, please . . . Lottie . . . , please?" he continued, lowering his voice.

"She went off with Della Dubois, yesterday afternoon." Laetitia's face became more serious at the mention of the name which was almost a curse in itself.

"And why exactly should she want to do that?" she sternly demanded.

"Oh, some bee in her bonnet about helping the girl to explore the Church crypt for clues to the identity of her father."

Somewhat embarrassed, Lady Lascelles lowered her head. She could no longer look Monty in the eye. It was obvious she was unsettled. "Not a very wise thing to do, I fear," she commented pensively. "I warned her about tangling with that harlot. The trollop will stop at nothing. You know that, Monty, don't you! Nothing!" At that point, she looked up, and their eyes briefly met again. There was an awkward, yet knowing, glance from Laetitia, which made Monty wonder how much she actually knew.

"We'd better think very carefully about our next step," she thoughtfully continued.

"Oh, OUR next step. So you're prepared to help me then?"

"Of course! We may not always see eye to eye, but you're the closest thing I've got to a real friend, I suppose. And you certainly need an ally now, Monty. Believe me!"

The Governor was quite touched by Laetitia's backhanded declaration of friendship. He began to realise that, despite their constant superficial rivalry, he must have regarded her in similar esteem. After all, it was she whom he had turned to.

"What the deuce possessed Daphnee to even go near that place, let alone with that woman?" reflected Lady Lascelles, slowly shaking her head. Monty sensed from the lack of resolution in her voice, that the idea was not totally unfamiliar to her. "Most ill advised. Still, it's done now. Damage limitation is the answer. We don't want a full scale alert. Drawing attention to that crypt would be most unwise. So, no search party! We'll have to keep it between ourselves and others we can trust."

"And who would they . . . " Before Monty could complete his question, Laetitia brusquely interrupted.

"Stop skulking at that doorway boy, and come in!"

The door, which was slightly ajar, was pushed open a little further as Alistair entered, red faced. He'd obviously been caught out. He was no match for his mother. But then, who was? "How much have you heard?"

"N . . . no . . . nothing, mamma," he responded, head bowed.

"You never were much good at lying, well not to me anyway. Same as your father! So, you heard it all then! May I remind you, Alistair, that it is exceedingly rude to eavesdrop, and sometimes exceedingly dangerous. Remember what you 'heard' last time you had no business to! Monty's eyebrows steepled inquisitively. "Oh, it's not relevant," Laetitia quickly dismissed, waving her hand. "Well, at least, not yet. Let's just say if, or when, I need to, I shall know how to use the pertinent information."

Alistair felt mortified that he had unwittingly betrayed his mother. On the occasion he told her what he had discovered about Elise being pregnant, she had been so compassionate towards him, so reassuring. Would she now ever value his confidences again?

"Come on!" suddenly instructed Laetitia, rising briskly from her chair and grabbing her hat and parasol. "We're off to Church!"

Chapter 26

Lady Lascelles banged forcefully on the door of Father Antonio's living quarters several times with the sturdy wooden handle of her trusty parasol. "Antonio! Antonio, are you in there? Probably under the influence again," she confided in the two men who had followed her without question.

"You won't get any answer," a breathless voice sighed heavily from behind. It was Harriett trundling up the pathway, looking as if she had the weight of the world on her shoulders.

"Why ever not?" demanded Laetitia. "He hasn't disappeared too, has he?" Monty winced as his ally announced his private worries as if she were on a parade ground.

"I do hope not. Why? Who's disappeared?" asked Harriett somewhat perplexed, unlocking the rectory door with her own key. Laetitia observed closely and raised her eyebrows. "Well I'm looking after him. He's had a terrible attack of gout again. He hasn't been out of the house for two days. Are you coming in . . . all of you?"

"We don't wish to intrude," spluttered Monty, by now puffing anxiously on his pipe.

"Of course we do! We have to. And this isn't a social visit," insisted Lady Lascelles.

"And here's me, thinking that Antonio's parishioners had come to offer him some pastoral care for a change," whinged Harriett sarcastically.

"Oh, I expect he gets more than enough of that from you, my dear," smiled Laetitia. "Now, to business!"

Harriett thought she'd better quit before she antagonised Lottie any more, and led the way to Father Antonio's private sitting room. Laetitia quickly barged ahead of the others, and wasted no time in prodding the dozing priest huddled on the settee. "Antonio, shake a leg. We need you!"

"I'm afraid we've got visitors," announced Harriett softly. "Are you up to it?" The dazed cleric looked up somewhat vacantly, displaying the after effects of over indulgence. After all, he had been forced to improvise with his own alcoholic medication while Dr. Tremaine still remained at his wife's bed-side on the main Island.

"Of course he is. He's only got a bad foot," replied Lady Lascelles with a total lack of sympathy. "And he wouldn't have that if he kept off the booze."

"Have a heart, Lottie ol' girl. A chap's got a right to a little tipple and some peace and quiet when he's on his sick bed," intervened a well meaning, but twitchy Monty.

"Well that odious instrument won't improve his health either, will it?" she rebounded, assertively removing Monty's pipe from his mouth and placing it precariously on the mantle shelf. Alistair cringed. His mother showed no signs whatsoever of mellowing with age.

"Daphnee is missing," began Lady Lascelles. "Apparently, she went with that tramp of a woman, Dubois, into your crypt, nosing around for details about the identity of her father. Surely you didn't give permission for this?"

Harriett and Father Antonio stared at each other in awkward silence. Their expressions betrayed their response. "Goodness knows what she will uncover down there. What in heaven's name possessed you?" demanded Laetitia in unreserved disbelief.

"Well, it was fortuitous that someone like Daphnee accom-panied her then, wasn't it," rebuked Harriett defensively.

"Let's just go down and find her, now," interrupted an agi-tated Monty.

"We wouldn't make it; well, perhaps the boy would," announced the priest, attempting to bring some order to the proceedings. "The passage leading down to the actual crypt is hazardous in itself. It's just too dangerous, unaccompanied."

"Ma, mamma," dared Alistair at an opportune moment.

"Be quiet boy! This is for grown ups!"

"But, ma, mamma, D . . . D . . . Della is..isn't . . . bbback either, is she ? Per . . . perhaps . . ."

It began to dawn on them all that Daphnee was a very resourceful woman, and must have known what she was doing when she agreed to such a venture. "Yes, yes, perhaps we are jumping the gun somewhat," pondered Laetitia more agreeably. "I suggest there is really no need to panic as yet. No doubt, Daphnee, at least, will be back shortly, I'm sure. We will convene at the hotel tomorrow morning for tea and, if there's still no news, well, we'll take action then."

No-one dared voice the obvious conclusions they had all independently arrived at, but it was evident from the darting glances circulating the room, that everyone's theories had now coincided. It certainly wouldn't be prudent, therefore, to jeopardise the outcome of a long awaited eventuality by becoming involved unnecessarily, or too soon.

* * *

Lord Meadows experienced a very uncomfortable night. He tossed and he turned, but he just couldn't sleep. It was alright for Lottie. Her cavalier attitude didn't allow for his feelings. He was the one who had to suffer. He was the one now pacing the floor at three in the morning, alone, sweating, and imagining all sorts of dreadful things. What if Daphnee didn't actually come back? What if any harm had come to her? The place just wasn't the same. Where on earth was she? Why hadn't she contacted him yet? They'd been through such a lot together, one way or another. Now wasn't the time to go missing. He needed her.

* * *

The morning couldn't come quickly enough, and at sunrise, the Governor was already up and dressed, and ready to set off for the hotel. He failed to notice the beautiful sky which had announced the new day, or appreciate Mother Nature's stunning surroundings, as he hastily quickened his step. He didn't hear the birds' chorus or allow himself the remedy of relaxation in the sea air. The gently, lapping waves on the beach and the comforting heat were of no consequence. Even the mutter of the awakening palms didn't attract his attention. He was blinkered. Finding Daphnee was the be all and end all.

"May I get you anything, Sir?" A young waitress timidly interrupted Monty's thoughts as he sat anxiously, and alone, in Reception.

"A coffee, perhaps. White, two sugars, thank-you," he answered automatically. "Oh, eh, Miss, have you seen anyone else arrive for breakfast yet?"

"It's rather early, but I'm sure they'll be here soon, Sir," she smiled, sensing the Governor's impatience.

"There you are Monty! Any news?" bellowed Lady Lascelles as she marched through the lobby, trailing her son like a puppy.

"Lottie, I've been here hours. Where is everyone?"

"Young lady, a pot of tea and crumpets for two, no make that three," she commanded obliviously, sitting down in her usual armchair. "So, I take it you are obviously none the wiser. Your face gives it away. Well, things take time, don't they?"

"Oh, do stop it, Fanny," instructed an approaching Harriett, as she unsuccessfully tried to control her yapping dog. "Bloody thing gives me a headache. I can do without it at the moment. Antonio is still unable to walk very far. He'll meet us back at the Church, if need be. Any news?"

"Any news? Any bloody news?" mimicked Monty. "Do you think I'd be sitting here if there were?"

"Don't fly off the handle, Monty. If you want our support, you'll at least be civil. Now then!" warned Lady Lascelles sternly, wagging her finger. The Governor opened his hands in friendship to a forgiving Harriett. "It's time to enlist the help of the others," proclaimed Laetitia, disregarding the moment of sympathy. "Young lady, get me the proprietors. Both of them . . . This minute!"

The poor, tongue tied waitress nervously dropped the breakfast tray she was carrying, before apologetically endeavouring to explain the prolonged absence of her employers.

Complete chaos followed. Startled by the clatter of the young lady's clumsiness, Lord Montgomery jumped up, overwrought with tension, looking as if he was about to have a heart attack. Harriett almost tripped over her whelping dog, as she advanced to support him. Lady Laetitia barked instructions to all and sundry, and Alistair just stood immobilised by the whole affair.

"Well now! That didn't bloody work, did it?" shrieked an extremely angry woman, at the top of her voice, from the hotel entrance. Furniture moved and fixtures shook, as she brashly advanced with the torment of a tornado.

Then there was silence. Slowly, everyone turned around in trepidation. Before them stood a very bedraggled, very volatile, but very alive, Della Dubois!

Chapter 27

With a face like thunder, it was clear she meant business and, as the small group of captive allies froze in fear, Della Dubois slowly, but surely, began her tirade of rage. "Thought she could finish me off by leaving me in that filthy rat hole, did she?" she seethed, shaking Monty by the lapels. "When I get my hands on her, I'm going to knock the bloody living daylights out of her, Governor's wife or no Governor's wife. What she did was attempted murder!" She lurched without warning into the flabbergasted bystanders.

A struggle ensued as everyone grappled to control the explosive Miss Dubois then, suddenly, the dinner gong echoed loudly through the hall, and brought everything to a standstill.

"I think someone had better tell me what the hell's going on in my hotel," suggested a calm, but firm, Sebastian. Raoul, Dimitri and Ryan O'Rourke were standing behind him, aghast at what they had just witnessed.

Della Dubois let go of the Governor, and by now, a little more subdued and showing obvious signs of exhaustion, slowly approached the four men. "They . . . left me . . . for dead," she started to sob. "They locked me . . . in that bloody dungeon . . . and left me for dead!"

The effect Della had on men, any men, was interesting to say the least. She was instantly made comfortable in an easy chair, offered a tissue and a stiff drink to stop her shaking, and then given the opportunity to tell her story in her own good time. Everyone listened intently to the events which had unfolded.

Reactions of those assembled were most revealing. Eyes met deviously across the room, and breath was held at each twist and turn. Everybody seemed on edge, for one reason or another, afraid of what was about to be divulged next.

Left stranded in the dark depths of the crypt, Della had managed to scrabble around the dusty ledges to find a small, dying flame, still flickering from a candle which had not yet been fully extinguished by the lethal blow of the draught from the slammed door. Gently, she had nurtured it back to life, until it was itself strong enough to give life to more substantial light.

"So how did you get out?" asked a mystified Raoul.

"The only way was to remain calm and composed. Gradually, I felt my way around until I noticed the flame of the candle being feebly drawn in a certain direction by a cold breath of air. I followed the beckoning breeze, almost in a trance, until I found myself facing a narrow crevice in the wall. At that moment, the candle blew out again. I had no means to relight it. I thought I was done for." She burst into tears again, and was immediately comforted by an ashen faced Dimitri.

"So what happened next?" O'Rourke had asked the question on everyone's lips. The others weren't going to ask. They were wary of showing undue interest.

Della Dubois wearily took up the tale again. "I peered through the crevice and thought I was seeing things. There was a very faint glint of daylight in the far distance. I scratched for dear life at the rock. To my amazement, the cave wall crumbled quite easily to the touch, so I decided to try to ease my way through. The gap widened the more I pushed. There was obviously some sort of passage on the other side that had been walled up by debris."

It was then that Monty began one of his nervous coughing fits, and Sebastian took the opportunity to fetch him some water and allow Della some further respite. Sweat trickled down her face. The others anxiously remained riveted like statues.

"Once I managed to get through the rubble, things were easy. I felt my way along the wall, until I could see full daylight, and smell the sea." She suddenly stopped dead. Looking Monty, Laetitia and Harriett straight in the eye, one after the other, she accusingly added, "I get the impression that I'm not the first to have tried to use this means of escape. But, I succeeded, didn't I!"

Lady Lascelles remained stone faced. Monty continued coughing, and Harriett just looked forlorn, as usual. Alistair was about to speak, but one glance from his mother shut him up before he had the chance to even try. Raoul sensed Sebastian was uncomfortable, but said nothing. Dimitri nodded to Della to continue.

"Anyway, the narrow channel eventually led to a secluded, little bay, surrounded by some craggy cliffs. Impossible to climb! Boy, was I glad to breathe fresh air again. Then, I must have collapsed, probably overwrought with joy and nervous exhaustion, all rolled into one, because later, I woke up with the sea washing over my body. My mouth was so dry, and I was so weak. I still thought I wasn't going to make it. I really did! Though I was dazed, I noticed what looked like some floating driftwood on the edge of the rocks. The tide was coming in quickly. There was no time to lose. It was a gamble, but I had just enough strength to wade out towards it." Della then once again became more agitated, and began to ferociously raise her voice.

"But it wasn't driftwood at all, was it? Oh no! It was a rowing boat, tied to an iron bar wedged in the rock. I wonder who left that there and why? More than just a coincidence, wouldn't you say? It must belong to someone! But don't worry, I'll find out who! I've brought it back with me and stored it somewhere safe. I know it saved my life, but just why was it there?"

"It's mine! There's no mystery. It's mine!" interrupted a breathless voice. They all turned around to see Father Antonio standing somewhat unsteadily in the entrance to the lobby.

"Toni, you shouldn't be here," gushed Harriett, as she rushed to support the priest. You were to wait for us at the crypt. Oh, you're shaking. Do sit down! Catch your breath."

Father Antonio placed his stick on a nearby table and painfully eased himself into a chair. Harriett immediately brought another to support his swollen red foot. "I go fishing sometimes. It's secluded there; a good place to fish, in peace. That's the reason the boat was there."

Lord Montgomery had by now worked himself up into a frantic frenzy, and could contain himself no longer. This time the boot was on the other foot. HE was about to explode! "Never mind all this nonsense; where's my wife? Where is she?" he shouted uncontrollably, as he angrily shook Della Dubois by the arms. She immediately pulled away.

"You should bloody know," she spat. "You set her up to get rid of me. You all think you're so bloody clever. Don't imagine, for one minute, I don't know about your plans to get me off the Island; all the whispers, huddling in corners, plotting and scheming. Everybody has always looked down their nose at me, because I'm not considered to be from the right background. Well, may I remind you all, I've got money now, and that makes me every bit as good as you, whether you like it or not!"

"If only it did!" sighed Monty to himself. "If only it did!" He then sank wearily into a nearby chair, and put his head in his hands in despair.

Lady Laetitia had also silently stood back for long enough. She was now ready to let rip. "Look, young lady, and I use the term loosely, hold fire with your insinuations and accusations. How dare you reproach us! You've no proof anyone means you any harm. The Island has put up with your antics lowering the tone for years. Why lay the blame at our door now? Guilty conscience? I'm sure we have nothing to do with your misfortune. More to the point, where's Lady Meadows? She was kind enough to go with you."

"Yes, but she had her own plans, it seems," Della barked back.

"Well, she's not here, is she?" argued Laetitia. "Save your recriminations until you can prove them."

"Wait a minute," interrupted Sebastian. "If she's not here, she must still be in the crypt."

"She shut me in! Weren't you listening?" shrieked Della Dubois, almost out of control again.

"And you know that for a fact, do you? You saw her do it? You checked the door, did you?"

"How could I? I've just told you, it was dark. I couldn't find my way to see. I heard it slam. That was good enough. I heard the key creak in the lock. It was a set up! Who else could have done it?"

"Well, perhaps that's what we had better find out. The poor woman may still be there."

"One thing, Miss Dubois," hesitated Monty, in a somewhat more controlled manner. "Did you by any chance happen to find what you were looking for?"

"Oh, Governor, you'll be surprised what I found," beamed Della Dubois enigmatically.

Chapter 28

The men were soon ready to undertake a rescue mission, having barely had the time to freshen up and deposit their belongings after their ordeal at sea. At least, the one night in port had afforded them some respite.

"I really must advise against this. It's a dangerous place, and you're unfamiliar with it. Wait for the professionals," pleaded Father Antonio, as he struggled to his feet.

"Every minute could make a difference. By the time we contact them, and they get organised, the poor woman could be . . . " Sebastian caught a glimpse of the Governor's pallid face out of the corner of his eye, and didn't complete his sentence.

"Well, at least let me come with you. I know the pitfalls," suggested the priest.

"Father, you're not well. You'll hold us up. Best you rest here," counselled Raoul, hastily putting some torches in a bag.

"I'll come as far as the outer door. I can make it that far," insisted an agitated Antonio.

They patiently waited as Father Antonio, supported by a stick, limped his way slowly behind them as far as the Church. Then they all proceeded to the side of the building hidden in bushes and brambles.

"There, it's just how I left it," remarked Antonio, pointing to the heavy outer portal which was still half open. "There's a passage way now, and another door. There should be a key in the lock. Go carefully, please."

Raoul pushed himself forward, closely followed by a determined Dimitri. Quite why the pool attendant seemed so purposeful made Raoul feel rather uneasy. Was it Lady Meadows he wished to save or something else?

"The key is still in there," shouted the leader excitedly back to the others. "And the door's unlocked." He had tugged it back with little difficulty. "Careful!" he firmly warned, as he suddenly stopped dead at the top of the steep steps. Dimitri had, in his haste, failed to halt quickly enough, and had quite forcefully nudged Raoul to the brink of an untimely descent. Luckily the banister of rope had prevented his fall. "I'm going down first!" he growled assertively, shining his torch into the face of a sweating Dimitri. "I'll call you when I reach the bottom."

"Be careful, Raoul," urged Seb, as he and Ryan O'Rourke held back.

"Lady Meadows? . . . Daphnee, are you down there?" The plea echoed around the cavern, rebounding off each wall. They all anxiously held their breath and waited for some kind of response. An eerie silence was all that greeted them. Raoul carefully shone his torch around the dingy, damp cave and then reported back. It doesn't look as if there's anyone down here. Bring the other torches. We'll have to make sure."

By now, Dimitri was again close behind Raoul. He hadn't waited to be invited. His eyes scanned the scene like a hungry hawk. Seb and Ryan O'Rourke then carefully negotiated the precarious stairway and provided more torchlight. "What a stench! This place gives me the bloody creeps," gasped Ryan, covering his mouth with a handkerchief.

"If you don't like the heat, get out of the kitchen," taunted Raoul with a wicked smirk. Dimitri found the wounding words amusing and sniggered.

"Let's remember why we're down here," said Sebastian seriously, bringing everyone to order.

They shone their searchlights in every corner, focussing mainly on the dusty floor. All of a sudden, a scraping sound made them all spontaneously wince. Sebastian's right foot had crushed something beneath it. "Oh it's only some old beads," he informed the others in a blasé tone.

"Those are more than just beads. It looks like someone's lost a Rosary, and quite an expensive one at that!" Ryan knowledgeably informed the others. Meanwhile, no-one noticed Dimitri edging back some canvasses stacked on the floor, so that they were now secreted behind a shelf, and out of view.

The breeze from the open doors leading outside brought a welcome breath of fresh air, as well as swirling up grit and dirt into their faces. "So, we get out of here now?" urged Dimitri, ushering everyone back like a sheep dog.

"Suppose so. She's not here, is she?" conceded Sebastian acceptingly.

"Now we're down here, I want a closer look round," insisted Raoul with an air of unwelcome intrigue.

"We haven't got time. The Governor will be waiting. We can't prolong his agony any more. Poor man needs to find his wife," argued his partner.

Making ready to climb back up the steep stone steps, Raoul unintentionally brushed roughly past the table in the centre of the crypt. His elbow inadvertently nudged a protruding heavy book which, in turn, toppled the pile of documents it lay on. He immediately leant forward to pick the papers up. His eyes blinked to focus, and involuntarily he gasped in shock at what was facing him.

An unnatural chill ran through his body as he carefully placed the document back on the bench, and shone his torch directly on it. The others had instinctively returned and huddled round. There, resting before them was what appeared to be the last entry in the Parish Records. A recent warning, shakily written in large letters of what they determined could only be congealed blood, gave them all the shivers:

"You will reap what you sow."

This was obviously a daunting threat, but was it aimed at someone specific, or anyone who dared to delve uninvited into the depths of the Church? More to the point, who was the scribe?

Engrossed in the puzzle, the men flinched in unison as the outer portal shut with a resounding bang. Like fish in a net, the rescuers instantly came to the inconceivable conclusion that they, too, had now been trapped themselves.

There was a deathly silence and a reek of fear in the air. A good ten minutes passed. Each man inwardly paralysed with fright, stared, in turn, into the eyes of the others, waiting for a reaction. Who would show weakness? Who would crack first?

The unbearable stalemate was suddenly broken with a thud, and then a creaking noise. "Are you o.k.? Anybody hurt?" Four torches simultaneously aimed their beams at the top of the staircase. They'd never been so pleased in their life to see a priest. "I'm sorry I took so long. I'm not as strong as I used to be. Hobbling down the first passageway took it out of me. The wind's getting up. That door sticks sometimes. It's very hostile to draughts. Have you found anything?"

"Well, not what we were looking for, that's for sure," announced Sebastian, slowly leading the way up the spiralling steps, parchment clasped under his arm.

The strong sun forced the men to momentarily shield their eyes as they met the safety of daylight again. Father Antonio's gaze immediately focussed on the document Seb had retrieved. "Not now, Father. I'll talk to you about it later, in private. It's rather inflammatory. I've told the others to keep what they've seen to themselves. Best get back to the Hotel and find Lord Meadows. Tell him the news, or rather lack of it!"

The anxious Islanders were sitting on the hotel terrace, patiently waiting. Grace Elisabeth had provided refreshments and sympathy, ensuring everyone was shaded from the soaring sun. Sebastian shook his head and shrugged his shoulders as they reached the pathway at the end of the garden. Montgomery did not know how to react. What did that mean?

"I don't know whether the news is good or bad, but your wife is not in the crypt. There's no sign of her."

"Of course there isn't. She's lying low. She thinks I'm dead," croaked a hoarse voiced Della Dubois, who was sitting chain-smoking, away from the others, with a large glass of neat gin in her hand. Grace Elisabeth stood over her, as if on guard, presumably to avoid any further confrontation. For reasons of his own, Raoul couldn't help but feel a new found sympathy for his housekeeper, and caught her eye with a reassuring glance. She seemed unusually uncomfortable.

Monty looked totally forlorn. He reached inside his jacket pocket and took out a rather tatty, black and white photograph.

"Haven't looked at that for years," he confided to the others, with a half smile. "Where are you ol' girl?" Tears welled up in his eyes. "Where the hell are you?"

He placed the picture carefully on the table, and gently straightened out the edges. "Can I have a closer look at that?" asked an Irish voice.

"Help yourself, my boy." Lord Montgomery offered the chef his private possession.

"But, I've seen her," he excitedly exclaimed.

"Of course you have, young man," barked Lady Laetitia, rolling her eyes. "She's the Governor's wife!"

"Don't be too hard on the boy; he hasn't been here long. He can't be expected to know everyone." Harriett came to the rescue.

"Well she's not just anyone is she?" responded the harridan in an exasperated tone.

"No, you don't understand," the chef babbled on. "I saw her . . . last night . . . on the big Island. It was her, so it was! She asked me for directions, so she did. She seemed in a daze. I t'ought she was ill or sometin'. She didn't seem to know where she was, or what she was doing. She wasn't even looking where she was going, that's for sure, because she bumped right into me!" He studied the photo again. "Yep, she looked a lot more bedraggled, and she was limping quite badly, but either that was her, or she's got a double!"

Monty's eyes immediately lit up. "Are you certain my boy? Are you positive?"

"Sure as I can be," replied O'Rourke, obviously pleased to be of service.

"That's good enough for me. I'll contact the authorities right away. Put out a missing persons plea. They'll find her. They've all met her. They'll find her!" Colour had returned to the Governor's cheeks and, with a glint in his eye and a spring in his step, he set off for his office to make the necessary calls.

* * *

"What in heaven's name is this all about?" a mystified Raoul pondered, after he and Sebastian had retired alone to their office. Both shuddered in bewilderment as they closely studied the parchment with the chilling warning scrawled in blood.

"Who knows? It's an omen of some sort, but whom is it meant for? Put it in the desk, Raoul, we don't want to alarm the others. Everyone's skittish enough as it is!"

Before Raoul had managed to hide the document, there was a knock on the door. Grace Elisabeth had come in with a tray of light refreshments. "I thought you could do with this," she smiled, as she placed the snack on the table. Her eyes fleetingly glanced at the parchment retrieved from the crypt, but her expression didn't betray any undue interest, so nothing was mentioned.

"Everything been o.k. while we've been away, Grace?" enquired Seb as a matter of courtesy.

"Fine, Mr. Sebastian. Everyt'ing has been jus' fine."

It was understood that, if ever both proprietors happened to be absent from their duties at the same time, Grace Elisabeth was next in charge. She was a valued employee and friend, and both partners had complete faith in her ability, and trust in her integrity. She, in turn, had the utmost respect for them. "Thank-you, Grace," they both echoed as she left the room.

By now, the rescuers were shattered and decided that a rest was next on the agenda. Everything had quietened down. There was peace at last; albeit probably short-lived! After all, according to the prophecy, someone was still at risk.

Chapter 29

"I'm not accustomed to being summoned," announced Lady Laetitia icily as she brushed by her host.

"Really? You still came though, didn't you?" was the sneering reply.

"Your illiterate scribble intrigued me. Just what is it that you think you have to say that would interest me?"

Della Dubois was about to chance her arm yet again, and undertake the biggest challenge of her, as yet, unsuccessful search for easy money, and most of all, respect. She motioned to her guest to sit down. "I wouldn't grace my backside with anything in this beachfront hovel, thank you," was the response through gritted teeth as Laetitia slowly advanced towards Della. She was a formidable woman, both physically and in status, but Della Dubois stood her ground.

"Tell me; what is the title of the grandchild of a 'Lady'?" she asked, with an air of innocence.

"I'm sure you didn't bring me here for a lesson on the aristocracy. Now don't waste my time." It never occurred to Laetitia to actually listen for once and consider the implication of the carefully worded question. Della Dubois just stood, smiled, looked Lady Lascelles straight in the eye, and waited for the penny to drop.

"Huh? It would almost be amusing, were it not so ridiculous," she snarled. "I suppose you're pregnant and you're trying to use my son as a scapegoat. Forget it! I've never heard anything quite so preposterous in all my life! You're an evil, scheming, little tart who has slept with half the male population on this Island, but not my son. The father could be anybody, rather like your own, in fact. If you think I'm falling for that load of baloney, you need your head examined. I'll bid you Good Day!"

"Oh, I'm not pregnant," she quickly volunteered, lounging purposely in the doorway to bar Laetitia's intended departure. "Well not yet anyway. I'm far too sensible for that. But . . . , I am sure it could be arranged . . . You see, I appear to be irresistible to any red blooded male . . . and being a very fertile woman . . . ," she boasted, pushing out her ample cleavage. "Well, let's just say, your son is no exception, believe me! In fact . . . he's had a little taste already . . . and he's just begging for more. You can't keep him to yourself forever, Lae . . . titia," she provocatively pouted.

This wanton display of cheap, shameless goading instantly provoked the desired effect. Nothing could have worked better! Lady Lascelles turned on her heels and breathed fire. "You go . . . anywhere . . . , ANYWHERE . . . near my son and I'll kill you. Do you hear me? With my own bare hands, I will kill you! NEVER, NEVER underestimate me!" A distinct click was audible as Della Dubois pressed a button behind her back.

"Well, now I've got you threatening me on tape. A little bit of careful editing here and there . . . I think I've just got even more substance to ask you to give me a little financial inducement to keep quiet, until my fortune arrives, that is."

Lady Laetitia went straight for Della Dubois' throat and there was a tussle. "I've been very, very restrained until now, but don't push me or you will regret it!" Della pulled away. She reached for a small camera waiting nearby.

"Some photos of the bruises on my neck. I'll . . . enhance them first . . . of course," she coughed. "It just gets better!"

An unflustered Laetitia realised that she was playing right into her blackmailer's hands and advanced again, towering over her victim. "You don't frighten me, and I don't make idle threats! Go near my son, or cross me again, and you'll find that out. Who's going to take the word of a little slut like you against mine? Think about it!"

With that, she carefully rearranged her clothing, checked her appearance in a nearby mirror and left the premises. Della Dubois watched, shaking, partly in fear and partly in rage. Perhaps she'd gone too far this time. Or had she??

* * *

The rattling shutter had managed to work its way free and carelessly crashed back against the antique wardrobe in the owners' apartment. The wind had increased and was certainly making its presence felt. Raoul rubbed his bleary eyes and squinted to look at the clock. It was midway through the afternoon, and Sebastian still lay sleeping peacefully. Their emotionally exhausting expedition was still taking its toll.

Once awake, Raoul decided to get up. He firmly closed the shutter once again, got dressed, and headed for the bistro in search of something to eat and drink.

"You'll have a long wait, unless you make it yourself," commented Kittie, who was sitting with Clarrie, at their usual corner table, doubtless looking for mischief to impart.

"Yes, we've been waiting such a long time," sighed Clarrie innocently. "There just doesn't seem to be anyone about."

"Sorry, ladies, what was it you would like?" apologised Raoul, realising he was actually going to have to prepare refreshments himself.

"Oh nothing thanks," replied Kittie, fluttering her eyelids. "We've had our tea. We're just letting things settle."

Ever on the prowl for distraction, Kittie's wandering interest was unintentionally drawn towards Alistair, busily scribbling away, in a secluded spot, behind a rather grand potted palm tree. He had made the unfortunate mistake of coughing and thus drawing attention to himself. An ideal target for good sport, the young man quickly realised that he was next in the line of fire, and clumsily collected his things to make a hasty exit.

Pushing his way past an advancing Kittie, he looked at his watch and politely nodded farewell without saying a word. "That lady is fast becoming a social piranha," grinned Grace Elisabeth, who had been watching events from the sidelines.

"I think you mean 'pariah'," laughed Raoul, automatically correcting her, "social pariah."

"Mr. Raoul, this time I know exactly what I mean," she dryly replied. "And there ain't a thing going on, on this Island, she don't know about, either, believe you me!"

"Grace . . . ?" Raoul hesitated before he spoke. "Talking about things on the Island; why are some of the gravestones in the cemetery unmarked?"

"Why, Mr. Raoul, what a peculiar question! And why ask me? I'm sure I have no idea," she responded disinterestedly, collecting Alistair's cup and saucer from the table.

He felt he may have inadvertently offended his friend with such a direct approach on such an unexpected and inappropriate topic, so he immediately excused himself. "Sorry, I expect you get fed up with people using you as the Island's fountain of all knowledge, but you have been here all your life."

"I sure have, but dat don't mean I know everyt'ing, now does it?" she responded, hands on hips, with a comical grimace. They both laughed. The uneasy tension had been broken. All the same, it appeared that such a topic was certainly not up for discussion!

"Where have you been?" demanded Raoul curtly, as Ryan O'Rourke noisily appeared through the kitchen swing-door.

"Having a break! I'm entitled, aren't I?" he insolently answered, looking purposely at the watch Raoul had found in Seb's trouser pocket, which had now mysteriously found its way back to the chef's arm. His employer held back.

"I suppose you are. But next time, don't take it when it's busy. Grace has been coping by herself." The housekeeper just rolled her eyes and shook her head, indicating there was no problem. They were just boys, full of testosterone, squabbling again.

* * *

The sound of thunder rumbled in the distance. "Looks like we're in for a storm," suggested Sadie as she surveyed the sky.

"Oh, I do hope not. The dogs do so hate it. They're really difficult to manage in bad weather. The wind is sending them scatty as it is," complained Harriett.

The ladies were relaxing in the beach gardens, with a cup of ice tea, and the intention of aggravating Della Dubois by occupying her favourite, secluded spot under a clump of trees. Sunglasses and scarves protected their delicate faces from the soaring sun, but their blouses and shorts did allow their arms and legs to benefit from the tanning rays. "Any news on your claim yet, Sadie?"

"No! And I wish Monty would pull his bloody finger out. If you ask me he's dragging his feet."

"Well the poor man's got much more important things to worry about now . . . , I'd . . . say." Harriett could have bitten her tongue before she'd finished her sentence. Sadie just glared. "Well, you know what I mean," she swiftly added, in an unsuccessful attempt to extricate herself.

Nothing and no-one was more important than Sadie's rightful fortune, and anything or anyone standing in the way would be removed, sooner or later!

"Good Afternoon, ladies!" Their peace was soon unapologetically interrupted by a stomping Lady Laetitia striding purposefully towards them. She sighed loudly, pulled over a wicker beach chair and sat down, obviously tormented by something.

"Everything all right, Laetitia?" asked Sadie, sensing it obviously was not.

"No, no, it most certainly is not. I've just had another run in with that damn tart." She suddenly stopped, and cautiously looked around. "Come to think of it, isn't this the spot where she normally likes to flaunt her wares?" Without waiting for a response, she angrily continued.

"Anyway, if she thinks she can take me on, she's got another thing coming!"

"Oh, what was it all about then?" asked Harriett, with an obviously practised air of innocence.

"That's immaterial, my dear. The point is she's bitten off more than she can chew this time!"

"Well, Laetitia, perhaps it's about time *you* got *your* hands dirty then, isn't it?" Sadie waded in with feeling.

"I suppose it may well be," she responded pensively. "I know I've held back as yet, but this time she's gone too far. You now have my full support in any scheme you choose."

"No, Laetitia! YOU now have OUR full support in any scheme YOU choose," insisted Sadie.

"Well . . . I can't be seen to be involved. Not in my position," she argued haughtily.

"On the contrary, I'm afraid now's the time. We've done our bit, albeit to no avail, as yet," Sadie earnestly reminded them all.

"You'll have to give me some time," decided Lady Lascelles, still deep in thought. "It'll all need to be water tight and in no way whatsoever possibly implicate me!" There was a loud, prophetic clap of thunder as, abruptly, she rose from her chair and, in a very resolved manner, began to head in the direction of the hotel.

"Do you think she means it?" asked Harriett with some degree of disbelief.

"Let's hope so. It's about bloody time!" Both the ladies then settled back into their own thoughts. As the palms rustled more and more ferociously, Harriett removed her sun shades and surveyed the clouding sky to monitor the weather.

"Watch out!" she suddenly shrieked, instinctively rolling off her lounger with unbelievable agility. A startled Sadie uncharacteristically froze, completely unable to move, like a rabbit caught in car headlights. A distinctive cracking noise still echoed through the air, instantly followed by a dull thud.

A bulky branch, precariously hanging from one of the trees in the garden, was apparently no longer able to cope with the increasing force of the wind, and had landed tip down, like a spear, inches away from the two sunbathers. Fortunately, it had miraculously missed them both. All the same, the shock had seemingly been most startling, perhaps enough to frighten someone to death!

Harriett frantically rummaged through her bag for her comforting Rosary beads, but mysteriously, found they weren't there! "Now where did I have them last?" she shakily thought out loud, mentally retracing her recent movements.

Dimitri, who had been trying to collect blowing menus and serviettes from the nearby terrace, had witnessed the incident first hand, and wasted no time in coming to the rescue. He instantly ushered Sadie and Harriett away from the swaying tree to relative safety. If it hadn't been for his swift and decisive action, both women could still have been in further danger, as the flailing cedar continued to struggle with the elements, and more branches fell.

Kittie and Clarrie just happened to be leaving the hotel at the very moment the commotion began. Heads down, holding on tightly to their hats, they had taken an unusual shortcut through the gardens to try and shield themselves from the increasing wind. Hearing Harriett's scream, they had naturally come over to see what was going on.

Clearly inspired by some excitement at last, the twins were ready to turn the insignificant affair into a full scale drama. This, however, didn't suit either Sadie or Harriett. It occurred to them both that, despite the whistle of the wind, their earlier conversation may have easily been overheard, especially by the Island's professional eaves droppers.

Now was certainly not the time for either of them to give the game away to anyone, so Sadie bravely decided to make light of the situation. "Laetitia's booming voice has got a lot to answer for!" she laughed, carefully observing the sisters' reaction.

Their bewildered response to the comment was sufficient to reassure the two friends that their would-be rescuers were completely ignorant of Lady Lascelles' earlier visit. The twins thankfully, therefore, couldn't have been in the vicinity long enough to acquire any harmful gossip.

Examining the evidence, Clarrie did, however, in her naivety, voice her observation that the break in the branch did seem rather clean cut, looking almost sawn to precision. This prompted Kittie to speculate whether the whole thing really was an accident.

Sadie had had enough of their idle chatter at that point, and suitably dismissed their ideas as utter nonsense, indicating the obvious ferocity of the wind. Nothing more was then said. She did, nevertheless, begin to wonder whether she and Harriett had innocently been in the wrong place at the wrong time, and therein perhaps foiled somebody else's attempt to literally put the wind up the Island's resident pain in the backside. Or was it merely a simple coincidence after all?

Chapter 30

Unfortunately, the weather hadn't improved at all by the following day. The clouds had thickened and the wind continued to blow, coughing up sand and dust, and making life rather uncomfortable for those going about their daily business in the open air. Thankfully, it was agreeably warm and the sun still successfully managed to make welcome, fleeting appearances.

In dribs and drabs, the fishermen had reluctantly gathered on the beach to assess the situation and decide whether it was worth their while to brave a day's work. Unable to agree, they allowed themselves to be idly entertained by an unfamiliar, plush speedboat, skilfully riding the wrestling waves. No respect seemed to be given to the perils of the sea, as the vessel arrogantly surfed through, at top speed, on its intended course. Finally manoeuvring into the jetty with the engine off, the boat drifted like clockwork and was successfully moored alongside.

A tall, well dressed lady in a grey suit stepped confidently down from the deck. She looked to be in her early forties. Her gleaming, auburn hair was tied back in a neat bun, and her eyes were shaded in dark, stylish glasses. Shielding her face with a wide brimmed, wine red hat, tilted to one side, she then tastefully removed her matching high heeled shoes before retrieving a briefcase from the boat.

Gracefully making her way across the beach towards the hotel, she did her best to avoid the swirling sand. The usual wolf whistles, commonly reserved for such feminine presence, were automatically silenced as a mark of respect for the lady's obvious sophistication. With a passing glance, she politely inclined her head and smiled pleasantly at her assembled male audience, evidently already in awe of her radiant poise and elegance.

Hermione Hemming-Harris rang the bell in Reception and patiently awaited a response. Some minutes later, Raoul aimlessly sauntered out of the office, whistling, hands in his pockets, as usual. His demeanour instantly improved when he set eyes on the beguiling and unexpected guest standing before him. "May I help you, Madam?" he asked, cheerfully and courteously.

"I do hope so," she answered, with an alluring smile, her face still half obscured. "I'm looking for a Miss. Della Dubois. Would you be able to help me?" Her impeccable English accent made her all the more attractive.

"Certainly," drooled Raoul. "She's a personal friend of mine."

"She's not listed in the telephone directory, so I came in person," the lady continued.

"Very few people on the Island have the telephone," Raoul explained knowledgeably. "It's such an intrusion. It usually means trouble, and spoils our idyllic lifestyle. Of course, one can pursue official or administrative services through the Governor's office, or by contacting the hotel." Raoul had noticed the stranger's brief case and had cleverly engineered his response to try and detect the reason for the lady's visit, but she gave nothing away and politely smiled once again.

"Thanks, that's handy to know!"

The hotelier seemed totally mesmerised and his inappropriate, fawning stare was only interrupted when the lady diplomatically asked where Miss. Dubois could actually be located.

"I'll take you myself," offered Raoul, without hesitation.

"That won't be necessary," replied the visitor, retaining her fixed smile. "I'm sure you have things to do. Just point me in the right direction please." Raoul nodded and gave unnecessarily detailed directions to the beachfront café. "I think I passed it on the way here," she patiently grinned. "Thank you for your help. Good morning!"

"What about a room?" Raoul quickly enquired, as Miss. Hemming-Harris began to leave.

"A room? Oh, I shan't be staying," she confirmed, and gracefully glided towards the exit.

"Who was that?" asked Sebastian as he came out of the kitchen, promptly followed by Grace Elisabeth.

"I don't really know. She didn't say," murmured Raoul, rather frustrated that he had been unable to glean any information about the reason for the enigmatic female's trip.

* * *

The gentle tap on the café door received no response. "You'll have to bang louder than that," offered a passing local, voluntarily doing the job with his heavy fist. "She's probably still asleep. Della? Della!"

"All right, hang on, I'm coming. Where's the bloody fire?" A heavily dishevelled Della Dubois, wearing none of her trade mark make-up, leaned out of the doorway, in just her bra and pants, and yawned, squinting in the unwelcome daylight.

"Hermione Hemming-Harris." The caller introduced herself, holding out her hand in a gesture of friendship. Della Dubois just grimaced. "I'm your lawyer, Miss. Dubois, or rather your late mother's. I've come from Mystique. There are things we need to discuss."

"Oh, Oh, I wasn't expecting you," she coughed. "Call me Della, by the way. Do come in." Chain smoking the previous evening had done nothing to soften her grating voice or the odour of her sitting room.

Hermione retained her unflinching smile, and her hat, as she entered a very untidy and dusty, airless parlour. Her change of facial expression prompted a reaction. "I'd open a window, but the wind is too strong," spluttered Della, almost apologetically.

"I'm sure we'll manage," reassuringly conceded the legal adviser, softly putting her perfumed handkerchief to her face.

While Della got dressed and made herself presentable, Hermione took the opportunity to inspect the premises more closely. Open bottles of wine, unemptied ashtrays and rotting fruit, quickly gave her an accurate picture of the type of client she was dealing with. "Drink?" offered Della, lighting her first cigarette of the day.

"No thank you and, with respect, my time is limited. We don't usually visit clients; they come to us. It was rather difficult to get hold of you, so this time, we made an exception. There are certain papers to be signed and witnessed, and I need proof of your identity before we release your finances."

"What? You mean it's been decided. The money is definitely mine?"

"Of course. There's no question about it!"

"But what about Sadie?" Hermione's face looked blank. "You know, her nurse. She contested the Will. She's the one who caused all these bloody problems."

"Oh yes, yes of course," she nodded, slightly flustered. "She doesn't stand a chance. She has no basis for a claim. No basis whatsoever."

You could have heard Della Dubois shout for joy at the other end of the beach. She immediately reached into a nearby cupboard, retrieved a dusty bottle of champagne, cracked it open and swigged directly from it, politely remembering to offer her guest a sip, which she gracefully declined.

"So, where are they then?" Della gleefully asked. She was duly met with an unresponsive stare. "The papers I've got to sign. I'll get some ID."

"Oh, yes, the papers. I haven't got them with me. We can't do that here. We must respect security and protocol. You'll have to come to my office on the main Island. I've got transport. We can go right away. Get your things."

Della looked crestfallen. Her fortune seemed short-lived. She didn't like the idea of leaving the Island at such short notice, but decided it was a means to an end. Miss. Hemming-Harris assured her it wouldn't take long, and she'd be provided with transport back, so she popped a few items in her bag and they prepared to leave.

Della Dubois was respectfully, but hastily, ushered out of her own home, and felt rather unsettled at the sudden speed of events. She reconciled her discomfort with the knowledge that bureaucracy was a time consuming necessity, and her high flying lady lawyer obviously had a lot to do, before she could release the money.

As they hastened along the beach to the jetty, a mild sandstorm was developing, courtesy of the prevailing winds. Hermione clung tightly to her hat and seemed anxious that her chic couture might be ruined by the dust. Indeed, her mood seemed to gradually change, and she became quite rattled at times, almost obsessively wiping the dirt from her jacket and skirt.

Both the women carried their shoes to quicken their step, and Della decided to tentatively engage her legal advisor in conversation, expressing concern about taking a boat in such unpredictably agitated seas. Miss. Hemming-Harris reassured her client that she was also a very experienced seafarer and that there was no need whatsoever to worry. "It won't be long before it's all sorted," she smiled again.

Della Dubois proudly took a comfortable seat at the back of the open top speed boat, and her multi-skilled lawyer replaced her hat with a headscarf, took the helm, and safely negotiated them out to the open sea. The further away from the Island they sailed, the calmer the seas became, and there was an interlude of pleasant, more tranquil weather. Della took advantage of the break and calmly sat back and relaxed.

Hermione eventually put the boat on auto-cruise, and joined her client at the back of the vessel, offering her an uncorked bottle of chilled champagne that she had already put on ice as a gesture of early celebration.

Della had a well known weakness for champagne and was soon guzzling away. She playfully remarked that Hermione hadn't shown her any ID and that, for all she knew, she could be being kidnapped. They laughed and began to strike up quite a conversation. Hermione now seemed much more relaxed, and began to chat more openly about herself.

"It's strange we've never come across each other before. I used to live on that Island many years ago," Hermione suddenly confided.

R. S. Charles

"Really?" asked Della, genuinely interested. "Before my time, perhaps. What made you move?"

"It was too restricting. I wanted to educate myself and get on, so I begged my mother to send me to boarding school on one of the bigger islands where there was more opportunity. The rest is history. I travelled abroad, went to University in England, and came back to Mystique to set up my own legal Practice. I've never married," she mused. "But I'm happier that way."

"So you're a successful, independent businesswoman now," Della enthused with a patronising air of support.

"Yes, and I've got my own self discipline and hard work to thank for it! I didn't need men, or anybody else's money, especially my mother's, to move up the ladder."

At that point Miss Hemming-Harris removed her headscarf and allowed her flowing hair to enjoy the light breeze. She basked in her own beauty. She was like a porcelain doll, untouchable, and Della got the distinct impression that, consequently, no man had ever dared try.

The conversation seemed to be turning a little sour, and with that, so was the weather. The boat started to rock again as it began to battle with the revitalised, raging sea. The sky grew darker, seemingly setting the scene for tragedy.

Della Dubois began to feel uncomfortable. Closely studying Hermione's now frowning face as they spoke, she sensed an unwelcome change of fate. It had been bugging her since they first met. The lawyer seemed to resemble someone she knew. She just couldn't place who.

Minutes later, for no apparent reason, Hermione switched off the engine, and the speed boat began to drift aimlessly. Della slowly realised that all was not what it seemed, and deduced just in time that Hermione definitely was the spitting image of her mother. She anxiously gripped a railing, and prepared to stand up.

A shiver ran through her body as she prepared to ask the inevitable question, to which she feared she already knew the answer. Della Dubois looked Hermione Hemming-Harris straight in her piercing, brown eyes, already tinged with obvious inbred hatred and contempt for women like her. A combination of bitter jealousy and pent-up sexual frustration were patently emerging from the depths of her carefully controlled persona.

"So, indulge me," Della nonchalantly began. "What is the name of your mother?"

"Oh, I think you know only too well. And it appears you also know my brother, intimately, it would seem. God, it's taken you long enough for the penny to drop, you conniving, blackmailing little bitch! You really are as crass and irritating as I was led to believe."

By now, both women were standing unsteadily on the rocking boat, ready for the ensuing struggle which without doubt had to happen. The only difference was that Hermione was already prepared, and the look on her face continued to reflect her true resentment. She stood sneering, now holding fisherman's netting in her hand. Her intentions were unmistakeable.

At the very moment she lurched forward to entangle her helpless victim, a giant, rogue wave intervened and exacted its own justice, enveloping the boat, tossing it like a toy. There were screams of terror as the vessel went out of control and fell prey to an angry, unrelenting sea.

Had Hermione Lascelles successfully done her mother's bidding, or was she, too, now lost in a watery grave?

Chapter 31

Back on the Island, the weather had certainly taken a turn for the worse. It had begun to rain, and the once carefree climate had now reduced its worshippers to scurrying little mice, dodging flying obstacles and the torment of torrential downpours.

In the Governor's office, Monty sat blankly staring at the wall. He was lost without Daphnee. At least he now knew she was safe and being well cared for, even if she had lost her memory. He was so thankful that they had made the effort to attend those boring ceremonial dinners on Mystique in the early years of his career as Governor. If it hadn't been for Ryan O'Rourke's fortuitous sighting and an eagle eyed fellow diplomat recognising Lady Meadows, his wife's whereabouts and well being may still have remained a mystery.

But Monty still felt distressed. What if his wife's memory didn't come back? What if she didn't remember that it was he whom she loved? What if she was never her old self again? All these thoughts trickled through his tortured mind. Of course he should have cherished her more when he had the chance, told her he loved her. But she knew that, didn't she? Surely, he didn't have to tell her. Perhaps he should have! God willing, he'd soon have the opportunity to make it up to her and vowed faithfully that he would. Monty then did something quite uncharacteristic. He lowered his eyes, clasped his hands, and began to silently pray. A tear trickled from his left eye, down his cheek. He had never felt such deep despair.

All of a sudden, his self torment was unexpectedly and rudely interrupted, when a temporary secretary entered the room, omitting to knock. In the half light she looked so like Daphnee, but perhaps that was just wishful thinking.

The Governor spluttered and covered his face with a handkerchief, as if to blow his nose. It wouldn't do for staff to see his pain. Without speaking, the young girl handed him a piece of paper. The look on her face made it obvious the news was not good.

It was a telegram. "Severe weather warning for outlying Islands. Stop. Extreme storms approaching. Stop. Possible long term duration. Stop. Power sources likely to be impeded. Stop. Contingency safety plans should be put into operation without delay. Stop. Met Office H.Q."

The Governor sighed. As if he didn't have enough to contend with. Now the weather was being awkward as well! The running of the Island was, however, his duty, so it was time to put aside personal worries and start to undertake his professional responsibilities.

Monty put on his Panama hat and white cotton jacket: it made him feel more official. It was crucial to give the right impression on occasions such as these. He turned the door handle and screwed up his face, preparing to meet the elements. Luckily, the rain had subsided somewhat, so he didn't have the handicap of struggling in the wind with an umbrella as he propelled himself towards the hotel.

Having made it to the terrace, the Governor reluctantly turned around, anticipating a scene of disagreeable devastation. But surprisingly, there seemed to be little real damage to speak of. A few branches had fallen off trees and the garden furniture was in disarray, but fortunately that was all. Perhaps, he tried to convince himself, it wouldn't amount to much after all. Thankfully, apart from irritating gusts of sand in the face and the deafening wash of the waves as they reached the shore and slapped the cliff edges, for the moment, at least, everything seemed tolerable

Then, the tinkling crash of glass bottles toppling over and smashing into pieces on the stone step beside him suddenly made Montgomery jump, and brought him back to reality. He once again needed to focus on his priorities.

The lounge area of the hotel was deserted; quite a contrast to the usual cliques of pampered guests milling aimlessly around looking for distraction. Sebastian and Raoul were both busily on duty at the front Reception desk, and immediately recognised by the Governor's demeanour, that he was not making a social call.

"Gentlemen, I need your help! I have received information from the Met.Office that the present storm is likely to become a lot worse and, however unwelcome, linger for some time. We need to put safety measures into operation and ensure that everyone remains sheltered and accounted for. If we act now, damage should be limited and there will be no need to panic."

"What do you want us to do, Governor?" Sebastian instantaneously asked with a solemn look on his face.

"Oh, don't worry!" interrupted Raoul with a blasé grin. "We've had all this before. It never comes to anything. It's usually a lot of fuss about nothing."

"Hopefully so!" coughed Monty, trying not to become flustered. "But one never knows. This one may just catch us out. It's as well to be prepared."

"Absolutely," enthused Seb. Raoul just rolled his eyes facetiously and carried on reading a French magazine which had been left in the bistro.

"We'll be alright, Governor! Didn't Seb tell you he was a boy scout?" he flippantly joked. "Anyway, haven't we had enough bloody drama to brighten up our lives recently? We don't want to be greedy. Surely we can't be due for any more?" he sourly added, in a more sarcastic tone.

"This won't be of our own making though, will it? We may have no choice this time," replied Monty, in sober reflection

"Sounds a bit like you're expecting some kind of retribution, Governor," suggested Raoul wryly.

"Not at all, Raoul! But fate's unpredictable. And you're right; things on the Island have not been harmonious of late. Far from it, in fact! For some reason, I just get the feeling that it may be . . . well . . . pay back time and we should fear the worst. But that's between us. Don't alarm anyone else to that degree. Perhaps I'm over-reacting. The last thing we want is panic."

Though Monty was unaware of it, Sebastian could see Raoul out of the corner of his eye, shaking his head and smirking, as if to mock the Governor's theory as the ridiculous ramblings of a tired, old man. He politely excused himself and pulled Raoul roughly to one side. "Look, he's under a lot of strain at the moment. You could at least pretend to be supportive. Where's your humanity, for God's sake?"

Pondering on what his partner had said, Raoul did begin to feel rather guilty at his cavalier attitude. So to make amends, he offered to personally ensure that everyone would be thoroughly briefed on the situation. He suggested that if people felt at all vulnerable, they were to come to the hotel for support.

It was also to be made known that, in keeping with tradition in times like these, as a last resort, if anyone wished to warn others of imminent danger, they were to go to the Church and ring the bell. The chimes would signal extreme peril, and call everyone to assemble in the oldest and safest building on the Island.

The Governor seemed pleased with the valued support of the hotel owners and left them to spread the news. He needed to be back in the office, available for any eventuality.

* * *

"Morning Ladies! You shouldn't be out in weather like this!" Sebastian greeted Kittie and Clarrie in mock admonishment as they arrived, windswept and bedraggled, in the hotel lobby.

"Life must go on!" concluded Kittie.

"Besides, we didn't want to miss anything," added Clarrie. Kittie gave her sister a withering look.

"Oops. I think I've said the wrong thing again. What is the matter with me lately? I seem to say whatever comes into my head," muttered Clarrie with a sweet look of injured innocence.

"Well, you're in the best place now," confided Raoul reassuringly. "And you can help too." He knew that imparting the latest news to the twins would be the quickest way to circulate it round the Island without much effort on his part; but he was seriously beginning to wonder just how eccentric Clarrissa actually was. The sisters excitedly ordered morning tea and listened intently to their special mission.

229

Laetitia Lascelles was pacing the floor. "Oh, d.d.. do sit dddown, mamma," encouraged her son. "Y..you're d..d.. dist . . . racting me. I'm t.. try.. trying to write."

"I've got things on my mind, Alistair. Things you know nothing about, nor should you," she quickly added before he asked the obvious question. His mother seemed very ill at ease. Little did he know, she was, after all, secretly awaiting news from her daughter? But as yet, wasn't it possibly too early?

Not possessing an abundance of patience, Laetitia could contain herself no longer. "I'm going out," she abruptly announced. "To the hotel; I need to use the telephone."

Alistair was not normally concerned about his mother's behaviour, embarrassed, yes, but he'd never seen her like this before. She seemed almost out of control. He resolved to follow, at a safe distance, just in case she needed him. Despite the brusque and belittling manner in which she often treated him, their loyalty and devotion to one another was unquestionable.

Challenging the heavy downpour outside, Lady Lascelles remained undeterred and laboured the short distance to the hotel through the storm, using her sturdy umbrella as a weather shield. "I want to use the telephone," she barked, banging the main entrance door behind her, and shaking the drips off her now misshapen umbrella all over the furniture.

As she approached the Reception desk, Sebastian swiftly turned the 'phone round to face her. It had been an instruction, not a request. "It's private!" she said curtly, motioning the proprietors to leave with a wave of her hand. Raoul just stared in resentment at the way he had been spoken to.

"I'm sure that we can find something else to do," smiled Sebastian obligingly, leading his partner away towards the bistro.

"That woman's going to go too far one of these days. We're not her bloody servants," scowled Raoul. He could feel one of his black moods coming on again. Since Jimmy had been away, his supply of medication had dwindled, and it was taking its toll.

"These are trying times," reasoned Seb.

"Oh that's right. Let her walk all over us, just like she does with everyone else. We at least deserve some civility, don't you think?" argued Raoul aggressively.

At that moment, they had the feeling that they were no longer alone. Alistair had secreted himself in the corner, and had heard every word. He looked rather shame faced and wriggled uncomfortably. "Sorry, Ali," shrugged Raoul in spontaneous self defence, "but your mother is becoming more and more difficult to tolerate."

"I know . . . , I kn . . . know," accepted Alistair, like a gentleman. "B..b . . . b . . . but sh.. she's j . . . just having a b..b.bad day. G . . . g..got something on her mmm.mind, I fear."

"Sebastian!" He had been summoned back into Reception. "What the deuce is wrong with this infernal machine? I can't get through." Seb offered to help, but when he picked up the telephone, there was no dialling tone. It was dead.

"The lines are probably down. We were warned this may happen. It's the storm you see, Lady Lascelles!"

"Of course it's the bloody storm. I'm not an imbecile. But my call is urgent, young man."

"I expect it's only temporary. Why not take some refreshment while you're waiting," he offered.

"Oh very well then! Tea, milk, no sugar," she responded ungratefully.

"Please!!!" growled Raoul under his breath.

Laetitia made her way towards Kittie and Clarrie who were engrossed in the free entertainment. "Something wrong, Laetitia?" asked an intrigued Kittie, with a smug expression.

"Nothing which concerns either of you!" she rudely snapped, as she proceeded to pull up a chair to their table. She obviously was in no mood to talk, so the three of them just sat there, in silence, looking into thin air.

Clarrissa was bored. She hated silence. She liked to chat, or at least be chatted to, so at the risk of inviting a dressing down she asked, "Have you heard about the storm?" in her child-like innocence. Laetitia just raised her eyebrows and, shaking her head, gave Kittie a disparaging look of disbelief.

"Is your sister going senile?" she sarcastically inquired. "It's hardly possible not to know about the bloody storm!" she then barked at Clarrie.

"She's not deaf, Laetitia! She's merely trying to tell you that they predict this one's going to be far more aggressive than usual! Rather like yourself at the moment!"

Kittie had triumphantly championed her sister. Clarrie liked that, and nodded in support, proudly preening herself. Laetitia looked away, but the message was getting through, and she inwardly resolved to check her behaviour. She didn't want to encourage any undue suspicion, after all.

Fifteen minutes of awkward silence passed. Laetitia then suddenly stood up. Both the twins winced, not knowing what was coming next. "I'll bid you Good Day, ladies!" she smiled, as she headed back to Reception. "Sebastian?" she called out, but in a much pleasanter manner.

"He's not here," growled Raoul truculently.

"Then would you be so kind as to please see if the telephone is functioning yet," she enquired, with unexpected courtesy.

Raoul was somewhat taken aback at Laetitia's new found manners and meekly did as he was asked. "I'm afraid the lines are still down, Lady Lascelles. Would you like me to come and inform you when they are in operation again?"

"That would be most helpful, young man. I'd appreciate that. Thank you!" Raoul stood open mouthed as she then nodded pleasantly and took her leave.

"Alistair! We're going now!" she bellowed as she walked through the lounge, not even turning a hair. Her son immediately revealed himself from his hiding place and hastened to open the main door for his mother, not in the least surprised that she knew he had followed her.

Chapter 32

H our by hour, the storm was gathering strength, and most people were safely sheltering in their own abode, reluctant to go outside. The once gently swaying palm trees were now wheezing in the gale force winds, unwillingly bowing in defiant duress. The tapping of rain droplets on windows had turned into a deafening crescendo of heavy hailstones, quashing the possibility of chit chat or conversation.

Back at the hotel, doors were banging as some remaining staff decided to take their life in their hands and try to scuttle home, despite invitations, and even well meaning instructions, to stay. The last to leave, as one would expect, was Grace Elisabeth. Thinking of others, as usual, she decided that she would be of better use supporting her elderly neighbours who would, without doubt, be frightened in such extreme circumstances.

The tinkling chandeliers were busily composing their own ominous music, but could barely be heard above the rattling windows and blustering blinds. Whistling draughts seemed to be invading every part of the palatial building, waking unwelcome swirling sands from superficially cleaned nooks and crannies.

Outside, poolside tables and chairs were being lifted into the air and blown around like feathers. Some of the carefully tended garden bushes had been totally uprooted and were well on their way elsewhere. Barking dogs were desperately defending their territory against the intruding tempest as the whining strains of the wind continued to howl through the struggling trees. One by one, the soggy sand dunes were gradually surrendering to the conquering sea as it slowly, but surely, angrily advanced, further and further towards a population in peril.

Sebastian and Raoul stood helpless in the hotel porch way, powerless to do anything but watch Mother Nature savage herself. "We ought to at least see if everyone's o.k.," eventually mouthed a frustrated Sebastian.

"What, and risk our own lives?" responded Raoul with a shake of the head.

"Well, we can't just stand here. We have to do something."

"Sebastian," smiled Raoul reassuringly. "Some things are even beyond your control. Why not wait until it's absolutely necessary. It may ease off." Seb looked distraught, but nodded in prudent agreement. There was no point in unnecessarily endangering themselves.

All over the Island, people were nervously being entertained by the freak storm which had forced them to stay cooped up indoors instead of enjoying their daily routine in the fresh air and warm sunshine.

* * *

Monty, still juggling his administrative duties and his inner angst, couldn't help but wonder how different life would be if such unsavoury weather were the norm. It began to dawn on him how spoilt they all were by their beautiful environment and climate, and how precious such a lifestyle was. His reverie made him oblivious to someone frantically knocking on his front door.

Sadie had wisely decided to shelter at Harriett's. Mrs Van Leiden's old house was taking the brunt of the bad weather, being so near the cliffs. She indignantly resented the storm for daring to interfere with her regular promenade along the beach with the dogs. That was her enjoyment for the day ruined again.

Harriett was on edge, sitting in the armchair by the front window. All she could think about was Antonio. He still wasn't well, and she wasn't there to tend to him. How would he cope, all alone? Little did she know that a bottle of his favourite port had lulled him into a deep, carefree sleep, his snoring competing admirably with the clamouring storm.

Neither of the women spoke. They were both deep in their own thoughts. The shadowy figure passing the window, obviously in great distress, was ignored. "Fancy going out in this weather! Some people just won't be told!" raged Sadie, too wrapped up in her own incarceration.

"How much longer are we to remain imprisoned by this blessed weather?" moaned Kittie, pacing up and down in front of their large bay window.

"Oh, I think it's rather exciting!" exclaimed her sister. "The lightning is just like fireworks." This obviously wasn't the reaction Kittie was looking for. She pursed her lips, annoyed that she might be missing out on some probable drama taking place elsewhere. Then, for a moment, her eyes lit up. She noticed someone desperately struggling to make headway outside, before ill advisedly sheltering under a nearby shaking tree.

"Somebody's out there, braving the storm. Why don't we go back to the Hotel?" she suddenly suggested.

"No!" Clarrie emphatically announced. "We shall stay here unless it becomes absolutely necessary to leave." Kittie was so surprised at her sister's unusual resolve, that she didn't pursue the matter further. She would just have to amuse herself by thinking up aggravating little ways to try and irritate her twin. But she would be wasting her time. Nothing could spoil Clarrie's child-like enjoyment of the spectacular performance of the enraged elements.

Lady Laetitia had engaged her son in a game of chess to while away the hours. She was, however, finding great difficulty in concentrating, and it was more than evident to Alistair, that her mind was still on other things.

"W . . . what's w..w.worr . . . ying you m . . . ma . . . mma?" he sympathetically asked, but was given short shrift, so he decided to keep quiet. She'd confide in him when it became necessary, he felt sure.

The passing silhouette of an obviously tormented human being, and the faint slump on their window as the wilting creature craved help, resulted in Lady Lascelles angrily pulling her curtains across. She muttered something about the stupidity of going out on such a night and the rudeness of interrupting her game. Alistair once more stared in disbelief at his mother's total lack of altruism.

Darkness was beginning to fall unusually soon. All anyone could possibly do was to prepare for an early night, hoping tomorrow would bring some improvement in the weather. What happened next, therefore, sent an unexpected tingling shiver down everyone's spine.

Clearly and loudly across the Island, the Church bell chimed, eerily silencing the simmering storm which seemed to appreciate the opportunity of a momentary rest.

This was the call everyone had hoped never to hear. It was the dreaded signal that the well being of the Island and its inhabitants was in utmost jeopardy!

Chapter 33

Sebastian and Raoul toured the hotel, ensuring that all the windows were properly fastened and doors were locked. Any terrace furniture remaining was dragged inside and shutters were securely closed. Luckily, there were only a handful of guests staying and they all belonged to the same party. The group was Island hopping and wouldn't be back for another two days, so there was no-one to evacuate.

As usual, Dimitri had already absented himself, so the only remaining member of staff was the chef. He joined the two owners in fortifying the hotel, before they made preparations to head for the Church. Protective clothing for such an expedition had never been necessary. Nobody possessed any. They just had to go as they were; in shirts, shorts and sandals.

Sebastian took charge and, thoughtful as ever, suggested that they should check on their regular patrons on the way, and escort them if need be. He knew that the native Islanders would never leave their homes, whatever the danger.

It was unanimously decided to seek out the women first. Presumably, the Governor could manage himself. After some discord about who was most at risk, first stop was Della Dubois' beachside bar.

As the men apprehensively approached, they realised the full force of the storm had already wreaked its havoc on the flimsy wooden café and the adjoining home. Windows and wicker blinds had been smashed by the impact of the treacherous waves, and one corner of the roof was still flapping helplessly in the gale force winds, before it eventually cracked and flew off down the beach in front of their very eyes.

Driving rain was making visibility worse, and the advancing tide caused the once idyllic beach to become a very unsafe and inhospitable place to be. Despite pleas from Sebastian to leave, Raoul still insisted on establishing that Della Dubois was not trapped inside. He banged frantically on the remaining doors, and as he struggled to the end of the terrace, he unexpectedly came face to face with a sinister looking, bedraggled figure, covered in a dripping wet blanket.

It was the Greek. He'd appeared from nowhere. After the mutual fright of their unexpected collision, Dimitri communicated by signs that the place was empty. Talking was impossible. The noise was deafening. Raoul motioned for the odd job man to follow and form into a pack with the other two. But where was Della Dubois?

Their next challenge was to successfully grapple with the hostile environment and reach Harriett Haversham's house. Once they'd made their way back to the pathway again, things were comparatively easier, though an errant branch managed to clip the side of Raoul's face and he'd started to bleed. At first, he took no notice, but the cut was rather near to his right eye and his vision was soon becoming unhelpfully impaired. He tightly grasped Sebastian's arm and relied on his partner to shield him from the uncompromising onslaught.

Candles were beckoning brightly in Harriett Haversham's front window. There was an obvious draught inside as the glowing flames were flickering wildly. The door opened before the men could announce their presence. Evidently, they were expected. Sadie pushed the door shut with Dimitri's help. He was not one of her favourite people, but her glare was half hearted for she welcomed his support. "What's happened to your face, Raoul?" she immediately asked.

"It's just a graze, I think. It looks worse than it is," he bravely replied.

"Sit down! It'll need seeing to," commanded the former nurse. "And watch you don't get blood on Harriett's furniture."

"I should think that's the least of our worries," commented Seb. "Anyway, where is she?"

"Well, that's what I'm worried about," began Sadie, appearing unusually flustered as she tried to concentrate on cleaning and dressing Raoul's wound. "I couldn't stop her. The woman's a fool! She insisted on going on ahead, to help Father Antonio. What on earth could she do on her own? I pleaded with her to wait, but you know what she's like as far as that man's concerned. She's got the notion that he's in great danger. I only hope she made it safely." Her face betrayed her obvious heartfelt concern.

"Be quiet!" Sadie again forcefully instructed her dogs. They hadn't stopped barking since the men had arrived, making it all the more arduous to try and converse. This time, the barks were different, more of a whining, as both the pets ran purposefully towards the front door.

Dimitri firmly believed that some animals have a sixth sense, so he followed. He heard a faint scratching and a whimper outside. With his weight behind the door, he slowly eased open the entrance and Fanny, Harriett's little Scottie, came scampering in looking very sorry for herself. She headed straight for Sadie, sat at her feet, looked up, and proceeded to inform her something was wrong by barking in a very specific way.

Sadie wasted no time. She galvanised the men into action again. They had barely caught their breath. "Harriett's in trouble," she sobbed. "I know she is. We've got to find her. I do hope all this worry hasn't brought on one of her turns, and she's not lying helpless in a ditch somewhere."

Despite the fact that Harriett exasperated her at times, Sadie really cared for her deeply. She was one of the only true friends she had ever had. Recently, it had been unusual to witness any emotion from the moody moaner that hadn't been terse or aggressive, so everyone sympathised and jumped to it straight away. The dogs were quickly tethered together on a strong rope and eagerly led the way out of the garden, panting as if it were a matter of life or death.

The first hurdle they encountered was not far up the sandy lane. A tired palm tree, unable to wrestle with the wind any longer, had just keeled over and was blocking their way. Sadie's wet face went even whiter when the dogs eagerly began to sniff beneath it. Was her friend trapped below?

"That just missed us!" shouted a barely audible voice from the relative shelter of some nearby shrubs. Two very unsteady figures emerged. It was Kittie and Clarrie.

"Thank God!" mouthed Sadie.

"Yes, that was what we thought," added Clarrie, rather feebly. They were obviously at cross purposes, but Sadie didn't enlighten them.

"Ladies, you should have waited for an escort. It's very unsafe for you to be roaming outside on your own!" observed Sebastian angrily.

"We've found that out!" Clarrie could barely be heard above the noise of the storm.

"Oh, we're tougher than you think," insisted Kittie. "Anyway, we'll join you now. Safety in numbers, ay? It's not far to the Church from here."

The twins held on tightly and formed a chain between Dimitri and Ryan O'Rourke. Clarrie actually surprised the masseur with the strength of her grip. It took valuable time, but they all managed to successfully negotiate their way round the aged dead tree, now stuck firmer into the wet sandy banks on either side of the path. Courageously, they then continued to fight their way onwards.

Noticing candlelight still burning in a house at the end of a long garden some way off the track, Sadie suddenly grabbed Sebastian's arm. "What about Laetitia?"

"Alistair is quite capable of getting his mother safely to the Church," was his booming, yet considered, response.

"I'm sure he is, but it's whether she'll do as she's told," shrugged Sadie with conviction.

"All right, I'll go," decided Seb patiently. "But, the rest of you carry on, and be vigilant. Things are flying out of nowhere."

Sebastian pulled himself along by grabbing anything he could until he reached Lady Lascelles' front door. He held on tightly to the old iron knocker and released it. He repeated the action several times before there was an answer. The door was pulled slightly ajar with the challenging instruction; "Identify yourself!"

Seb realised his dirty, wet appearance made him by now almost unrecognisable. "It's me, Lady Lascelles. It's Sebastian." The door opened further, and Seb almost caught his heel in the gap as it was swiftly shut behind him.

"Can we help you?" asked Laetitia, looking rather dumbfounded. "Rather inclement weather to be visiting, isn't it?" Sebastian mentally counted to ten before he reacted.

"It's not safe for you to be here. Didn't you hear the bell?"

"Nonsense, this is my home. I'm not abandoning it. Don't be absurd, man."

Noticing Alistair looking very ill at ease, sitting on the stairs, Seb took his life in his hands and moved closer to Lady Lascelles.

"Look!" he began, through gritted teeth. "I have risked my personal safety to ensure that you are both going to find the only secure shelter on the Island. For once, do as you are damn well told. Get ready and follow me."

Flabbergasted that anyone should dare address her in such an improper manner, Lady Laetitia suddenly realised the apparent gravity of the situation. She reluctantly submitted and nodded to Alistair to comply with Sebastian's instruction. Meanwhile, the hotel owner roughly ripped some curtains off their rails and put them around her shoulders. Alistair followed suit.

Huddled together, they slowly but surely trudged the short journey up the remainder of the hill, dodging rolling shrubs and debris of all kinds coming the other way. Grateful to reach the Church gardens unscathed, they briefly paused to get their breath back under an unsteady, creaking, wooden archway. Wet and windblown, Laetitia felt most undignified, openly exposing what lay beneath her, as yet unchallenged, usual veneer of sophistication.

The heavy Church door had been slightly wedged open with a boulder, allowing just enough room for people to slip through one at a time. Draughty, damp and dingy, the atmosphere inside was chilling and ghostly. The smell of incense wafted through the air, enveloping everyone in a soft cloud of protective haze. The sound of hand bells being rung near the Altar and the mutterings of comforting prayers drifted unconvincingly to the back of the Church. The only light to grace the revered refuge came from the large, flickering candles dotted around the building, creating sneering, grotesque shadows on the Holy walls. The bizarre ambience resembled the curious aura of a dream, or perhaps worse, a nightmare.

Somewhat temporarily removed from reality, the group took time to get their bearings and lingered uneasily in the entrance hall. Sebastian scanned the congregation and tried to account for everyone. "Where's the Colonel?" he suddenly panicked. Everyone's face looked blank. There was no wheelchair. They had forgotten him. The one person who probably most needed help, and they had forgotten him!

Seb automatically went to leave, but Raoul grabbed his arm and looked him tenderly in the eye. "He'll have to take his chances now, like the rest of us. It's too far. He probably wouldn't have left his home anyway. We may need you here."

Acclimatising to the eerie atmosphere, Raoul's eyes suddenly lit up when he saw the back of a woman wearing a distinctive turban hat, kneeling in one of the pews. "I knew she was back!" he mumbled to himself, rubbing his hands in grateful relief. "I just knew it!" As if reading his thoughts and feeling the presence of his piercing stare, the lady coyly turned around and gave him a knowing smile. But to his utter disappointment, he had been sadly mistaken. It clearly wasn't Edith, just someone who looked like her. Raoul's heart sank once again.

"What about Harriett?" panicked an obviously restless Sadie. Raoul smiled reassuringly and pointed to two hooded figures in cassocks, kneeling, praying at the Altar. "She's with Father Antonio. She's fine!"

"Oh, thank the Lord you're all safe!" came a heartfelt whisper from a side door. There stood the priest, hand in hand with his wife.

"But who's . . . ?" Before the question could be answered, one of the shrouded figures slowly stood up and gracefully climbed into the empty pulpit.

"Vengeance is mine, sayeth the Lord!" The familiar voice boomed above the howling winds and unceasing rain. The fearful worshippers, taken by surprise, raised their heads and directed their full attention to the direction of the frenzied warning.

There was an audible gasp, as the hood of the cloak was slowly removed, and the identity of the accuser was revealed.

Chapter 34

The unsolicited omen echoing from the pulpit came from the lips of none other than Grace Elisabeth Hickory. But, why did she feel the need to preach fire and brimstone? Cold shivers went simultaneously through Raoul and Sebastian. Such behaviour was totally out of character. Her sense of propriety was unrivalled. Embarrassed and aghast, they waited with baited breath, inwardly dreading what was to follow.

The much loved and respected Islander launched her prophecy with such feeling that this moment must have been brewing inside her for years and years. She certainly had a new found eloquence. She must have practised and rehearsed what she was about to reveal over and over, to perfection. Everyone was about to meet a different woman. Even the elements outside seemed to temporarily cower in anticipation of her impending story.

"I remember the last big storm which tormented the very soul of our Island, twenty years ago. Like now, we were a true community. Everyone looked out for everyone else. We put aside petty squabbles, dislikes and quarrels, and we stood together, as one, against the might of Mother Nature. It was not for us to question God's intentions or search for rhyme, reason or blame. It was just our turn to be tested, to see what we were made of. It was the very core of man's humanity to man on this Island of paradise which came into question."

By now, the spellbound congregation was beginning to fidget and react uneasily. Many looked bewildered, some looked unnerved. Others showed signs of impending humiliation. But why? Obviously, the historical events to which Grace was referring were starting to strike a chord in the hearts of some of those who had lived through them.

"During that occasion, when God chose to challenge us, everyone was saved, or so most people thought. There was, however, one young Island girl, barely eighteen years of age, with a story of her own. She loved life and she lived it to the full. She was a sweet thing; but her innocent naivety was often misinterpreted for promiscuity, and some of the men on this Island took full advantage of that. They flirted, they talked of romance and filled her head with all kinds of jibe, before they eventually used and abused her. These were powerful men, men she respected, men she felt duty bound to please. She was, of course, sworn to secrecy about everything which went on.

But on this Island, talk is cheap, and it wasn't long before jealous wives and girlfriends, sisters and mothers, heard the tales of the whispering palms and looked for any opportunity for revenge. Not on their husbands or boyfriends, brothers or fathers, but on the innocent Island girl who knew no better!

These women, unable to face up to their own short comings, made her life a misery. They spat at her in the street. They uttered profanities which should never be heard from a woman's mouth. They all but destroyed her zest for living. Yet she managed to rise above the hypocrisy of those who sought to grind her down because she was different."

To some now, the tale was becoming clearer. Buried in the mists of people's minds, old wounds were beginning to uncomfortably resurface. Shuffling figures restlessly squirmed in the shadows. Eyes were lowered to the ground. Forbidden glances over the shoulder flew from one side of the Church to the other.

"Time has now passed, but nothing has changed. In your own way, you are all still sinners. You are all no better than those you feel you have the right to judge. Lies, deceit, lust . . . , greed, envy, mistrust . . . , revenge, infidelity, bearing false witness; life on this Island continues to revolve around sin just as it ever did!"

Cowering looks of guilt and shame furtively spread from one to another. Accusing comments, in hushed tones, bounced around, as those present began to examine their own consciences and yet still point the finger elsewhere.

"When the fateful storm came, the young girl was at her most helpless, stranded outside on her way to visit her sick mother.

Along the way, she pleaded for shelter at the homes of those she had previously pleasured. Each time she met with hostility. Door after door was shut in her face, always by the woman of the house; women who didn't have the courage to face up to the truth. Some were too wrapped up in their own self righteousness to even acknowledge the presence of the poor creature in need, in the first place.

There was not an ounce of pity, not a morsel of sympathy, not a breath of compassion. The time had come for ultimate revenge. The Island's shameful sinner, the innocent girl who cast a guilty shadow on those she felt it was her duty to please, was about to be taught a lesson.

Weak and without food or clean water, she sheltered for days in unseemly, abandoned hovels, crushed by the storm one by one. It was only when she managed to reach the Church, locked to avoid looters, that she found her way into the depths of the crypt and took solace in God's basement, praying for forgiveness.

Either by chance or design the door to that refuge fell foul of the storm. She was too frail to push it open. She lay in that dungeon until she perished, alone and in fear. Even when the storm had subsided, her underground grave was conveniently ignored, and the bushes outside allowed to grow wild."

Sebastian and Raoul looked at each other in complete dismay. Were those tears in the eyes of Laetitia? Or were raindrops still lingering on her cheeks? Was Sadie so remorseful that she couldn't lift her head or look anyone in the eye? A faint Harriett had already slumped onto Father Antonio's lap. He sat solemnly, white faced, next to a visibly distressed Montgomery. Both men stared blindly ahead towards the Cross on the Altar, searching for consolation.

"And now, here's the bit you don't know, none of you. The sick mother she was desperately trying to reach was ME. The vulnerable, young woman you sent to her death was MY daughter. Yes . . . she was my . . . daughter!"

Grace's voice faltered as the full impact of her revelation shook the very foundations of the Church. "I have always served you well, all of you," she began to sob. "I have always known and kept my place. Why did I have to lose the only thing that was precious to me? Why was it MY daughter who had to suffer the consequences of all the wilfully unacknowledged sin on this Island? She was no more a fallen woman than many others who live amongst us. So, why her? Why didn't anyone help my baby . . . , my poor little girl?" she now pitifully wept.

Father Antonio rose to his feet and began to painfully limp to the front of the Church. The other hooded figure remained kneeling, head bowed and covered. Before he could reach her, Grace renewed her venom. "I had to track her down," she shrieked. She was now out of control. "It wasn't until weeks later, that I, myself, discovered her lost, decaying, incarcerated body when, out of desperation, I could think of nowhere else to look, so I explored the ultimate shelter, the House of God.

My little girl was almost unrecognisable. It was only her necklace . . . just a simple gold necklace . . . Alone and in dazed grief, I had to find the inner strength to physically remove her body from the crypt myself," she wailed, "and, in the darkness of the night, bury her, in an unmarked grave, on the edge of the cemetery, the place where she now resides either in torment or peace. Please, God, rest her soul! God rest . . . her pitiful . . . , innocent . . . , little soul."

By now, Grace was almost on her knees, drained of emotion, a broken woman. That fine, upstanding, highly regarded Islander with the beaming smile and the heart of gold, had been reduced to a quivering, crying wreck. The storm outside seemed insignificant in comparison. The shame of the Islanders was there, for all to see, on their guilt ridden faces.

Listening to the heart rending tale, Sebastian and Raoul had drifted through depths of despondency and emotion they never knew they possessed. After all, Grace Elisabeth was part of their life. Yes, she was their employee, loyal and supportive, but first and foremost, she was their dear friend. They had grown to love her in their own special way, and surely she felt the same. Yet, in the entire time they had known her, she had never once betrayed an inkling of the burden she had been carrying. So they didn't really know her at all, did they? And that was perhaps the hardest thing to stomach.

It troubled them greatly that she hadn't felt able to confide in them. Why hadn't she given her closest friends the opportunity to offer much needed solace and compassion, to help heal the wounds, before this spectacular public disclosure. Did this mean she didn't trust them?

Raoul also found his myriad of confusing thoughts being gradually drawn into a blurred web of even more puzzling intrigue. No matter how much he tried, he couldn't remove one hurdle from his racing mind. Just how did Grace Elisabeth know the events directly leading to her young girl's death in such graphic detail? On her own admission she had stumbled on the tragedy too late, coping with the aftermath entirely alone. So, if there had been no final, tearful good-bye between mother and daughter, who else was involved?

Chapter 35

A s the full impact of Grace Elisabeth's revelations was sinking in, people were desperately trying to salve their own consciences. Could anyone be completely free of guilt? Life invited sin. Was it humanly possible to have the strength to avoid it altogether?

Outside, the storm seemed to have once again renewed its vigour, with even mightier, accusing blasts of howling wind and pelting rain penetrating through the narrow access into the Church. Several of the rattling, ornate, stained glass windows suffered minor damaging cracks, but battled on courageously against a force possessed. Even so, everyone instinctively clustered closer to the middle aisles to avoid harm from eventual possible defeat or surrender.

Fork and sheet lightning intermittently illuminated their blessed sanctuary, only to be followed by ever closer bangs of angry thunder.

Kittie and Clarrie quietly shuffled to a pew nearest the pulpit. Little did they know, worse was yet to come? The congregation tried to retain its composure. It was difficult to imagine what was more frightening, the emotional or physical threat to those present.

Father Antonio felt it was time to take control. Everyone was looking to him for words of guidance and absolution, reconciliation and forgiveness. Patently shaken by the events which had taken place in his own Church, he made an uneasy move towards the platform of private and personal prayer.

Before he could reach the dais, the cloaked figure in front of him, who had remained tranquil and reverent throughout, slowly rose to full height, and stepped chillingly up into the pulpit.

There was a gripping feeling of suspense and apprehension as, bold and upright, and still shrouded in robes, the unknown worshipper carefully pulled back the hood from the cassock. Unnerving gasps of horror and desperate cries of anguish spewed out as the looming apparition coldly announced the spine tingling words; "I am the face of retribution! Now it's MY turn!"

It was none other than Della Dubois.

No-one could predict what was coming next. Father Antonio reluctantly returned to his seat, stunned, and instinctively shielded Harriett with his arm. Sadie sidled closer to the priest for spiritual protection. Her clairvoyant 'gift' had certainly not prepared her for the potentially unthinkable forebodings she was about to face.

The look on Laetitia Lascelles' face showed that she, too, now feared the worst. Alistair, with a weird twinkle in his eye, had to support his mother as she automatically stood to challenge, but, for once, was lost for words and had to sit down again.

Facing what was about to unfold with unrelenting trepidation, Monty gasped desperately for air. He clutched his pounding chest, visibly struggling to comfortably breathe.

Firmly gripping the back of the wooden bench where the others sat, Sebastian and Raoul stood steadfastly together. Neither knew quite how to react in what they imagined to be such an inconceivably surreal situation. Next to them, unable to comprehend the unfolding spectacle, Dimitri broke into an uncontrollable cold sweat and, disorientated, backed shiftily up against a nearby wall. Unnoticed, O'Rourke had recoiled like a frightened rabbit into the tempting safety of the sinful shadows.

The twins huddled together for mutual support. Kittie's eyes lit up with excited anticipation. There was drama in the air; drama more awe inspiring than any storm. Clarrie remained composed, with the inane grin of a simpleton on her face. Had she really any grasp of what was going on?

Della Dubois looked down on them all, literally and now figuratively. She stared at each one in turn; a stare that pierced their very souls. The tantalising temptress had something to say and her captive audience was going to listen, like it or not!

"I hope you've all enjoyed these tiresome little games we've been playing lately," she began, nonchalantly looking at her carefully manicured nails with an insulting air of disinterest. "You see, it was all a means to an end. Someone had to show you all the error of your ways before it was too late, and it fell to me to do it."

At that point, one of the battling windows finally gave in and crashed into smithereens at the back of the Church. Everyone jumped in panic. Della Dubois remained calm and focussed, waited for silence, then continued.

"Only one person on this Island has ever had any genuine time or respect for me; someone who first had to earn the trust and respect of everyone else; someone who was often so deep in grief, as a result of the unspeakable events within this community, that she could have been forgiven for wallowing in self pity and closing her eyes to the world forever. Instead, she was prepared to forgive. But she could never forget.

Without question, this person is the epitome of a true neighbour and real friend; never judgemental, always ready to help others, neither seeking nor expecting favours or advancement in return. She is a remarkable human being, an example to us all. And you have just heard her sorrowful story. So where do I come in?"

At that moment a roar of thunder and a dazzling flash of lightening bounced off the window beside the pulpit and bathed Della Dubois in a luminous, shimmering glow. Her aura was commanding uncompromising attention.

"Some years ago, merely by chance, or maybe it was fate, I unwittingly discovered Grace Elisabeth's plight while I nursed her during a short illness. She had a fever. She was delirious. And just like today, all her inner angst was triggered uncontrollably to the surface.

When she recovered, I broached the matter. Obviously embarrassed, she passed the episode off as the ramblings of a sick woman. She clearly didn't wish to relive the agony; she wanted it to remain buried deep inside. Nor did she want revenge. But I was different. I did! That day I made a vow. Sooner or later, I was going to get even on her behalf! You see, I had all the right credentials to do the job!

So, I engineered history to repeat itself. I anticipated a different outcome this time, of course, hoping you'd live and let live, in the light of past misdeeds. But, I was wrong.

Slowly and surely, I became a threat to your cosy, yet hypocritical, privileged, little society. Jealousy once again, provoked many of you to feel threatened or unjustly offended, and human nature kicked in with a vengeance.

I wildly enjoyed what life has to offer, in a manner you couldn't approve of, but would secretly love to fully experience. I laughed out loud, flouted convention and didn't care who I upset with my so called anti-social behaviour.

I was only too aware that such an outward, flamboyant show of forbidden pleasure would displease you and disrupt the so called 'moral code' of the community; a code you all choose to ignore when it pleases you.

Predictably, the women took the lead and the men turned a convenient blind eye. You hatched your little plots with your witches' covens, conducted whispering campaigns and dreamt up pathetic plans to rid the Island of me, one way or another."

Again, Della mercilessly glared at them all in turn, but this time, with an air of contemptible disbelief. "Funny, wasn't it, how every single one of your little schemes backfired? Didn't it ever occur to any of you to consider why?" she reproachfully shrieked. "Well, perhaps it's now time for the high and mighty of this precious little Island to learn something . . . You've all been conned!

I've played each one of you like a pawn in a game of chess. You see, I orchestrated the whole thing, and I was always one step ahead, thanks to you all, my own unwitting, whispering palms.

You gave yourselves away so easily; unguarded tittle-tattle, open windows, careless notes, unattended diaries, clandestine meetings. It was just a question of finding the skeletons in your closets or your Achilles' heels and then exploiting them in any way I could. It was so simple!" she accusingly condemned.

"So, this is the epilogue! Has there really been any harm done? Well, that's for you to decide. No-one's actually dead. But some of you have been to hell and back! And have any of you really taken the trouble to consider why those who 'left' the Island under mysterious circumstances have not yet returned? Some have been away rather a long time, wouldn't you say? Let's just put it down to an influential diplomat who owed me a favour or two.

Alicia, Daphnee and Maggie are all languishing on Mystique, recovering from their various ordeals. True, Elise is still in a coma, but there's hope, so I'm told. And, Laetitia, even your evil, conniving daughter, who is secretly as brow beaten as your son, has been rescued. Though God knows she didn't deserve to be."

At that moment, the strongest pillar of the community let out a pitiful cry of relief and cradled her head in her hands.

"Sadie and Harriett, I've enjoyed my mind games with you, especially. You've both been taken to the very boundaries of your emotional limits, and that's good enough for me. Yes, I'd say, all in all, the women on the Island got just what was coming to them.

And as for the men? You couldn't remain dispassionate for long! True to form, feminine wiles got you all involved, in one way or another, enticed you in to the dubious proceedings, the web of desperate deceit. You all more than deserve the backlash and humiliation you've suffered too!"

Della's gaze then suddenly zoomed to one of the small side chapels shrouded in darkness. "Edith . . . ! If that *is* your name! You can surface from the twilight now, as well!" she disparagingly commanded. "I know you've sidled back to your fate. I'm sure Interpol would love to know where you are! The 'accident' you had at home was nothing to do with me, by the way. Somebody else got there first. It was just meant to be a warning, I gather, from some of your unsavoury friends, to come clean about false evidence you gave to incriminate an innocent man. But, feisty as ever, you had to turn it into a fight. Well at least you've got guts, but that was your downfall! You had no chance.

Luckily, Jimmy Tremaine knew all about you. He was your saviour, even though you condemned his brother! But remember, Edith, people in glass houses shouldn't throw stones. One day someone might find out who you really are!"

A petite figure in a turban hat confidently emerged from behind one of the cold, stone pillars, looking unruffled, chic and sophisticated, and gracefully sat down, head held high with a dignified, sneering smile and vehement look of stylish antagonism.

"The only real tragedy was poor Mrs Van Leiden. You all treated her like an outcast too. Unfortunately, her unexpected and untimely death just made things go a little more easily, gave me further possibilities I hadn't really counted on. Fortuitous fate, you might say! But she could have been in league with me. The Will? A father on the Island? You're going to have to work out whether it was all true." Della Dubois fixed her vengeful eyes in the direction of her adversaries and then ranted at the top of her voice, "Now, let HE or SHE who is without sin, cast the first stone!"

Outside, at that point, a sudden moment of serene stillness surrounded the Church. All was tranquil. The storm had subsided. But, in the blink of an eye, without warning, came an almighty thunderous bang, accompanied by simultaneous bolts of lightning.

The tempest had now reached fever pitch and culminated in a direct strike on the helpless Church tower. There was one, loud, echoing ring of the bell, and then, instantly, the belfry crumbled and crashed unapologetically through the rafters below.

Beams fell, pillars tumbled, glass shattered, and the sacred refuge was now wide open to the unforgiving skies. Agonising screams of horror and pitiful cries of fear were soon muffled by the deluge of falling debris, and then, deadly silence returned.

Below lay carnage; complete and utter devastation. The eavesdropping storm had become judge and jury, rightly or wrongly, and finally brought its own ultimate form of divine justice.

* * *

This mysterious Island still has many more intriguing tales to impart. Will any whispering palms survive their destiny to pass them on, or will the stories remain untold, buried forever in the sanctuary of souls?

LaVergne, TN USA
02 February 2010
171788LV00002B/11/P